Jellicle Girl

STEVIE MIKAYNE

ISBN 10: 1622533011
ISBN 13: 978-1-62253-301-5

~~~~~~~~~~~~~~~~~~~~~~~~~~~~~~

Cover art and interior formatting by Mallory Rock

Edited by John Anthony Allen

Evolved Publishing LLC.

www.evolvedpub.com

For Lynn. Because you always took a stand

—even when you had to be seated.

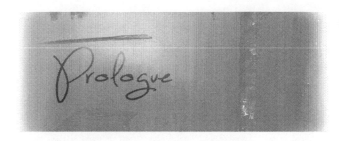

Prologue

I was in my running phase.

I ran everywhere; couldn't get there fast enough—or rather, couldn't get *away* fast enough.

Thank God you don't have to wait until adulthood to choose where you live in Canada. Hit sixteen, and you're sprung.

Three days past my sixteenth birthday, I slammed the door of my mother's grey, stone home for the last time. The knocker rocked on its hinge, squeaking indignantly against the metal door. I felt the vibrations in my arm, rooted to the spot for a moment by my own audacity.

Then I ran.

I ran and looked over my shoulder, almost tripping over the curb, as if she'd come after me. As if she'd actually put down her paintbrush and open the door of The Tower long enough to notice her daughter was gone. What would I have done if she'd actually noticed? What if Heather had got into her car and come raging down the street, hissing out her window for me to get back in the goddamned house? Would I have gone back with her? What if she had opened her arms and cried, wanting to apologise for everything—the silent contempt, the quiet but screaming disapproval over everything I had become?

Would I have let her?

No.

It was far too late for that. I needed her even less than she needed me—which was not at all.

I could almost convince myself.

Because it was my running phase, I hadn't exactly planned this out. I'd packed what I could carry—a backpack, and a little duffel bag full of clothes. The rest would have to stay. Even what was mine didn't belong to me. What was mine was Heather's, and taking Heather's things would be stealing.

No choice. I was drowning alive in there.

The day had come when I'd found myself sitting in my corner window seat, frozen to the ledge, unable to get up to turn off the white noise on the radio in case I walked right out of my body. I hugged my knees to keep them attached to me, and rocked and rocked into the wall to prove I could feel it. Even one more minute in The Tower would cause me to melt into my head.

With time enough to pack only a few things, I imagined myself turning into that python that swallowed an alligator, and exploded. I had to keep running or the beast in my gut would claw its way through my organs and flesh and kill me. I wasn't crazy, just terrified of myself—of my own obsessive mind that never seemed to shut off.

Jackie was supposed to have fixed this for me. She'd promised, knowing I couldn't handle slipping back undercover in this house after that summer. I'd breathed fresh air and stretched out my cramped muscles until they hurt. And I'd laughed. Crunching myself back into Heather's tiny box would kill me.

It would be like living in a house infested with black mould, never turning on the lights. As soon as you see the tiny infectious spores, you can never again pretend it's safe. You have to run, or die slowly—being poisoned by your shelter. Inevitably, that decision changes you. You become someone else.

No sense blaming Jackie; it wasn't her fault. Everything that happened that summer was like a series of glass brick interlocking in front of me. I never thought to be afraid, because it was so beautiful. It seemed so harmless.

Now, those bricks have allied to build a sheer solid wall in my path. I can't go forward, and I can't return. Stuck between two versions of myself, I don't know where to sketch my outlines.

I am Grizabella, on my way to the Heavyside Layer. I just haven't arrived.

Obviously, I'm a little obsessed with Cats, the musical. When I was about thirteen, my mother took me to see it live at the theatre. I sat riveted as this old, straggly cat—the beauty queen of her day—limped around the stage, while the other cats hissed and shunned her. When the first chords of Memory started streaming out of the orchestra pit, and Grizabella opened her haunted mouth, I sat stunned, tears streaming down my face. She had such a beautiful voice, such a beautiful hope. All she wanted was to be perfect again, to be beyond reproach and shame. She wanted what I needed, and in the end, she got it.

She got her Jellicle Transformation.

From that day in the red plush seats of the domed theatre, I knew my happiness relied on my own Jellicle Transformation. A fairy tale ending. Perfection.

The day I left The Tower, I still believed it would happen to me. I could erase the events of the summer and glide into the perfect, normal version of myself that was waiting for me on the other side of the bridge. I just needed air. Space. A big fat toke would also have been helpful, but I didn't have one. I wandered around the neighbourhood for a few minutes, drifting half-heartedly down to the bus that would take me to the subway.

For a few hopeful moments, I imagined myself in my own apartment, decorated with the best from IKEA, making peanut butter toast in an overpriced cherry-red toaster. Of course, I was about to start my junior year of high school, which meant no job, and no skills to get a job. As the daughter of a successful artist, I'd never had to work, and Heather had never considered telling me to try anyway. That gave me time to do my own things, a nice plus, but her motivation was probably more self-centred. It would have ruined her image for her daughter to dress in a McDonald's uniform.

Reality set in fast—fast enough for me to start panicking.

Even if I did get a job, no one would rent to me. And working full-time would mean missing school. I could coast through most of my regular classes with minimal effort, but that wasn't the problem. My university bridge courses required attention. I could not blow off those classes the same way.

The bridge programme was my school's answer to a class for gifted students. The Hole, as an academic school—the primary reason Heather had put me there—didn't actually have the money for a separate Advanced Placement track. The whole school performed ahead of the regular public system academically, but some kids were just so gosh-darn brilliant that the teachers decided they should advance even further, and become even more socially awkward and elitist, than the rest of the school. So they shoved those brilliant grade 11 kids into grade 12 classes, and then let grade 12 kids take a few first-year university classes.

When they threatened to put me in the bridge programme, I didn't say no. I had my own reasons for accepting. Of course, once they figured out I actually wanted to be in the programme, they started with the conditions: only if you can handle your freedom; only if your grades in the first-term prep courses are good, and only if you go to our stupid mandatory guidance meetings to help you adjust to the *burden* of being *gifted*.

I didn't give a shit about being gifted. I just wanted to get out of school, out of The Tower, and start my life!

That goal had kept me sane all this time—and it was even more important now. If I stopped working toward it, everything would stop. Momentum was crucial; stick with the plan. I couldn't afford to lose that chance. I couldn't afford to live on my own. But I still couldn't go home to Heather and The Tower.

With all these conflicts stretching the limits of my cracking sanity, I found my favourite spot on the tremulous concrete bridge that overhung the train tracks by the ravine, and hoisted myself onto the ledge. My backpack sat rigidly beside me, stuffed to capacity with all my notebooks and my laptop—everything my mother must never read. My duffel bag sagged into the orange metal cage that surrounded the bridge. There was hardly anything in it. I didn't care about clothes or makeup or hair accessories the way the Fairy Queens at school did.

I didn't really fit anywhere—not with the Queens, the nerds, the athletes, the chem-heads, or the music geeks. I could talk to everyone, and everyone talked to me, spilling their secrets into my lap like jellybeans from the 'guess how many' jar. It was amazing what people would tell you if you didn't ask, if you sat quietly sketching, scribbling, staring out the window, cracking a slight smile at bizarre jokes people told one another. The thing was—I could so easily have been a freak. But I wasn't. No one made fun of me—probably afraid of what I'd say. I just didn't fit in with anyone enough to want to hang out on the weekends.

Not that Heather would have let me anyway.

I leaned against that orange metal cage and closed my eyes as a train thundered up the tracks beneath me. Those engineers always glanced up to check for jumpers. Every time a train passed, I thought the same thing: the wire cage wouldn't be impossible to climb.

I could walk to the end of the bridge, where the sidewalk started, and hop over the bar to the other side. I could shimmy up carefully, walk the ledge on the other side, inch my way over, and wait. Wait for the whistle; wait for the thundering and just let go. Trains. There was another way to do it.

I thought about it often. Sometimes I would come here early in the evening and sit, watching. One time, I actually stood over the cage, peering down. The conductor blasted his whistle at me and practically scared me right off the edge. I didn't stand up for awhile after that.

Mostly, I came to the bridge to meet my cousin Kate at the top of the hill. We coasted down on our rollerblades with orange-flavoured slushies in hand. Kate and her mother—my dad's sister—lived three streets over. Heather never talked to them, but Kate and I were in the same year—different schools—and had a lot to say during our semi-covert meetings. We looked a little bit alike, and talked the same, and were pretty good friends even though we hadn't met each other until middle school. We shared an indescribable urge to escape, though we never could articulate exactly why. Every time we went out, we stopped on the bridge and screamed as hard as we could as the trains roared past. Then, exhausted and hoarse and sick from all the sugar, we'd coast down the rest of the hill and collapse in the park under the huge willow trees.

But it wasn't Kate I was thinking about that day; it was Jackie. I missed Jackie, even though she'd never been here with me. Even though I'd never sat on the bridge with her, screaming at the invisible conductor in the train. Would she have liked it, or would she have just called me crazy?

I was crazy... no doubt about it. But she was crazier.

I wanted to cry the day I left The Tower, but standing on the bridge, trying to let the tears come, it dawned on me: I couldn't cry anymore. Not that I shouldn't—I couldn't.

This knowledge sprouted a horrible feeling in my chest, like the weight of thousands of pounds of water all around me. The feeling grew stronger as passing cars marked the passing time, but I couldn't do anything about it. I couldn't do much of anything at all, actually. My glorious freedom had rooted me to this concrete block, because even with my miraculous emancipation, I remained stuck in a sixteen-year-old body with a sixteen-year-old's job skills, with no way to support myself and go to school at the same time.

Shit. Shit, shit, double shit. Now what the hell am I supposed to do?

When I finally thought about him, I laughed out loud. He was such an obvious solution—so perfect, and yet so forgettable. Funny that it took me so long to think about him.

He was like the mirage you see on the horizon when you're driving down a straight black road on a sweltering day. It seems very convincing—the haze of water in front of you—but as you drive closer, it gets farther and farther away. Look at it directly, and it disappears altogether.

Maybe it wasn't so funny that I forgot about him. After all, I saw him once a year, maybe twice at best.

After three hours on the bridge, and an extra-large slushie emptying itself by rapid degrees into my overfilled bladder, I trudged over to the other side of town and took the key from the leg of the barbeque at my dad's house. He was in Turkey, snapping pictures of strange animal and mineral phenomena.

It would be weeks before he knew I'd moved in.

Chapter 1

The early-morning sun pricks my eyelids, forcing them open. I blink awake and groan. My stomach lurches with the memory, the guilt and the horrible anxious feeling that sits on me until I pop an Ativan to make it go away.

God, is it morning already?

My hands quiver—something that happens the day after a major episode. And last night's episode was definitely major. Sometimes I wonder how hands so small can inflict the kind of damage they do. They're no longer a child's hands. I'm seventeen now, old enough that the police can't come to my door, trying to push me out of my father's bachelor pad because he doesn't actually live here. Today is Thursday: 470 days since I left The Tower, 485 days since I last saw Jackie, 441 days since Dad figured out I live with him. Well... live here. He's in the South Pacific somewhere. I think. Maybe that was last month?

The coffee-maker chimes to tell me that it's working. *Thank God.* While I wait for my first cup, I run the water in the kitchen sink and stick my arms under the icy late-winter stream. It soothes the sting, and numbs me. The familiar coffee scent percolates through the kitchen as I pat my wrists dry, apply anti-bacterial salve to the new scab lines and dress them in light gauze. Today's another long-sleeve day.

I need to feel something for shit's sake, or I'll never stop. I shake my head and bite my lip. *There, I felt that.*

In the sunroom, the distressed leather furniture is already hot, so I choose a chair shaded by the oak bookshelf. The coffee is strong enough to shake away the perpetual haze around my senses—if only for a few seconds. I wish it tasted the way Nabob looks on T.V. commercials, so rich and dreamy. But I'm always disappointed. It never tastes good—not as good as Jackie's at least. I don't know what her secret is—to coffee or life. I wish I could ask her.

The rooms around me are silent, and for once I actually want a conversation with someone instead of the endless monologue inside my head.

First period starts at 7:57. Even though the start time is asinine, I sincerely try not to miss class. But once in a while, even with an alarm to remind me, I can't get there. On those days, I sit and stare out the window until it's too late to go.

Time slips. I drop it on purpose sometimes.

I fidget, trying to drink my coffee. It's the same thing every time I wake up in this mood—as though worms are crawling all over me, inside my legs, up my back. I would dance them out, but that only makes it worse. It's useless to even try to work on essays this morning; the computer would go out the window.

I slam my coffee mug down on the table, creating a mug-sized tsunami dangerously close to my half-written English essay. "Shit!" I leap up, grab a handful of paper towel from the kitchen and sop up the mess. *That does it. I should have stayed in bed this morning. What the hell is the matter with me?*

Jackie would understand. Jackie.

I take out a blank, cream-coloured piece of paper from the shelf where I keep my nice stationery and ponder my collection of fancy multicoloured pens. Teal looks good. This will be no ordinary missive. No need for a "Dear Jacqueline"—she never cared about the etiquette of letter writing at all. Sometimes I wonder why I bother.

Jacks, I wish you were here. I miss you like hell.

Love, Beth.

The first time I met Jackie, she was sitting on the top bunk of the tent we shared with two other girls. She'd pulled her fine dark hair back into a loose braid, and crossed her legs at the ankles as she leaned against the post that stretched from the floor to the tent's southern peak. A pen stuck out from the side of her mouth, and she frowned at the book in her hand—an ancient hardcover edition of *Anne of Green Gables*—which barely supported the foolscap she was using to write a letter.

"Hey," she said, one corner of her mouth turning up. She always had this look like she knew something about your life that you were just about to discover. She took the pen from between her glossy lips—who wears lip gloss at camp?—and said, "Do you have a postcard? My mother gave me this legal paper to write on. As if I'm going to write more than five words. 'Hi Mom. Camp's the same.' Maybe I'll say 'Love, Jackie,' but why bother? Who else is going to write her on foolscap?"

I grinned. "You're in my bunk."

"Oh yeah?" She cocked her head at me and smiled. Her tanned skin glowed, and her rich brown hair waved down her back like a chocolate fountain. Her eyes were this strange violet colour. I didn't know eyes could be violet. "C'mon up then," she said, "I'll paint your toenails."

I dropped my gear, and climbed up onto her bunk. It didn't feel at all weird, slipping off my flip-flops and propping my feet on the pillow in her lap. She just smiled and reached for the nail polish.

She painted them dark pink.

Chapter 2

The phone rings more jovially than usual, which alerts me to the fact that it's my father even before I scramble to the living room to press the "talk" button.

"Hi Dad."

"Hi Scribbles." I grin. *Damn it!* He sucks me in so effortlessly—a phone call, a card—he should change my nickname to "Sucker." He doesn't really care when he asks, "What's going on in the big T.O.?" But I answer as if he does.

"Not much. How's Fiji?"

"It's gorgeous. It's summer over here."

"Do you know how much longer you'll be there?"

"Only a few days, but I'm heading to Australia for three weeks after that. Want to come over?"

Make light of everything. That's our rule. "Yeah right," I say. "If I didn't have a life I might consider it." It's fine for him to offer, but I don't know how he'd react if I ever accepted.

"You're not lonely, are you?"

What? Since when did he get wise? "Of course not. Who could be lonely with the big screen T.V. and all your pleasant neighbours?"

"What pleasant neighbours? Has Mrs. Continisio been up with spaghetti?"

"Twice a week, Dad. Twice a week. Not that I don't appreciate it, but honestly... what would it take to get some lasagne?"

Dad chuckles. Mrs. Continisio has been feeding him since he moved into the terrace house above her ten years ago. One day when I was about thirteen, during one of my infrequent visits, she came over with the most amazing lasagne. It smelled *so* good, and the taste has haunted me ever since. I ate it for dinner, and went to bed dreaming about the garlic and herbs. In the morning, I crept downstairs, fully intending to finish the lasagne for breakfast, but found Dad sitting at the kitchen table with the pan and a fork, putting the second-to-last bite in his mouth. He saw my face, and held up the last forkful to me... but I shook my head.

No. One bite would never be enough.

And ever since then, it's been spaghetti.

"So how long till you're home?"

"Well, after Australia I have a quick stop in Paris, then I'll be in Athens for two weeks, then I'm coming home for a few days."

At least a month and a half, then. "Sounds like fun." I try not to sound peevish.

"What are your plans?" he returns, as if there are infinite possibilities.

"Oh, I don't know... I'm considering staying in Toronto this week, and then next week, probably Toronto, and then, if I like it, Toronto again!"

"Glad to see you haven't lost your sense of humour, smart-ass," he chuckles. It's nice to hear him laughing; he hasn't called in a while. I enjoy our verbal tennis matches twice a month. If we talk more often we run out of jokes, and our game becomes awkward.

"How's the boyfriend?" he asks.

"How do you know I have a boyfriend?"

"Well, you usually do. Who's the flavour of the month?"

"Mike. If you must know."

I pause for a moment and consider the things he should be asking: Do you have enough money? Is there anything you need? Are you going to school? How are your grades? Do you think about throwing yourself off a bridge more than twice a day, Beth? Because that could really signal trouble....

Nada. Not a one. Not even, Are you having safe sex? Any normal parent would ask these things, right? I suppose I should be grateful, but really, I'm just pissed off.

But my anger only lasts about three seconds, and then he suckers me in again. "Hmmm. Well listen, I was walking through some of the stores here, and I found something you might like. I'm sending it for your birthday, so watch the mail, okay?" Damn it, I'm actually smiling—despite the fact that, for once, he's way

11

ahead of schedule, and I'm forced to wonder if he even knows when my birthday is.

"What is it?"

He laughs. "Yeah right."

"Hey—a girl's gotta try." *Better get off the phone.* It's getting hard to keep my voice up.

"Don't blame you. Okay kiddo, gotta run."

For a second, everything piles up on the tip of my tongue— school, my latest string of boyfriends, the sex, the drugs, the suicidal thoughts... Jackie—but at the last second I snap my mouth shut. "Okay, Dad. Talk to you later!"

"Bye, Scribbles. Take care." The click of the receiver jolts the pit in my stomach. Slowly, I put the phone back in its charger. *He's in Fiji, huh?* That's farther than usual—not that it makes much difference where he is. The money keeps popping into the bank, and I keep spending it on groceries and lingerie.

He'll get home eventually, intending to stay a few weeks, but he'll get bored long before that. He'll pretend that he's not waiting for that phone call—the one that will spring him from the daughter who looks so disconcertingly like his ex-wife. And when the phone rings at some ungodly hour, he'll say he's disappointed that we can't spend more time together, and he'll be on the next flight to Africa.

It should upset me more, the fact that my dad and I never connect, but it's been this way as long as I can remember. He's always been absent from his own life. He likes things that way. It prevents anything serious from clouding his good time. Jump on a plane, bum around with the locals, snap some photographs and develop them in a makeshift darkroom using whatever supplies you can get your hands on—some of which are definitely not to code, and could probably kill you—then sell them to magazines at prices that will pay for your next plane trip. That's his life. And the number one rule: don't stay too long. And never long enough that you want to stay longer.

I'm a little lost after I hang up with Dad. I find myself touching things around the living room, staring glassy-eyed for a few moments. On the wall hang some of his better shots: a bull elephant lumbering toward a ruby sunset, a towering redwood tree, a shiny blue bug that used to scare me as a kid. Would I ever be interested in snapping pictures? Probably not. Pictures of people are more interesting than random animals and plants. I touch the frames around my computer, wishing the paper inhabitants were flesh and blood. Jackie, my cousin Kate, Simon—my best friend from middle school. They're all smiling, joking with me from behind the glass, captured in that second when they ran through my life, happy.

Except Heather.

My mother's picture troubles me. Her haunting eyes overshadow the others' smiling faces, watching me move around the room. A clip of semi-precious stones holds back her dark hair. You can't see the clip from the picture of course, but I watched her design and make it. She went through a phase when she abandoned paint altogether. Beautiful broaches, hairpins and necklaces filled every free space in the house for a while. She made a necklace for me once—amethysts and rose quartz with a chain of brushed nickel. She inscribed my name onto a funky metal piece in the centre—I still remember running that metal through my fingers, jagged and cool. When I left The Tower, the necklace stayed behind. *Did she throw it away?*

I look at her picture for a long moment, trying to figure out why both my parents have withdrawn into their own little worlds, as far from me as possible.

The picture sits in my hand, mute. Heather's face is an enigma—impossible to read—as if she's concealing a great secret. Maybe she knows something about me, about my Jellicle Transformation. Maybe that's what she wants too, for me to float up to the clouds like Grizabella on her magical staircase, and be reformed as a beautiful, charming, normal young lady that no one can help but love. Maybe she'll want me then.

Elizabeth, please don't chew your nails. You look like a chimpanzee.

Shaking this pointless nostalgia out of my head, I force myself to concentrate on the time. *Don't be late again.* Outside, bright winter sun gleams off piles of salty snow in a direct assault on my retinas. I almost tramp on a homeless woman tucked over a hot grate in a grotty sleeping bag, a torn woollen toque barely containing her wild hair. I have a peculiar desire to stop for a moment and snap a picture—a black and white Polaroid for my bathroom mirror. *This is where you're going if you don't get a fucking grip!*

The grate emits puffs of foul odours—or maybe it's the homeless woman. Who can tell? I dare myself to look down into the bowels of the city as I march onto the slits of metal. What if one was loose? What if, after thousands of people thundered over it every day, one of the screws came undone? The grate wore too thin? The concrete around it crumbled? What if someone got swallowed whole in the sewer? Would they come out transformed? Is that how the Jellicle Transformation happens? I stand still for a moment, jump a little, daring the grate to take me.

It doesn't.

Five minutes later, I shuffle through The Hole's draughty lower corridor to my locker. A tall guy wearing a red sweatshirt almost ploughs into me as he leaps to catch a sandwich someone's tossed.

"Could you maybe not step on my feet, Jason?" I snap. "I have Stuart Weitzman shoes on here."

"Sorry," he mutters. His eyes flick over me—so quickly anyone else might have missed it. But I'm looking for it, counting on the boys to tell me my disguise is working: pretty girl from head to toe.

"Hey. Are you really not back next semester?" He catches my arm.

"Not if I can possibly help it."

"Too bad." Jesus, he sounds sincere.

"Really?" I smile at him. "Wouldn't you get out early if you could?"

He cocks a grin at me. "Hey I don't blame you. I'll see you at graduation then?"

"Sure," I say. "Save me a seat." Jason's a nice guy— mostly. We've even gone to a few dances together. It's not that I want to avoid him exactly. I just prefer not to get too close to anyone. Makes things less complicated.

"Get out of the way, you fucking queer," says a voice to my left. For a second I freeze, my stomach lurching into my throat, but they're not bullying me. In fact, they're not bullying anyone. It's just a pack of girls harassing their "best gay" Steev. I overheard the three of them in the library talking about "immersion therapy." Apparently the more you hear something, the less sensitive you become to it. They're taunting him to protect him, to toughen him up.

Bizarre trio.

I force myself to breathe, and calmly pull a book from my locker.

Here's a thought—let's just all stop using that word and no one will have to be "immersed" at all!

I straighten my dress and shove away from the lockers, pushing my book deep into my side bag.

Two more weeks until Christmas break, then I'll never have to see this place again. It took some coordination, but I managed to get both co-op and bridge courses at Toronto University in my last semester.

All off site.

Thank God!

No one's told me yet where I'm co-oping, but I really couldn't care less, as long as it isn't here. As if in answer to my unspoken question, the guidance office opens ahead of me, and out comes Mr. McArter, a forty-something ex-coach who creeps out all the senior girls—we all call him McFarter behind his back. He could have been handsome twenty years ago, but his arrogance far exceeds his charm, which may be why he's got into some trouble lately.

"Ms. Sarandon. Could you come in here for a moment, please?"

"Sure." I follow him past the resource table into his cluttered and vaguely malodorous office. Obviously, he has a penchant for tuna sandwiches....

"Ms. Sarandon," he grins.

"Mr. McArter," I respond flatly. His grin fades a little, but he recovers well—splaying his large callused hands over my file, and feigning the "I'm concerned" look that guidance counsellors must practice in the mirror. I've seen it so many times before that I can sense it coming even before it flashes across their features. "I'm concerned," they say, because.... But the because doesn't really matter, since they all have a variety of ridiculous reasons: you live alone; your father has essentially abandoned you to gallivant across the universe; your mother is a recluse and worse, an *artist*; you do your own grocery shopping, Beth; you wear long sleeves in the summer time; you don't talk to the other students; you're frequently late for school; you never participate in class; your intelligence scores are off the charts, but your grades are in the mid-80s; how will you adjust to life at university...?

McFarter shoots them all at me—like rotting paint from an automatic paint gun. The last one is by far my favourite. Every other high school in Toronto—in the world, for that matter—salivates hungrily for the day when the senior class graduates and they never have to see them again. But The Hole seems determined to insinuate itself into *my life* for as long as humanly possible.

"Beth," McFarter's voice barely passes through my wall of repressed rage, "we see no reason to hold you back—"

Hold me back! Who the fuck does he think he is? He can't hold me back. I'm finished. I'm out of here! I'M DONE WITH THIS PLACE! In my head, I'm sliding his neck under a dull-edged chop saw, but I keep my face perfectly composed. I've practiced it all my life; composure is one of Heather's rules.

"We'd like to set you up with support during your six months in the bridge programme. Particularly in light of the fact that you won't be returning here for any classes."

This was entirely deliberate, you moron. I wouldn't come to you for guidance if I was deaf and blind and about to walk in front of a goddamned bus!

"I plan to complete my guidance requirements," I say. My voice is so flat it could slide right under the door. Too bad my body couldn't slide under there with it....

"We believe you need a bit more support than a few guidance visits," he says smoothly.

"Is this mandatory?"

"We think it's for the best, Beth."

"Who is we?"

"Ms. Almont and I both feel—" Ugh, God. Almont—also known as The Vice. She's the vice principal who once caught me smoking weed on the roof of the school. Of course it's her idea.

She thinks I'm totally emo and disturbed. I think she's a sexually-confused control freak.

"Whatever," I interrupt. "How long do I have to do this?"

"You'll be required to meet with a university counsellor during the first week of your semester. He or she will likely want to see you every week or so. The university will be in touch with you when they've found a match."

I would like nothing more than to reach across the desk and smash his too-large, too-silver glasses into his eyes. A brief vision of him clawing at the glass shards in his corneas calms me down enough to ask, "Has anybody bothered to find me a co-op placement for next term?"

"Co-op?" He looks genuinely surprised. And yet he knows I'm not returning next semester. It truly amazes me what people fail to put together. "I didn't realise you were registered for co-op. We announced all the placements weeks ago." *Which you would know, if you condescended to make friends,* he does not add.

"Evidently not," I reply icily. *I have friends, damn it. I just don't like them enough to lie in one of their little rings, gossiping about school activities while someone shoots a picture.*

He shuffles his papers. I stand and glare down at him, daring him to say something more. "I'll see what I can do," he mutters. As soon as he looks down again, I barge out.

Chapter 3

Dusk. The city grows quiet as the last streaks of pink disappear into the deep blue ink of nightfall. The lights are out, and the day has ended—not only for me, but for most of the city. At this time of night, I trot easily down into the subway station without having to fight a tide of frenzied business people whose rush will toss me over the yellow line and onto the tracks. The day's struggle has ended. And this mood allows me to stand still and listen to all six voice messages with only minimal cursing.

First message: "Hi Beth, just calling to say hi. It's really nice out, so I thought..." Mike. *Great.*

Message skipped. Message erased.

Next message: "Hey Beth. Haven't heard from you in a few hours..." Mike again.

Message skipped. Message erased.

Next message: "Beth, it's Maureen from the Beverly House group home. Just calling to schedule your orientation. The number here is...." *Ah. So that's where my placement is going to be. Nice of McFarter to let me know.*

Message skipped. Message saved.

Next message: "This call is for Beth Sarandon." *Well, you've got the right mailbox then.* "This is Nancy Sullivan calling from the Bloor Street Mental Health Centre. I'm affiliated with the bridge programme support services for Toronto University. Please call me back to arrange a time to meet." I frown over that one. *Is this the counsellor I have to see? Christ on a bike! McFarter doesn't bother to get me a co-op placement, but he sure doesn't waste much time getting me a shrink....*

Message saved.

18

Next message: a hang-up. *Sorry that the voicemail was such a surprise to you. Sometimes that's what happens after the phone rings and rings and nobody answers.* Message erased.

Next message: "Beth, it's Kate. Call me." My cousin. Lovely. *Thank you for being succinct.* Katie gets things. It's one of her many charming qualities, and one of the reasons she's the only member of my family whose number is in my contacts list.

Message erased. There are no more messages.

Best news I've had all day. I chuck the phone into my handbag and wave my transit pass at a very bored looking booth-man with myopia. More than likely, I could have shown him Muhammad Ali's transit pass, and he wouldn't have batted a cataract.

The underground Second Cup beckons me with the smell of foamed milk and espresso.

I don't even have to say "Latte, please." The guy behind the cash register just punches it in and takes my money. The usual barista is gone. Instead, a girl my age swirls milk under the steamer, grimacing as the machine spits and whistles. What would possess a girl to have so many piercings on her face? And is that a tattoo behind her ear? She has spiked blonde hair and, I notice as she turns to grab another pen, wooden spacers stretching her earlobe.

Wow.

Girls like that fascinate me a bit. I wonder what it would be like to dress like her—to wear my secrets out in the open. Is she really that free with herself, or are her piercings and spiked hair as much a disguise as my makeup and high heels?

She hands me my latte without a word. But as I walk away, I have a strange feeling that she's watching me.

My dad lives in the far west end, which makes the trip freezing and inconvenient in the winter, and sweltering and inconvenient in the summer. The subway ride is actually good for me, though. It gives me a chance to think, forces me to sit still for fifteen stops. I can order my mind on the subway. If I'm lucky, that serenity will stay with me after I alight, but most of the time it doesn't. It's like popping an Ativan—an artificial relaxant that only masks the turmoil, pouring a smooth slick of oil across the raging waves. My mind still churns, but from above, it doesn't seem so bad.

19

As soon as the jail-stone wall of the subway station greets me, so does the knot in my stomach. For a moment, I force my thoughts onto errands to keep from being consumed by the anxiety in my chest: *I haven't gone grocery shopping yet, and there's nothing in the refrigerator. Even less in the cupboards. My dad's credit card bill is still lying on the table, unpaid. Mental note: do that* first thing tomorrow.

It's no use—the anxiety pushes through: *And I have to call back that stupid support counsellor. Goddamn it. Why do guidance people think they have to hold your hand held every step of the way?*

Sometimes you have to feel things on your own. The pain, the insecurity, the nostalgia. The shame. The guilt.

Mostly, the guilt.

It's always there; even the most skilled therapist in the world couldn't make that go away. I have to put my hand out to the wall and feel its coldness before I can walk up the stairs.

We sat by the edge of the lake, our backs against an old canoe, far from the view of the counsellors on deck—which is why we could get away with smoking the joint we'd smuggled down to the lakefront. The seclusion and the lily pads and the squelching of the frogs in the reeds—all of it was hilarious at that moment. Not only because we were high, but because we were free.

We were Junior Counsellors in Training: one year up from being campers, but two years away from full-fledged counsellors. My birthday wouldn't arrive until the end of the summer, making me fifteen while most of the others—Jackie included—were sixteen. Normally, being youngest didn't bother me, but that summer, most of the friends I'd made in previous years had spent the school year together, and they cliqued like a mass of lake fronds. Luckily, Jackie had arrived. No one joined camp in J.C.I.T. year, but Jackie always did things nobody else considered.

J.C.I.T. year meant no more assigned activities, no campers to look after—yet—and almost no supervision. We'd spent two weeks paddling canoes out to the middle of the lake and sun-tanning while reading new magazines and munching Nibs.

"Has your mother always been such a head case?" Jackie asked, passing me the joint without looking at me.

I took a short toke—Jackie had a higher tolerance for the stuff than I did. I hadn't asked her where she'd got it. Better not to know.

"No," I replied slowly. "She only started getting crazy when I was seven or eight. I mean, she always scared me. But when I was little it was because she screamed all the time. Later, she just...."

No need to finish. Jackie knew all about the problem between Heather and me. Contempt. One of the tenets John Gottman describes as the "Four Horsemen of the Apocalypse." When one person finds no redeeming qualities in the other, does nothing but criticise, complain and try to change that person, the relationship will not survive.

Heather sensed my flaw, a pervasive stain on the base canvas of my identity, and tried to get at it from every angle. But no matter how much turpentine she used, or how many palates of paint she smeared over it, the blotch spread like a port-wine stain over a baby's face. There was only one solution: the Jellicle Transformation I'd been praying for since Grizabella floated away on that staircase.

Jackie just nodded and squeezed my hand. Funny, that didn't creep me out at all.

I know it's part of the programme, but I really don't want to do it. I hate guidance. And something tells me this is going to be more like therapy. I don't need therapy. I mean, I know it's not normal, what I do, but won't I just outgrow it eventually? Honestly, who's ever heard of a fifty-year-old cutting herself? Not me.

That appointment with the university shrink they've set me up with is mandatory, even though I doubt it will achieve anything practical. I thought about therapy when I wanted to stop. Last summer. When Deet called and asked me to come back to camp for S.C.T.J. year, and I realised I could never show up like this. I almost made an appointment then. But cutting doesn't scare me now like it used to. I could continue this way indefinitely really. It still freaks me out a little when my hands move without my brain telling them to, but I've accepted it as part of myself. A monster writhes inside of me, and I can only kill it by slicing through my skin.

I just think about it like this: everybody has self-destructive behaviours. Some people drink too much, some people smoke, some do drugs, some have promiscuous sex, some barf their guts out when a crumb of food hits their stomachs. I don't have any of those problems—I just watch my blood seep into the sink. How is that worse than anything else people do? In fact, it's almost preferable. A clean shallow slice, instant gratification, and then it heals. Alcoholics can't say the same about their livers, can they?

Wish you were here, Jacks. I miss you like hell.

Love,

Beth.

Another Christmas morning spent in the company of Charlie Brown and the Grinch. At least there's popcorn, and a chocolate log cake from the really expensive bakery downtown. Dad's credit card paid for that—which he doesn't know yet—but it's his own fault for being on the Great Barrier Reef over Christmas. I hope he's warmer than I am. Actually, no. I hope a really awful ice storm hits Australia, even if it is the beginning of summer down there. I've avoided calling back that Nancy Sullivan woman. It's the holidays. She probably won't be working anyway.

The furnace has died, and I don't know who to call to fix it. So I'm sitting in three pairs of socks, two hoodies and gloves, with a heating bag around my neck and a huge quilt on my lap, when the doorbell rings. I consider not answering, but it might be Mrs. Continisio. If she's brought me pasta, I won't have to get out of my blanket fort to make dinner. Who cares if it's spaghetti again? I won't even think about her lasagne—the crushed tomato and garlic, the layers of homemade pasta, the herbs and the parmesan.... I'll just close my eyes and imagine that the spaghetti is lasagne, and be grateful for the dinner.

My wool socks slip-slide against the polished hardwood on my way to the door. I peer through the peephole. Mrs. Continisio!

I whip open the door, grinning. Our neighbour's dark hair tumbles around her shoulders—she's either going grey or is still dusted in pasta flour. She holds out a glass tray for me and smiles broadly as she pats my cheek. "Merrya Christmas, Eliza," she says, and her hand rests for a moment on my pink face. "Your cheeks—they're cold. Are you all right?"

I nod, avoiding her eyes. The smell of sauce wafts through the tin foil atop a square pan. *Square! It's lasagne!* I almost kiss her.

Chapter 4

A repairman has come by and fixed the heat by the time I'm ready to leave for my first day of co-op at Beverly House. It turns out the yellow pages has a section called "Heating." You choose an ad you like, call the number, and someone in navy coveralls arrives to fix the problem. If I'd known that, I would have called days ago. Luckily, the pipes didn't freeze. Apparently that's bad. I don't know anything about furnaces, I told the repairman. Probably shouldn't have said that. But as the Visa bill won't arrive until next month, I'll have to wait to see how much damage my admission of idiocy has done. *Another point in the case against seventeen-year-olds living alone while their parents tour foreign countries.* My feet still haven't thawed out properly as I slip on a pair of black leggings, knee-high boots, and a long red sweater that hugs my curves. Long earrings, a spray of delicate perfume, and a touch of eye makeup completes my disguise.

I squint in the mirror. When did my hair get so dark? Pictures of my childhood reveal a honey-blonde kid—with a perpetually furrowed brow—but lately, my hair's turned something closer to Heather's maple-syrup shade. Do I look like her? A lot of people remark on the similarity, but she says no. I certainly didn't inherit my dad's large features or rugged charm.

Jackie once compared me with pictures of my parents. She glanced from one to the other, scrutinising my mother's intense eyes, my father's easy smile. She looked up at me on the bunk, then back down at my parents.

Heather's heart-shaped face, Dad's short curly hair, Heather's pale skin, dotted with tiny freckles over the nose, Dad's dimples— I was a composite of both of them, an emulsion.

Jackie shrugged her slender shoulders. "Neither," she pronounced. "You look like yourself."

I smooth a few frizzed hairs down with hair gloss, and then grab my purse, ready to face the day.

The white-sided townhouse on Beverly looks like no one has bothered with outdoor maintenance for several years. *What did you expect from a group home?* Cracked eaves troughs tilt off the old grey roof, and shrubs in the side yard sprawl wildly. Long cracks line the driveway like tributaries springing from the large pothole in the centre. I gingerly mount the sloped front steps and ring the bell.

"I'm Lizzie. I'm almost eight," says the squirt behind the screen door. A baseball cap sits backwards on her head, covering long brown hair that could use a very patient combing. She holds up a kaleidoscope to her eye, and starts twirling it. "You look funny," she says. "But you're still pretty upside down."

She's not very big—in fact, she looks more almost-six than almost-eight. Her too-big, blue and green shirt with its faded Power Rangers decal just adds to the incongruence.

"I take it you're not going to let me in," I say.

"Nah. Can't open the door to strangers. You might be someone's real mom who's not allowed in here." Her tone is neutral, but her insight is unsettling.

"Good point," I shift my weight to my other foot. "I'm Beth, by the way. Short for Elizabeth."

"Hey! That's my name!"

"I figured."

She drops the kaleidoscope and stares at me. Her face is streaked with something that could be dirt—maybe chocolate. "You mean we have the same name?"

"Guess so."

"That's weird," she says.

Footsteps crash down the hall, and a smiling twenty-something woman appears, pushing her way through hockey equipment to get to the door. "Sorry, guys," she says. "I was up to my elbows with the plunger. You must be Beth." She unlatches the screen, and Lizzie scoots out of the way to let me in. "I'm Maureen, the counsellor in charge."

"Hi there." I shake the warm, slightly damp hand she offers. *God, I hope she's washed it since the plunging.* The screen door draws so tightly against my backside that it could easily catapult me inside if I let it go.

Maureen stands a little taller than me, with thick light hair pulled into a messy ponytail and baggy jeans that give the impression she's just lost twenty pounds on a crash-diet. Her face is ruddy and freckled, and she obviously doesn't like makeup, but her smile is huge—almost as huge as her feet.

"This is Lizzie. She's seven," Maureen kicks some goalie pads aside to make a path for me.

"Almost eight," Lizzie mutters.

"She'll be eight in a few weeks," Maureen adds.

"We're having a party," Lizzie's face stretches into an excited grin. "I get to choose the cake."

"What kind do you like?" I ask.

"Chocolate," she replies, as if there is no other possible answer.

"Hm. Me too. But I like mine with rainbow icing and candy on top."

"Really?" her eyes widen in awe. "You can put candy on a cake?"

"Sure you can. My dad does it all the time."

Lizzie's face clouds. "My dad's in jail," she says, heading down the hall. "He's not coming to my party."

"Shoved her head into a shitty toilet and flushed," Maureen whispers as I take my boots off and follow them deeper into the house.

"Why?" I whisper.

"Could there be a reason for that?" she mutters. I blush. Of course not. What a stupid question.

"C'mon, let's go," Lizzie shouts impatiently from somewhere ahead. "I'm friggin' starving."

Maureen swings through a door and into the kitchen. Compared to the dark hall, the lights in here could grow a crop of weed overnight. I blink several times, temporarily blinded.

"Lizzie, where'd you learn that word?" Maureen demands. The washing machine chugs then screeches, its cycle finished.

Maureen immediately pounces on the laundry, turfing towels and facecloths into the dryer. Lizzie looks down at something on the floor, and squashes it with the toe of her filthy sneaker. Better not to ask what that was.

"From Kenny," she says.

"Yeah, well, you're too little to use rude words. Wait until you're eight."

"You mean then I can swear all I want?"

"Then you can swear all you want."

Lizzie grins.

"Under your breath," adds Maureen. "So no one can hear you. In the bathroom, in your closet, under your covers at night, and when you're hiding during hide-and-seek you can swear yourself breathless. And if you actually take a bath—God forbid—I'll even let you swear out loud."

Lizzie slumps down onto one of the long benches that line the plain wooden table. "I'm hungry! Can we have a snack, now?"

"Have a seat, Beth," Maureen says. "You might as well enjoy these last two minutes of peace. The kids'll be home soon."

I slide in next to Lizzie, and she frowns at me before shifting herself slightly farther away. *Sorry kid. Didn't see your giant personal space bubble there.*

Maureen throws together a plate of cheese, crackers and fruit that looks like it would feed a starving regiment, and puts it down in the middle of the table. Lizzie grabs a handful and munches steadily. She's eaten a quarter of the plate before Maureen notices. "You think maybe the other kids might want some?"

"Probably," Lizzie helps herself to another cracker.

"You want to leave any for them?"

"No. They never leave any for me."

"It's true. Poor kid's practically fading away to a shadow! If it weren't for the bright blue hat, you might miss her altogether."

Lizzie looks at me out of the corner of her eye, like she's wondering if I'm going to make fun of her too. Maureen tickles her and she smiles grudgingly—then giggles.

"You go ahead and eat while you can, Liz. Soon it's back to grabbing the crumbs off Kenny's plate."

"What crumbs?" Lizzie says drily. "He licks his plate."

Suddenly, it sounds like a subway line has been rerouted through Beverly and up to the front door. "Moe! MOE! I forgot I had hockey today!" A boy's voice roars in desperation.

"I'm in here, Kenny. Come talk to me." A stocky young boy bursts through the door, almost knocking into the table, followed by a girl of about twelve, her thin face pink from the cold. Concealer does little to mask the dark circles under her brown eyes.

"Moe, first you have to get Rachel off the bus," she says. "Gina's trying, but she's doing that grunting thing."

Maureen brushes by both kids, and the front door squeaks shut.

"This is Beth," Lizzie points to me, obviously pleased to know something they don't. "She's a new student counsellor."

The girl eyes me steadily, the boy from the hall stepping up behind her. Neither smiles.

"That's wonderful," mutters the girl. "Another student to sit around staring at us."

"Why are you here anyway?" the boy asks. "You want to grow up and be a social worker or something?"

Before I can answer, they look at each other and gush in unison, "Such a *noble profession*." Obviously this isn't a new party trick.

"That's Monica and Kenny," Lizzie says. "Kenny eats his boogers. And he always wears the same socks. If you're wondering whose feet smell, it's Kenny."

Kenny gives her a withering look, but otherwise seems undisturbed by her matter-of-fact insults.

"And Monica's his sister."

Monica rolls her eyes and slumps against the wall. I try to smile at her but she looks at her hands.

"Hey Kenny," Lizzie pipes up, her eyes bright. "I've got one."

"Yeah right," Kenny replies, though he looks a little intrigued. "Betcha you don't."

"Betcha I do. It's like this: 'DASHING THROUGH THE SNOW, ON A PAIR OF BROKEN SKIS. OVER THE FIELDS WE GO—'"

"'—CRASHING INTO TREES,'" Kenny finishes.

Lizzie bangs the table. "Crapola!"

"That's been around since I was a kid," Monica informs her.

"What's the score now, Mon?" Kenny asks.

"You'll have to look. But I think it was thirty to forty-two last time I checked."

"I still have a twelve point lead," Kenny says. Lizzie just sets her jaw.

"How long has this contest been going on?" I figure I'd better take this trio by the horns if I'm going to get to know them.

"Three months," Monica says with a scowl. "Who knew there were that many idiotic songs in the world? And trust these two to try to collect them all."

Kenny turns his attention to wolfing down a handful of crackers and cheese. Monica ignores the snack and walks past us to the staircase. "I'm going to change," she says.

"Wait! Mon, will you please take me to hockey?" Kenny says around a mouthful of food. "I really don't want to miss it tonight."

Monica sighs and turns around. "Why didn't you just get off the bus when you were supposed to?" Her waiflike frame wavers. "You know you always have hockey on Mondays."

"I just forgot," Kenny says miserably.

"Kenny has ADHD," Lizzie says. "It's not his fault he can't remember where he parked his brain." For once, Kenny actually looks hurt, but Lizzie's jaw is still set in that defiant jut. Monica's face softens.

"Yeah, all right. I could use the exercise anyway. Ask Moe if it's okay, and I'll meet you back down here in a few minutes. Don't forget your equipment, because I'm not doing this twice."

Kenny nods, and bolts to the front door. "Moe! Moe!" he yells outside. "Monica's going to walk me over to the arena, okay? Okay? Thanks!"

It sounds like Sonic the Hedgehog is whirling around the front hallway. "Crapola!" he groans as something crashes to the ground.

"What was that?" Lizzie yells.

"Me!" comes Kenny's muffled reply. "I tripped on my stupid boot!"

Lizzie rolls her eyes and helps herself to another handful of cheese and crackers. "Damn it!" Kenny explodes.

"Kenny, for God's sake, can Rachel and I at least come in the house?" Maureen's exasperation is evident, even from here.

Lizzie giggles, and crumbs of Ritz fly out her mouth.

"Gross!" I say, pulling the plate away. "Don't get your spit-coated crumbs all over the food."

She giggles again, but covers her mouth this time.

Monica glides back into the kitchen. She avoids even looking at the snack tray as she picks up her coat from the bench. "Are you ready, Kenny?" she calls.

Kenny pokes his head in the door. "Yeah. I've got my coat and boots on... and my bag."

"Did Moe say it was okay?"

"Yeah. It's okay, Moe, right?" Kenny stands holding the swinging door like it's going to collapse without his support.

"What's okay?" Maureen's voice comes from the front hall.

"IF MY SISTER TAKES ME TO HOCKEY!" Kenny enunciates slowly, as if Maureen were deaf and more than a little delayed.

"Oh yes, that's fine." Kenny ducks under Maureen's arm as she trips into the kitchen. "Are you going to homework club while you're there, Monica?"

"Yeah, I think I will." Monica gathers her bag. "That cute tutor is there on Mondays."

"Well, you just keep your flirting to a few batted eyelashes okay?"

The waif almost smiles.

"Let's go," Kenny stumbles to the front door. Something thumps to the floor and squeaks. "Oh, geez—sorry Rachel. I didn't see you there."

"C'mon Rachel," Maureen sighs. The door slowly swings open, and a little girl with huge hollow eyes tiptoes in. Maureen puts a protective arm around her as she rocks back and forth on her tiptoes. She grunts, her face bunching into a tight ball. "All right, you guys," Maureen calls. "Get out of here before you're late. Be back by five—no later."

Something wallops the ground as they leave. Maureen just rolls her eyes. "Goodbye, goodbye, goodbye!"

Lizzie eyes Kenny's hockey stick leaning against the fridge. An internal debate writes itself over her tense features: wait and see if he notices, and then watch Monica yell at him, or run his stick out to him. She must feel bad about her ADHD remark because... "Kenny!" she bellows, leaping up. "Wait!"

Suddenly, it's just me, Maureen and the little hollow-eyed girl named Rachel. She glances my way, and scrunches up her hands and face, making a horrible grunting noise—she sounds like a constipated parrot.

She takes a step toward the table, as if she wants to pass into the living room, but instead rocks back and forth on her heels, stepping forwards and backwards, that horrible noise intensifying. Maureen watches for a moment, then plants herself in front of the table, a physical barrier between Rachel and me. Finally, Rachel rocks forward and uses her momentum to toe-walk into the living room, where she shuffles slowly from one side of the entertainment centre to the other, touching each movie. "Is she autistic?" I ask in a whisper. Maureen shakes her head.

"Maybe. She definitely has some sort of delay, but maybe also PTSD."

"Posttraumatic Stress? But she's so little."

"Would you believe she's older than Lizzie? She's a refugee from Afghanistan. Her parents were killed in a car accident just after they arrived here about three months ago, so we don't know how much of her behaviour is delayed development, and how much is stress. The social worker comes once a week, but so far, no one's got close enough to even hazard a diagnosis. She kind of just wanders around."

"She goes to school?"

"Yeah. She's got an assistant in the classroom. We don't know how much she understands."

"Does she speak English?"

"She doesn't speak. But I think she understands some. She comes for dinner and everything."

Lizzie bangs back into the kitchen, followed by a tall girl with wavy blonde hair and a deep frown.

"Gina, meet Beth. She's our new student counsellor," says Maureen.

The girl puts a hand on her hip and glares at me. Her green eyes could cut diamonds. "Whatever," she says and stalks past me to the stairs. "She's here for what—four months?" She doesn't even look back as she runs up the stairs. Sometime later, a door slams. Maureen sighs and tiptoes to the threshold of the living room to watch Rachel.

"Gina's thirteen," Lizzie says. "She'll be in high school next year, so she's not allowed to stay here. She has to go to a youth home."

"Has she been here a long time?" I ask Maureen.

Lizzie prattles on as if I asked her the question. "Two years and three months. She counts it on a calendar in her room. Her parents got a divorce, and then her dad moved to Finland. And then her mom got a new boyfriend, and Gina didn't get along with him. But then her mom married him anyway, and he did bad things to Gina, and—"

"Lizzie!" Maureen says sharply. "If Gina chooses to tell Beth her life story, that's her business. Why don't you stick to talking about yourself, okay?" She moves to the sink and starts stacking plates and cups in the dishwasher with record speed. A pink cup tumbles from her hands, and I brace myself for the shattering glass. Luckily it hits the floor and bounces. Acrylic.

"Fine," Lizzie says grumpily. "She already knows all about me anyway. I'm almost eight. I'm in grade two. I got to miss stupid math class today because I had an appointment with the stupid social worker. But then I got to come home early, so I guess it was worth it. I want a doctor kit for my birthday, but nobody is going to get me that because everybody gets the same thing for their birthday when they live in a group home."

"Yeah? What do you get?" I ask, wondering how this little spit of a thing got to know so much.

"A stupid card with everybody's names on it, and a chocolate bar."

"Do you think maybe you could use another adjective, Liz?" Maureen says.

"What's an adjective?"

Maureen sighs. "Like, 'stupid.'"

"I already told her it was stupid. Weren't you listening?"

I hide a smile. Maureen vigorously wipes down the kitchen table with a pungent cloth. Vinegar?

"How many years have you got a chocolate bar?" I ask.

"Dunno," Lizzie gets up. "But I didn't have my last birthday here, right Moe?"

"That's right. You came in the summer, Liz, remember? And we went to the pool on your first day."

"Oh yeah," Lizzie grins sheepishly. "I almost drowned. Maureen didn't tell me it was the deep end."

"You told me you knew how to swim!" Maureen objects as she grabs a laundry basket from the living room and dumps it on the vinegary kitchen table.

"How could I know how to swim when I'd never been to a pool before? Anyhow, I've been here since last summer. But I was with my mom before that. And in another group home before that. But I'm going home soon. Right, Moe?"

"We'll see, Liz. Want to fold?"

Lizzie shrugs and carefully avoids any underwear as she gingerly picks out a pink top. I grab a set of holey jeans. "Well, Mom has to go to parenting classes for six months, and then she has to promise that when Dad comes out of jail, he's not going to live at home with us, and then I'm allowed to go home. So, that's soon. I won't be here for my next birthday, right? Definitely not."

"Probably not," Maureen agrees, creasing and folding with expert efficiency. She easily manages four items to my one, not even hesitating over the boys' boxers. "Though I figure you could do worse."

"Yeah, maybe," says Lizzie. "But I could sure do better than a chocolate bar too!"

"Hey!" Maureen jumps up, throwing the last set of shorts into the basket. Lizzie squeals and dashes up the stairs. "I already have your chocolate bar picked out!" Maureen runs after her, stopping to scoop up the laundry basket on her way. "It's the smallest one I could find. It's DIABETIC too!"

With all the noise, I don't hear the front door open. But when I look up, a boy, who's probably around ten, stands in the kitchen watching me. His skin is the colour of a Tootsie Roll, and the neat braids of cornrows in his hair stop abruptly at the edge of his scalp.

"Who're you?" he says in a voice that's too low and deep for his age.

"Beth Sarandon. I'm new."

"Yeah? What happened to d'old girl?"

"Who, Maureen?"

He nods.

"She's still around. Upstairs. You live here?"

"Maybe." A tiny smile plays around his full pink lips.

"What's your name?"

He shrugs, "Depends." He walks slowly past me toward the sagging stairs.

"Fine with me," I reply mildly, "if you want to name yourself after adult diapers."

"Say what?" he turns around and frowns. Suddenly, he laughs, showing a wide mouth full of perfect white teeth. His deep brown eyes crinkle at the sides. I can't help but grin back—the effect of his smile is amazing. He looks sideways at me. "My name's B.N.E."

"As in 'Break & Enter?'"

He laughs again. "Nah. As in Brian Nicholas Emerson."

"Pleasure," I say, extending my hand. He makes a fist instead, knocking his knuckles against mine.

"You're one weird dude," he mutters, amusement still hanging around his eyes. "How long you here for?"

I pick up a magazine and leaf through it, giving him a sideways smile. "Depends."

Chapter 5

I started at F.U. this week. It's enormous. It took me half an hour to find the Psychology building, then I got lost again looking for a coffee. My intro class is Existential Psychology, and there's another girl there from the bridge programme—she goes to an arts school across town that I've never heard of. Not the same school as you. I kind of like her, at least enough to sit next to and chat with every once in a while: she's not blonde, she doesn't wear pink track suits, and she can form a coherent sentence. Plus she's a victim of the stupid guidance/support programme too. We had a lot to discuss the other day while we waited for someone to unlock the door to our classroom. Her name is Juliana.

Wish you were here, Jacks. Miss you like hell.

Love, Beth

Today Juliana wears a frilly patchwork skirt, a too-tight tank showing more than an ample amount of her generous chest, and a crocheted hat. Tiny gold bangles band both her arms from wrist to elbow. I have a pretty good idea what those are hiding. She wears neither a sweater nor a coat despite the accumulation of January snow on the ground. *Maybe she lives on campus somewhere.*

35

We take our seats at the back of the room where we can avoid Professor Mirtica, whose presence intimidates even the most intelligent students. I ease my books open and poise my pen, trying to act like a normal university student.

"Have you been to the shrink yet?" Juliana asks. I shake my head. Still haven't called her back. I have a wild hope that my file will fall through the cracks, and Dr. Sullivan will forget about me.

"It's not so bad," Juliana says. "Kind of like therapy, but free."

Juliana's actually been in therapy—a lot. Her arts school schedules a block of time for students' "Personal Issues." What a farce. If everyone knew I had enough Personal Issues to fill a time block, I'd kill myself. That's another one of Heather's rules: *Don't ever give anyone power.*

Problems are secrets, and secrets give power to others, which is why we keep them to ourselves.

Juliana must be smart, though, to get into this programme despite all her curricular counselling.

"What did your shrink say?" I ask.

"Well, he said that because I was in real therapy, I didn't have to go to the support programme. This is good, because I don't have time for both, and I need my happy pills." She grins.

I grin back, but shake my head. The occasional Ativan is as far as I go. "Who started you on that anyway?"

"Two shrinks ago," she says. "He didn't even have to prescribe it. He could've just split his stash with me!"

I smirk.

Juliana pokes me as the professor walks in. An instantaneous hush falls over the class—impressive. Dr. Mirtica exudes an understated authority that makes her seem older than she looks. But then again, Native women rarely show their age as much as white women do. On T.V., I've seen some Nation leaders in their sixties who still have raven hair to their waists. I don't know if Dr. Mirtica belongs to a band, but I do know she's involved with the First Nation Student/Elder programme at the university. It's cool to see the Elders walking around campus. Some of them wear traditional clothing; some even bring dogs. There's just something about that whole Grandfather-in-buffalo-skin advising the punk-rock-tattooed-Youth-with-an-iPod-in-his-ears that makes me wish I had an Elder.

The professor's face is delicate and precise, like the rest of her. She walks into the room quickly and sets down her notes. I can't help but stare as she glides around the lecture space, gathering her supplies into neat piles. No expression crosses her face, even when she speaks.

"Check out the boots," Juliana breathes. Knee-high, black leather.

"Wow," I whisper.

As usual, she's impeccably dressed. Her clothes never show an unwelcome crease or spot or run. Short black skirt, black sleeveless top, silk scarf.

Juliana shakes her head. "Isn't she beautiful?"

I just nod.

"What does it mean 'to be'?" Professor Mirtica's voice is so low that she almost whispers, and yet everyone is listening. I smile. That's her strategy—whisper so people have to lean forward to hear. Don't try to control them out there; draw them into you.

She glances up at me. Her face may be expressionless, but her eyes flicker with secret fire. I consider whether I'd want to see what's hidden in the depths of her clear dark gaze, but before I can decide, her eyes flick away.

Thursday evening brings my second shift at Beverly. My co-op placements mirror Maureen's schedule, which means that in addition to Thursday nights, I also get Saturday morning co-op hours. Joyful. But at least I have a placement.

The house is eerily quiet as I make my way up the creaky front steps.

"Hello!" I call.

"Just wait in the kitchen." Maureen calls from upstairs. Raised voices echo down the staircase and something slams. Furniture? Doors?

I step down the hall and into the kitchen, and see Kenny and Lizzie sitting at the table in uncharacteristic silence.

"Hi," I whisper, because it seems like the right thing to do.

Lizzie frowns, but gives a little wave. Kenny blows quiet bubbles into his chocolate milk and avoids my eyes. In the next room, Rachel flakes out in front of a Disney movie turned down low.

"What's going on?"

"Monica's in trouble," Lizzie says. "She stayed out overnight, and that means she goes back down to zero."

"Zero?"

"It means she can't stay here with me anymore," Kenny blurts out. His nose is red and his fists are curled up against the tabletop.

The front door bangs and Gina hurries into the kitchen. She catches sight of Lizzie and Kenny sitting at the table and stops cold. "What?"

"Monica's back to zero," says Kenny miserably.

Gina sinks down into the head chair, which is the only upholstered piece of furniture in the kitchen. Dark corduroy—probably hiding years of stains—covers its cracked wooden frame. "Shit," she mutters. "Sorry Ken. I told her not to leave last night, but she really wanted to go to that party with Dex. She snuck out and wasn't back this morning when I woke up."

"It's not your fault," Kenny says, his eyes downcast. "She should know better."

"Explain zero." I say.

They all look over like they've just remembered I'm there.

"It's like back to basics," Gina says, forgetting for a second to be hostile. "Most of the kids here come from a behaviour programme. We move up a level for every milestone we pass. Like, I started out at a detention centre for substance abuse. Then I got moved to a treatment home where the other girls were in a programme too. Then I got moved here, to a residential home. But if I ran away or did drugs or drank, then I'd be moved back down to zero, and I'd have to go back to the detention centre."

"And who would send you there?"

"Moe. She's the head counsellor."

"Right," I reply, trying to hide my amazement that a thirteen-year-old could already have been in a detention centre for drug use.

The slamming noise sounds again upstairs, and Lizzie shrinks into the wall.

"Want to go out on the porch?" I ask.

She considers for a second.

"Maybe I can find a popsicle in the freezer?"

She nods, and I take her out the front door with a purple popsicle in tow. She slumps onto the bottom step—painted mud-red with an industrial plastic paint that's chipping heavily at the sides. The wind chill makes it feel like −10 out here, but she doesn't seem to notice, despite her thin blue coat. I split the popsicle against the stair and hand her half.

I hold mine up and say "cheers." She looks at me for a second, then bangs her half against mine, smiling for the first time.

"So, any chance Monica won't have to go?" I ask. Even though Lizzie's the youngest, she seems to know how most things work here.

She sucks her popsicle for a moment. "First time?" she says, more to herself than to me. "Maybe she'll get a second chance. But she'll definitely be grounded. And if she drank beer or something, or smoked, there's like, 'no room for negotiations.' It's just that Kenny really needs her."

"It's nice that they're together at least."

"Yeah. I wish my big sister was here with me."

"You've got a big sister?"

"Yeah. Her name is Meggi. Well, really it's Marguerite, but she doesn't like that. She's fifteen. But she's in the same detention centre as Gina was. She's not allowed to go home though."

"Because of her behaviour?"

"Uh-huh. She does meth. And she drinks vodka. And she gets into lots of fights at school. Once another girl broke her wrist, and she bit the other girl's thigh so bad that the other girl almost died because she lost all her blood, and she was in the hospital for a week."

"Wow."

"Yeah. She's not very nice sometimes, but I still want her here instead of in the detention centre."

"Well, maybe one day she'll move up some levels and be allowed to come," I say.

"Maybe," Lizzie says doubtfully. "C'mon, let's go inside. Maybe Moe decided about Monica. "

We go into the kitchen where Gina has moved to the bench across from Kenny. Lizzie crawls up beside him and reaches for the chocolate milk, trying to pour herself a glass with her clumsy little hands.

Gina grabs the handle. "Let me help you before you spill it all over the place." Lizzie makes a grumbling noise but allows the older girl to help her. The only place left to sit is the grimy corduroy chair. I know in the split second before my butt hits the upholstery that something is wrong. Kenny and Gina both glance my way, hiding shocked smiles. A warm liquid seeps into my skirt, and I jump up with a gasp.

"What the hell was that?" I splutter.

Maureen tromps into the kitchen, her gaze zeroing in on the large wet patch spreading across the back of my skirt. Kenny and Gina both duck their heads as Maureen immediately sizes up the situation. "Bathroom's down the hall. Got a change of clothes?"

I can't even speak—I barely manage to shake my head.

"Gina will lend you something," Maureen says pointedly. Gina avoids my eyes as she bolts upstairs.

I step into the bathroom and lock the door, then peel out of my skirt and underwear, and gingerly bring them to my nose. Urine. *Those little bastards peed on that chair, and I sat in it!*

Trying not to gag, I saturate a facecloth in warm soap and water, and scrub my skin until it tingles. Christ on a bike! It's the most disgusting thing I can imagine. *Who the hell does that to someone?* The water is barely tepid, and the cold on my butt makes me shiver. A shower would be the best solution, but I'm not about to get naked *here. I'll take whatever clothes that little shit Gina brings me, put them on, and get the hell out of this place.* Catching communicable diseases from sitting in someone else's piss is not worth a high-school credit. *McFarter will just have to find me another placement!*

Someone taps on the door, and I open it a crack. Gina holds out a pair of jeans and a set of silk pyjama shorts that look like women's boxers. I expected her to be smug—even laughing—but her face is completely straight. "The boxers are brand new—"

I grab the clothes and shut the door in her face.

It's been years since I've worn jeans, or any sort of androgynous clothing, in public. That summer, Jackie and I spent ten weeks in cut-off shorts and messy ponytails; and it became clear that nothing would be the same again....

I pull on the clothes. Hazing sure has changed a lot since the days of the Sound of Music. Freulein Maria got a pinecone on her chair. As I recall, she covered for the little wretches and punished them with guilt. I get disease-ridden urine soaking into my clothes. And somehow, I don't think guilt is going to work on this lot.

In the kitchen, the corduroy chair has been removed, and the kids slouch around the table. "They're not copping to it." Maureen glares at the two offenders as I hover in the doorway. Kenny swallows hard and looks at Gina, who is staring straight ahead, face blank. "I'll have to ask the others tonight, and if no one confesses, this whole house is going to be on restriction. Of course, at least one of the residents is already on her last chance."

The threat is clear: if Monica hasn't been demoted to zero yet, then this latest offence, paid for by the whole house, will put her there. Lizzie shakes her head and rolls her eyes, but she doesn't speak up—even though she knows they're guilty as well as I do.

"I'll get you a plastic bag for your clothes," Gina gets up from the table and rummages through a cupboard. I lead her into the bathroom, one part of me wanting to smack her, and the other part curious about why she isn't gloating. I don't have to wait long to find out. "Listen," she whispers, "I'm sorry. I only wanted to cheer Kenny up. He was so upset about Monica, and you know, since he's a boy and all, he likes fart jokes and pee...."

Oh. Is that what cheers up young boys? I force myself to concentrate on the crime. "Where the hell did you learn something so disgusting?" I snap, but I've lost some of my venom.

She shrugs sullenly, and crosses her arms over her chest. Suddenly, I realise I'm looming over her, a good six inches taller. Her attitude makes her seem bigger than she is, but she's tiny. Frizzy blonde hair she hasn't learned to straighten, soft eyes looking somewhere in the vicinity of my shoes—she's barely even a teenager. Her chin juts out defiantly, and the unbelievable content of her life hits me once again. She could have seen the pee prank in any number of places.

"Gina," I say, softening a little. "Where?"

"At my other foster home, the behaviour one, the other girls told me about a trick they'd played on their counsellor, who was driving them to an appointment. When she went inside, the girls took turns peeing on the driver's seat. And then she came and sat in it, and she didn't even notice right away." Gina bites her lip, as if stifling a smile, and I shake my head. If it hadn't happened to me, it might have been funny. A *little* funny.

She frowns. "I didn't think about how gross it would actually be. I just thought it would make Kenny laugh."

"Did it?"

She nods, a smile creeping to the corners of her mouth. "Yeah, while he was peeing on it. And then after you sat down—but only for a sec. Then he realised your skirt was really nice, and that he'd probably ruined it, and hurt your feelings. Also, that he could get in big trouble."

"He probably doesn't care about that so much, especially if Monica is back to zero. Maybe he wants to go with her."

Gina shakes her head. "No one wants to go back to zero. But...."

"What?"

"Well. I have one warning already. And Maureen knows Kenny didn't think this up by himself."

"So you're on the brink too?"

"Sort of."

Something about her frankness makes me want to relent, to give her—and this placement—a second chance. These kids probably don't get a lot of those. Besides, starting over at this stage in the semester is going to be tricky. This one seems to be the bottom of the barrel as it is....

"Well is this it?" I demand. "Or are you planning some sort of hazing ritual for after dinner?"

"No," she says. "There's nothing else."

"Fine." I stare straight into her clear blue eyes. "I'll tell Maureen that I have a bladder control issue and that my Depends leaked." *How many times are adult diapers going to come up during this placement?*

Gina snorts, then clamps her hand over her mouth. "Sorry," she whispers.

"But this will never happen again. Got it?"

She nods.

"Because I plan to stick around. And I'm going to be cooking your food starting next week...."

And then, just to horrify her a little, I hork a wad of phlegm into the sink.

Her eyes widen.

"Just remember that I make the *best* milkshakes."

Chapter 6

Jackie used to say that we're all useless at something, but we spend so much time pointing out other people's faults that we don't bother to make ourselves change. We don't want to notice the fact that we're lousy drivers, or have terrible English or barbaric table manners, so we point at other people instead. Jackie never did that. Well, sometimes she laughed at me, but always in a way that made it clear that she was on my side.

"What do you mean you've never been to a party 'like that'?" she asked.

"Heather doesn't let me go to parties," I said, smiling wanly. I could admit things like that to her.

We'd sprawled out on the old swim dock at the southernmost part of camp. Most campers used the new dock with a slide and diving board that had been built a few years ago, so only the staff used this one—and usually only at night. We had the place to ourselves.

"What, does Heather keep a shackle around your ankle so she can hear when you stagger out the door?"

I smile. "It's a hidden GPS system, actually. Highly sophisticated. It's here, right behind my left ear."

She actually looked!

The sun blazed right above us, closer to the water than ever. We had already tanned to a deep golden brown from our three weeks on docks and in boats, so we no longer bothered with sun screen.

"Shit, I'm sweating," Jackie wiped her forehead with the bottom of her tank top.

"Here," I took one of the clips out of my hair, and motioned for her to turn around. She scooted over on the dock so her back was toward me, and I twisted her dark waves around my finger and wound them into a messy knot at the top of her head. I pushed the clip through the dense bun.

"Thanks," Jackie said, blowing the hair out of her eyes. "So why aren't you allowed to go to parties?"

"I don't know. Maybe Heather doesn't want to be bothered picking me up? Not that she'd even know I'd gone."

"So why don't you just ask?"

"Better to avoid asking her for things. Asking would remind her that I'm there, and I like that she doesn't realise it most of the time."

"So, what do you do?"

"What do you mean what do I do?"

"Like when you want something. Do you just do it and hope she doesn't find out?"

"Sometimes."

"And sometimes you just forget about it?"

"Yeah. If she knows I want something, she'll make me walk on eggshells to get it. Or, she'll let me think I have it, then take it away at the last minute. I don't want anything that badly."

"Shit. That's fucked. She put her arm around me. "You know what? You don't live that far from me. We'll make a plan, start getting you out into the real world."

I grinned, and a nervous shiver stole over me, despite the heat of her hand and the mid-July sun.

Actually, I'd lied. I had wanted some things really badly—mostly when I was a kid. By the time my teenage years rolled around, I'd figured out that what I wanted most was freedom from Heather, and since I couldn't physically get away from her, the next closest thing was mental freedom. Most of the time, I just asked myself: would you rather have thing x, or skip it and not give Heather the chance to take it away? Slapping down Heather's power always won out.

Except once.

Of all the things I could have wanted, don't ask me why *this* was it. I may have mentioned my penchant for melodramatic musicals?

During auditions for a school play, I'd somehow landed the title role in *Annie*. Getting a leading part had never occurred to me when I'd auditioned, and I certainly hadn't counted on the teacher insisting that our parents sign the rehearsal schedule.

I couldn't lie. The commitment was just too extensive to be covered by a string of excuses; Heather would've caught me for sure.

I came home that night, my heart pounding in my chest as I clutched the thick rehearsal folder in my hands. Heather and I hadn't gone through this song and dance for a long time. I made a point of being independent. My mother thought my classmates' parents were strange for throwing money at them—for clothes and CDs and nights out for dinner and movies. I had no use for spending money, she said, because she'd get me anything I needed. Of course, I had stopped asking long ago. Babysitting on the weekends earned me enough money to get most things for myself, but not nearly enough to keep up with my friends. I said no so often that soon, they stopped inviting me out.

I waited until after we'd eaten—my mother picking at her filet mignon, absorbed in something else, as usual. My fork squeaked as I speared a new potato. The meat was too rare—it made my jaw ache. "Elizabeth, please don't chew like a truck driver," Heather said tiredly.

I swallowed my mouthful noiselessly. My mother abhorred common behaviour. Of all Heather's rules, *Be a lady* was the most important. Her comments had become so rote that she was probably unaware she'd said anything at all. She might have said any number of things in the exact same tone. *Do not sit with your legs crossed at the dinner table. Put your napkin on your lap. Stand up straight. Quit tugging at your clothes. Do not clomp through the house like a construction worker. Be delicate. Put on a decent dress. Take your hair down from that ridiculous ponytail and pretend to be a human being!*

I set my knife and fork side by side, and slowly slid the schedule over to Heather. "Mom, could you sign this please?" I tried to speak in a strong voice.

"What is it?"

I held my breath as she picked it up. "I was cast in a play at school."

"A play? Which play?" Was she interested? Incredulous?

45

"*Annie*," I whispered.

"Please don't mumble, Elizabeth."

"*Annie*," I repeated, my voice sharpening.

"*Annie?*"

"Yes."

"Elizabeth, you know you're not permitted to participate in extracurricular activities without permission."

I held my breath. My heart lurched painfully in my chest. If my mother found out that I'd auditioned after school instead of coming straight home, I'd be grounded. It shouldn't have bothered me, considering I'd spent the past three years grounded. But I still hated the feeling of being in a straight jacket. Having to stay in my room, no walks outside, no television. No meals downstairs—the one consolation. Sometimes I wondered if Heather grounded me just so she'd have the supper table to herself. No phone privileges—not that I had anyone to call anymore. Once, I answered the phone while I was grounded. Why? Because it was ringing. It wasn't a friend, though—it was Heather calling to test me. Then she grounded me again for using the phone without permission.

"When did you have time to audition?"

"Auditions were held during lunch."

I'd trained myself to look her right in the eye whenever I lied. But to do that, I needed to prepare the lie ahead of time, and actually sort of believe it myself. All that afternoon, I'd envisioned myself with a brown bag in hand, munching a ham sandwich while rehearsing the script.

She looked the rehearsal schedule over. I couldn't read the look on her face. Amusement? Jealousy? Disbelief? I had stopped being able to tell. When she returned it unsigned, I gritted my teeth and ripped it up into tiny pieces.

The next day, I told my drama teacher that I wouldn't be participating in the play.

She frowned in genuine surprise. "Why not?"

"Because my mother won't sign the form." I felt no compulsion to protect Heather. My loyalty to her had disappeared. I'd learned that telling the truth gave me control over her image in the minds of other people—and I wanted that control.

46

The play went on, and I swallowed my misery as best I could. I watched rehearsals from the balcony at the side of the stage, telling myself how corny—how stupid—it all was. People in ridiculous costumes belting out cheesy songs. Just dumb.

I had almost convinced myself that the play would flop when one of the regular cast members got sick the week before production. When the drama teacher asked me to fill in for her, I nearly said no. But the word wouldn't form on my tongue. My heart leaped into my chest.

"It would only be one rehearsal, Beth. It's not a large part. Do you think your mother would allow you?"

"I—I don't know."

"Do you want me to ask her?"

I shook my head. "No. No thank-you. I'll do it myself."

Another stone-cold silence during dinner. "Mom, Ms. Andrews asked me to understudy for one of the orphans in the play. It opens next week, and the role is small, but it's important. There's only one rehearsal. And the play runs for three nights."

"What was your grade on your Biology test?"

How did she know about these things? Did she log onto the school website daily just to monitor my study schedule? "I don't know yet," I mumbled.

She glared at me. "If you think that by failing Biology and Chemistry that I will allow you to take more music and art classes, then you're sadly mistaken."

Because math and science have got you so far in life?

"If you don't bring that grade up to an A by Christmas, you will drop Dramatic Arts."

Fuck you, I said inside my head. "I know," I said out loud.

Secretly, I think she wanted me to fail. That's why she pushed me so hard. And of course, the more she pushed me, the less I listened. Some kids fantasised about success—of being a prefect, of making a sports team— but I fantasised about failure, of coming home and gloating, "Look, an F! A real, genuine, 'I'm stupid' FAILURE! I tried and I *failed*, and there's nothing you can do that will make it better, because I'm just *that* much of an idiot!" God, what a relief that would have been.

Alas, I did possess some skill in Biology, and just enough pride to loathe falling behind my classmates. The next day, I found out I'd managed an A on that Bio test, and my mother agreed that I could understudy in the play.

"You'll need to get yourself to and from rehearsals," she said, focusing on her palette as she mixed paints. "I don't want anything to do with this."

Fair enough.

I told her a friend would drive me from school, and took the subway home after rehearsal.

On closing night of the play, I ran out of the dressing room, looking for a costume person to help me out of my Fifties garb, and glimpsed Heather in the hallway, a dozen pink roses in her arms. I stared at her for a minute, just out of sight, trying to make sure it was really her. She'd come the night before to see the play. Why was she there again?

"Mom?" I said. She handed me the roses and smiled tentatively. I pushed the whole bouquet to my nose, drinking in their sweet, luscious smell. "They're lovely," I kept my eyes fixed on the blossoms—I didn't want her to see the tears coming unexpectedly to my eyes. "Did you see the play again?" Had she finally realised that I loved Theatre? That I was good at it?

Her words were darts that popped my fragile balloon.

"Of course not. It was long enough the first time."

She walked out the front door and toward the car. I ducked back into the costume closet, blinking back tears.

"Nice flowers," said a cast mate as she dabbed at her face paint with witch hazel.

I handed her one, but kept the rest for myself.

"What the hell?" Jackie sputtered when I finished the story. "Your mother is seriously cracked."

I just shrugged.

"Do you want to go in?" Jackie pointed at the water.

"Sure," I answered, stripping down to my tankini—very nearly a one-piece bathing suit, but saved from total prudishness by a little strip of skin showing at the waist. I was slender enough at fifteen, but would still never wear anything like Jackie's white string bikini that tied at the hips. The tiny triangle swatches barely covered the perfect curves of her breasts. She had "blossomed" over the summer. Healthy camp food, lack of exercise, and lazing in the sun: a perfect recipe for gaining breasts and hips. I looked away before she could catch me staring.

She watched me curiously as we dangled our toes in the water, letting our bodies adjust to its coolness. "Beth," she said with a serious look on her face.

"Yeah?"

"Have you ever been with a guy?"

"Like... kissed a guy? Of course. I go to an academic school, not a monastery!"

"Yeah, I heard about you and Jacob last year at the dock dance, making out until they turned the spotlight on you."

I blushed. How did that story keep getting around?

"I meant, like, *been with* a guy."

I stared at a school of minnows darting under the dock. *Sex? God. Why did everybody always want to talk about that? Why did they assume that if you liked somebody, you were having sex?* Truth be told, I had been with a guy—I had lain there while Jacob took my bra off, fondled me, rubbed on top of me until he'd come all over my underwear. I'd spent half an hour in the bathroom afterward, cleaning off the stickiness and the smell, and ended up stuffing my underwear inside an empty toilet paper roll in the garbage. I hadn't said no. I hadn't even *thought* no. But as much as I thought I wanted it at the time, the next morning I'd woken up hating myself—and hating him for doing that to me.

Jackie must have thought I was embarrassed, so she didn't press me any further.

"What about with a girl?" she asked after a moment. A little smile crept along the corners of her mouth. What would make her think that? Her scanty bikini passed through my mind, her increasingly short shorts.... *Was that on purpose? Did she think I liked that? Did I like that?* I looked up and caught her gaze.

49

I shook my head.

"Never?"

"Never. Have you?"

"Oh, sure," she replied, like it was the most natural thing in the world. Was it actually true, what girls say—all girls learn with girls?

"How... many times?" I asked, trying to mirror her nonchalance.

"A few."

"Like, kissing?"

"Yeah. Kissing. You know, like, everywhere."

"Really." I said it flatly—afraid that if I made it a question, it would come out as shocked. And I didn't want Jackie to think me a prude.

"Yeah, of course. Don't your girlfriends do that?"

I shook my head. "I don't think so."

Jackie laughed and put an arm around my shoulders. "Oh, my poor little innocent Beth," she giggled. When she stood up, the spot where her hand had been felt strangely cold. I put my own hand over it as she dove beautifully—without a ripple—into the bottomless lake.

Chapter 7

I'm jamming my feet into black pumps when the phone rings. "Christ on a bike," I mutter, sprinting back through the hall to the phone. "Hello?"

"May I speak with Beth, please?"

"This is Beth." I hear the impatience in my voice; I should have left for class ten minutes ago.

"Beth, this is Nancy Sullivan calling from the Bloor Street Mental Health Centre. How are you?"

Shit. "Fine thanks."

"Beth, I have a spot opening up next week, which I'd like you to fill if you can make it. It's at ten o'clock on Tuesday. Do you have a class then?"

My mind races to come up with an excuse, but her sentence ends before I've thought of anything. "Uh... no," I stammer. *Fuck! Why has articulation suddenly deserted me? Way to go Dr. Sullivan—catch me off guard. Nice first move.*

"Good," she says. "I'm afraid that I don't work on campus. It involves too much travelling. I have my own practice here on Bloor. I apologize if you were expecting something different."

"Oh, that's okay." I try to picture the cross street.

"Do you think you can find your way here?"

"Probably."

"Great. Okay. I'll see you next Tuesday." *Shit!* I had hoped to avoid this a little longer—altogether, actually.

I hang up the phone and run as fast as I can to the door. Now I'm really late—and, worse, the therapy anvil has dropped. *Fuck The Hole and it's ridiculous mandatory support. Do I look like I need to be supported? Sometimes neurotics* like *to be neurotic, damn it. Sometimes being neurotic is* okay!

Tuesday morning. As I head out the door for my appointment with Dr. Sullivan, I'm anxious about leaving the house in this colossal mess. Four days' worth of dishes sit piled in the sink; clothes spill out of the laundry hamper; the refrigerator contains half a jar of vanilla icing and a bottle of ketchup—not to mention the fact that I haven't done any readings for class—and now I have to waste time going for unnecessary "support."

I review my plan. I'll simply go in, meet with her, and explain that I appreciate the *astronomical and profoundly irritating* effort the school is making to help me adjust to university, but that I'd really be fine without it.

Getting on the subway, I notice the homeless people more than usual, their eyes glassy and faded, or darting about, terrified of things no one else can see. They mumble to themselves or shout belligerently at passersby while nursing grimy bottles. It's pathetic. Most of them are mentally ill. If they'd go to the hospital, they could get treatment. That's what shrinks do: treat the really mentally ill, not mildly neurotic university bridge students who just haven't yet developed the skills to live in the real world!

Nevertheless, I arrive at Bloor Station, anticipating a ten-minute walk to Dr. Sullivan's office. Soon, the sun will start to glare off the high rise windows, and the smell of the dumpsters will give everyone a vaguely green and pinched look as they pass by. But at 9:45 in the morning, the light is still shallow and white. The snow that dusts the twigs of the mature maple trees hasn't yet melted, and people are still caffeine-induced enough not to use their elbows as weapons.

The Bloor St. Mental Health Centre should be nestled somewhere between St. Paul's and Campbell. I almost miss it, expecting a modern building. But no. It's an old Georgian house.

A faded brass plaque by the front door announces Dr. Nancy Sullivan: 105. The corner of the metal is dented, as if someone has taken a very small hammer to it. I imagine little elves with construction tools....

No doorman or Info desk waits in the foyer—nothing that offers any information at all, save for a wall lined with pamphlets on everything from HPV to coping with a schizophrenic parent. The hall splits before me—left or right. I go left.

A stab of anxiety twists my chest, so I press my hands together and compose my face.

This morning I went for the "casually sophisticated" look: dark skirt, brown leather boots, a tight-fitting teal sweater and silver jewellery. I debated over the earrings, but decided that a decorated ear lobe is always preferable and put them on.

I find suite 105 and stop to sprinkle some baby powder on my hands—can't pretend to be calm with clammy hands. They're dry as chalk as I open the door.

The anteroom is empty, but the door to the adjoining office is ajar. *No, a door is a door... a jar is a jar.* Simon and I used to tell each other that joke over and over as kids. I can't see much from my position, but a quiet voice answers when I knock. "Come in."

I recognise it immediately—wry and full of gravelly warmth. I'd better be careful, or I'll start to like this woman. It takes me a moment to find her over by the bay window at the far end of the room, staring out into the front garden. She looks to be in her early fifties; two combs pull back the wide curls of her soft, grey hair. She raises a cup of tea to her lips with an unhurried air that makes me feel I'm interrupting a spiritual meditation. Her smile is serene—amused—as she turns toward me.

Oh, shit! That's a wheelchair!

"You must be Beth. I'm Nancy Sullivan."

I'm trapped. Even standing by the door, civility bars my escape route. My breakout speech—thanks for making time for me, but I feel that other students would benefit more from a place in this programme than I would—dies on my lips. I've come in, disturbed her, and to leave at this point would scream para-phobia. *What if she takes it personally?*

"Come in, Beth," she gestures to a nearby chair. I pick my way carefully over the plush area rug, worried that I'll trip or do some other foolish thing. I stand awkwardly in the middle of the room. *Should I offer her my hand? Maybe she can't shake hands. That would be embarrassing. What the hell? I'd better take a breath or I'll start to look uncomfortable—which would really make me look like an idiot.*

I sit on the edge of the armchair across from her and cross my legs.

"Did you have any trouble finding your way here?" she asks.

"No. It was fine."

"Ah. That's good. Usually we try to meet the students on campus, but I stopped doing that a few years ago."

I would make my clients come to me too if I were in her position.

"So... Beth. Is it Elizabeth? Bethany?"

"Elizabeth."

"Ah. My daughter is Bethany. We call her Beth too."

I smile. She's disarming: spirited but vulnerable. Her eyes dance with intelligence, like she knows the secrets of the universe and finds the rest of humanity amusing.

"So, you're taking courses at the university."

I nod to show that I'm paying attention. She's like a lawyer, asking only the questions she knows the answers to.

"Any idea what you're leaning toward?"

"Not yet. I hope to have a better idea after my first few courses."

She adjusts her sage shawl, lifting it higher on her shoulders. "In my experience, the university bridge programme is very good. Are you enjoying it?"

I meet her peculiar eyes, blue flecked with green. Despite the baby powder, a slick sheen of sweat coats my palms. I feel exposed, stupid....

Whoa. Get a grip. She doesn't deserve special treatment just because she's disabled. Put that exit strategy in place.

"I'm happy to be in it. But I don't understand why I need to see a counsellor just to go to university classes early. If I was a first year student, they wouldn't make me do it, so why is it required for students who fast track?"

"Because of the suicide rate," Dr. Sullivan says matter-of-factly.

Wow.

"Students get into their first year away from home, with no support system, and find they can't take the pressure. I wish more schools would participate, but most won't even offer the bridge programme. You're lucky your school is so involved."

I just smile and nod. *Lucky* is not the word I would have chosen.

She continues, "Rather than drop young students into school on their own, only to have them drop right back out, we support them through the first semester. We help them get acquainted with the school, and with the freedom and independence that university brings."

"I'm already pretty independent, Dr. Sullivan." *On guard,* I remind myself. *Talk to this woman like she's a stranger on the subway. Don't reveal anything.*

"Well, then I guess you'll find university more exciting than scary."

"Yeah, I think so."

She smiles. She could be a lot worse. I stare out the window, and she lets the silence hang. I won't be tricked into filling it. Instead, I watch the intersection—people coming to and from the park on the opposite corner. Carrying coffees and guiding their children onto monkey bars.

Finally, she speaks. "What would you like to talk about, Beth?" She asks this as if offering a menu of entrées. We could contemplate the existence of white holes; compare the relative brilliance of Einstein and Shakespeare; discuss the current government administration, the education and health systems; or "Hey! How 'bout those Leafs?" Why bother talking? She already knows what my problem is.

McFarter and The Vice have undoubtedly put it in their report. They circle me like rabid vultures, waiting to pounce on any morsel of weakness. That time when The Vice caught me on the school roof smoking up, I'd taken off my sweater and stood there in a t-shirt. I never bared my arms in school, obviously, but it was hot, and I thought I was alone. The Vice glanced at the criss-cross tallies from my wrists to my shoulders and swallowed hard. The next day, McFarter asked to see me— did I want to *discuss* anything with him? Since then, they've made it their personal mission to interfere in every possible aspect of my life—*so* charming.

"I sense that you're hesitant to talk to me," Dr. Sullivan says gently. "Is there a reason for that?"

"Reason?" I echo. "No. No reason." *Shit. She thinks the wheelchair is putting me off.* I wish I could tell her it's not, but I'm too damn Canadian to say anything so forthright. *Above all, be polite* is practically a mandate in this country.

"Good," she says. "So, what do you do besides study?"

A long question-answer session begins: where is my co-op placement? Really? That's interesting. Too bad about the hours, but good that I like the work. Do I live with my parents? Oh? Is my father home often? Why not? What do I plan to do when I've finished university? Have I given any thought to my major? What would help me decide? Do I have a boyfriend? What's his name? That's interesting. What about my mother?

The clock on the mantel reads 10:58. She's not keeping proper track. Therapists' hours run fifty minutes, and it's been fifty-eight.

"Time's up," I say.

She looks at her watch. "It is."

I stand, smooth my skirt, and try to figure out how to say goodbye so she knows it's final.

"I'll see you next week," she says. "Tuesday at ten."

I walk home distracted, moving without seeing, not even aware of having boarded the subway. The last thing I expected was to remain the full hour, let alone be forced into another appointment! How did this happen?

Same as the first appointment—surprise tactics.

To be honest, Dr. Sullivan might be right: I probably do need help. But you have to let someone in on your secrets if you want them to help you, and there's no way I'm telling this shrink anything.

Chapter 8

Mike, my boyfriend, functions more as a verbal appendage than a fixture in my life. Adding "my boyfriend and I" to casual conversations helps me appear normal, but in reality, I avoid him as much as possible. Lately, I've brushed him off for an entire week with, "Oh, sorry—paper due," and, "Not tonight, okay? I'm really swamped with my placement," before running out of excuses.

My dad refers to Mike as "flavour of the month." We've actually been dating a lot longer than a month, but if I tell Dad things like that, he starts to fumble awkwardly around conversations.

I met Mike at the 7-Eleven down the road when he grinned at me over the slushie machines. I reasoned that his intense focus on the optimal ratios of orange and green sugar meant that he probably lacked the mental capacity for rape and murder. We chatted. He was a senior at my cousin Kate's school; he hated English and French, but liked Chemistry and Phys. Ed. He was cute, but not too smart—exactly what I was looking for.

Even before I open the door I can sense that he's here. Inside, he's kicked his shoes against the wall by the front hall closet, and the door to my bedroom hangs open. My teeth grit involuntarily.

"Mike?"

"Hey dude," he calls. "What took you so long?"

He's sprawled on my bed.

Mental note: move hide-a-key from leg of barbeque ASAP. I glance at the book lying spine-up across his chest. "Jane Austen?"

"You must really love her." He gestures to a bookshelf full of her work.

"She's a required taste." I kick off my shoes and flop down next to him. "I have to take her for an entire semester."

"Why?"

God, he can be dumb. "For my English requirement? At T.U.? They didn't have Mediaeval Poetry or I would have signed up."

"Uh huh." He puts his arms around me and leans in for a kiss. His dark, feathery hair brushes my forehead.

"You need a haircut."

"You volunteering?"

"If you pay me."

"Thanks. I can hack it off myself for free."

I laugh. His unpredictable humour is what I like about him—if I like him at all. Can you like someone and resent their presence at the same time?

I flop face-first on the bed, like a toddler protesting a nap. His hands warm my shoulders and back as his lips brush my neck and down my arms.

"Don't," I whisper.

"Why not?"

"I have to sleep."

"So sleep."

His lips move across my shoulders and the front of my neck, and he gently turns me over so he can kiss my face. I feel his breath hot against my cheeks, but try to stay relaxed and neutral. No use. Something about his closeness—his smell and taste and the roughness of his fingertips—chafes me.

His hands close over mine, and he kisses my fingers, one by one. I keep my eyes shut, press my face into his chest.

I should want this. I *want* to want this. The pressure of my hips straddling him, his hair slipping through my fingers: breathless and impulsive pleasure.

But I can't.

"Stop," I whisper. "I'm really tired. I have to get some sleep."

"Sleep," he runs his hand down my spine and pulls my leg up over his. "I'm not stopping you."

I can feel him hard against me, still, quiet. I relent, just to keep him guessing. He's brave, this boy. Some days, I'll turn my back on him and stomp out; other days, I'll stay. But no matter what I do, he always comes back.

I run my hand down the small of his back, and he gasps. This is what normal people do, right? The least I can do is turn my mind off and help the Transformation along—will my body to enjoy it.

He slips my shirt off, fingers my bra strap. I run my hands under his sweater, over his arms, around his belt line. He moans, very softly, then pulls his sweater off and throws it beside the bed. He runs his hands over my stomach, kissing me, pulling me toward him. I shiver. I want to let him have his way, but something inside me screams for him to stop. His skin is so warm. Insistent. He rolls on top of me and presses his hips against mine. He wants me to know how much he loves being with me.

Our clothes come off. He opens a condom and puts it on, then leans over me.

The friction of our bodies makes my head swim—and as soon as that happens, the cold ball in my chest starts spreading. He groans, face twisted, lip red between clenched teeth.

I hate him.

With a ferocious gasp, he's still.

He doesn't waste much time—a quick minute to take a breath, then, "let me..." he says, kissing my stomach, his lips moving softly down, down....

I almost let him. Almost. But I can't. I'm afraid it won't feel like it's supposed to. Like it did with her.... I can't risk knowing for sure.

I push him lightly so he rolls over, then hop off the bed and wrap an old throw rug around my body. He sighs and flops down into the pillows.

*You just made
yourself shut down
when other people
tried to wind you up,
like one of those
self-propelling
cars from
McDonald's Happy Meals.*

59

You just brushed them off—
with that
your-insults-make-you-look-stupid
kind of expression—
without ever being mean
or seeming embarrassed.

You liked yourself
enough to
keep to yourself.

But why did you
like me the way you did
when I was never sure...?

I can't describe how much I love waking up early on Saturday mornings to get to my co-op placement—though frankly, I ended up with better work experience than any of my classmates got. They're stuck slinging celery at grocery stores, while I, at least, learn to cook. As promised, the kids haven't pulled any more hazing rituals, and when the others noticed Gina playing nice, they decided to behave too.

Mostly.

Lizzie's standing on a stool, watching me make her birthday breakfast of scrambled eggs, toast and bacon, when Maureen appears from the living room.

"Sleep well?" I ask.

"Not at all," she groans.

She sets the table while I man the stove. Rachel and B.N.E. will sleep in; the others have plans for the morning. They're not about to waste a single second of their precious weekend. Predictably, the bacon brings Gina and Kenny down from upstairs. Lizzie runs to the table to grab the first glass of orange juice as Monica sidles in from the hall. She's been on restriction since her big night out, and part of her programme includes attending meals.

Kenny leaps into his seat with a loud *whoop* and promptly knocks Lizzie's orange juice down her front.

"Aw, Kenny!" she wails. "This is the only clean shirt I have!"

"Sorry, Lizzie," Kenny moans. He mops at the orange juice with a soaked napkin.

"Kenny, come and get a tea towel," I sigh.

"Honestly," Gina yanks open the fridge door, "I think we should start rationing the food *before* it gets to the table. I'm sick of having my breakfast dumped all over the fucking floor!"

"Gina, language," Maureen warns from her post at the end of the table, where a plastic chair has replaced the corduroy one.

Gina rolls her eyes and throws herself onto the bench. "Well, I guess I'd better get something to eat before Kenny decides that all the *freaking* food should follow the *freaking* orange juice!"

"Pass the *freaking* orange juice over here." Lizzie holds out her empty glass. Gina pours her some more, with less of a scowl than usual.

"Happy birthday to me," Lizzie mutters.

Monica brings me the plates, and I dish out the breakfast. There's plenty left on the stove for the late-risers. I squeeze in by the wall next to Monica, who picks at her meal while Kenny shovels in his breakfast noisily and promptly helps himself to more.

"How much can you keep down?" Maureen whispers.

Monica shakes her head, half wary, half defiant. "I don't know."

"How have you been doing lately?"

She looks away.

"Okay." Maureen pulls her plate away. "Half a piece of bacon, half a piece of toast, and three tablespoons of egg. Is that okay?"

"No bacon," Monica says firmly.

"How come?"

"Because," she says, fixing Maureen with a look that clearly indicates she's an idiot, "there's like 300 calories in every piece."

"Fine." The bargain is struck. Maureen partitions the plate and hands it back.

As soon as everyone has finished eating, Maureen leans over to Lizzie. "Hey Liz, I have something for you." She takes out a long triangular object from under the table.

Lizzie smiles cautiously. "Is that my birthday present?"

Maureen passes it over, and Lizzie grabs it with two small hands. Slowly, she tears the wrapping paper. It's a 750-gramme Toblerone.

"Holy geez," Lizzie whispers. "It's almost as big as me."

"And it's not diabetic either," Maureen grins.

"Thanks, Moe." Lizzie's still smiling, but behind the prism of chocolate, a tiny cloud of disappointment darkens her eyes. Maybe she hoped that Maureen would bend the rule just a little for her birthday—possibly into something made of black pleather with a stethoscope inside.

The kids present Lizzie with a giant card that they made themselves. As I help her sound out the messages, she catches sight of a plastic grocery bag in my lap. "Is there something in there?" she asks, biting her lip.

I smile. "Yes, but it's to borrow not to keep." Maureen hides a smile. Favouritism, in any way, would create problems, so I know not to bring an outright gift. But Lizzie is the youngest. And it's her birthday. And she deserves not to be disappointed.

"It used to be mine, but I don't need it anymore, and I thought you might like to use it until you're old enough to pass it onto someone else." Lizzie tears open the grocery bag and yelps in delight.

"It's a doctor kit! Look, Moe! It's got a real stethoscope! Here, Beth... can I listen to your heart? C'mon. Come closer. No. Sit still!"

"I am sitting still," I protest as the plastic disc scrapes across my sweater. "My heart's on the other side, Liz."

"Oh," Lizzie grins sheepishly and readjusts. "Sorry. Oh there! I can hear it! That's so cool! Thanks Beth. Is it really yours?

"Yeah, why?"

"Well, I figure you wouldn't snot on it like someone else might. Right Kenny?"

"Lizzie," says Maureen.

Kenny sticks out his tongue. "Better watch out. Or I'll cram that thing full of boogers!"

"No you won't!" shrills Lizzie, and she scampers upstairs with the medical bag stuffed up the front of her shirt.

After breakfast, Monica and I clean up the kitchen and head into the television room to "hang out." We use this term for the hour we spend together after meal time. She stands quietly, looking a little green. Her stomach struggles with digesting food— it has skipped that process for some months now.

"Monica, how are you doing?"

"I feel disgusting," she snaps.

"You're looking good," I reply. She rolls her eyes, but chooses to sit on the couch with me instead of the chair on the other side of the room.

"*Beaches* or *Steel Magnolias*?"

"I don't care. *Beaches*, I guess."

Beaches always reminds me of myself and Jackie. Best friends— connected at the heart, the head and the soul. When C.C. and Hil fight over the makeup counter, my gut twists every time. One conversation can change everything. One fight. One wrong line can ruin a friendship forever. I hate that part. It's almost as bad as the ending, which, thankfully, we never get to. In fact, if I didn't know we'd switch off the video long before Bette Midler started belting out that horrendous "Wind Beneath My Wings" ballad, I'd probably throw the DVD player off the roof.

Chapter 9

Tuesday morning at Dr. Sullivan's office. For the briefest moment, I considered killing myself to get out of this appointment. That'd really throw her for a loop. Bet she'd never see that coming.

"So, Beth, how did you sleep last night?"

"Like a corpse." Her eyebrows lift slightly.

We've resumed our positions in the alcove, our chairs at opposite ends of the V. We stare out the window, watching the rain seep into the new-sprung grass, like we have for the past five weeks. She waits for me to say something meaningful, and I refuse to say anything at all. I'm just marking time. They can make me come, but they can't make me talk.

The drizzling rain has made my hair curl—which I hate. It's also made my mascara run. All in all, I look less than my best, which puts me in a dark mood.

For a long time, Nancy says nothing, simply watching the park over the road. A couple of dykes walk down the grey pavement hand-in-hand. One is heavier than the other, but both have short, spiked hair and round, masculine faces. Heat creeps into my cheeks as people stare at them, and I hide my tightly balled fists in my lap. A teenage boy does a full-out double take and cat-calls something. I can only guess what it is.

With one hand enclosed in the other, I flip him the bird. But the heavier woman flashes him a wide smile. It transforms her face, making her instantly attractive—a smile makes any woman feminine, whether she likes it or not.

In a second, she gathers the teenager in her arms, hugging him hard.

Only then do I notice his blonde dreadlocks, his rainbow running shoes.

Nancy watches me curiously. I know I'm blushing and swallow hard. *Why do I always assume the worst? What would I do if someone screamed insults at me on the street?* They never would, because they'd never know. *Mental note: pick up a hair straightener tonight.* Nothing says *girl* like long straight hair—flattened, and glossed into submission.

"Beth, tell me why you don't need support," Nancy says suddenly. *Support.* In all our sessions, she carefully avoids the word *therapy.*

I smile frigidly. "Because I don't, Nancy."

"Your co-op placement is going well?"

"Just fine."

"Beth, normally people who enjoy working with troubled youth, as you do, are experiencing a great deal of pain themselves."

I didn't really have a choice in my placement—though I suppose I could have refused it. But in any case....

"What does that say about you?" I say.

She shakes her head but doesn't look away. Any other therapist would have followed up with, "So why are you here?" But she remains silent. We both know that's a ridiculous question. If the school didn't require me to come, I'd be out the door and down to the mall by now.

"Are you creative?" she asks.

I shrug. "I suppose so."

"In what way?"

"Poetry, mostly."

She nods, but doesn't seem surprised. "Are you any good?"

Am I any good? I've never really thought about it. I don't do it to be good. It drives me—I have to accomplish something tangible every day to prove that I've been here.

"No," I say neutrally. "Not really."

Her breath catches, and her delicate fingers grip the armrest on her wheelchair. She closes her eyes, bites her lip.

"Nancy?"

Tears seep from the corners of her eyes. My stomach clenches. This isn't the way things are supposed to go; she's supposed to be the one helping me. Her arm flies out, like an errant missile, and rattles a glass on the windowsill. *What the hell?* I steady the glass with my finger, afraid to touch her. I pull a tissue from one of the many boxes scattered around the room, and sit back down gingerly, hardly daring to move the air around her.

She swallows; her breathing deepens and her eyes open. I hand her the tissue, and she blots her cheeks, still biting her lip.

"What do you see? Outside?" she asks finally. Her voice is quiet, but carries a slight edge.

I follow her gaze to the park across the road, the Second Cup on the corner, the pedestrians moving across the sidewalk. This isn't Hollywood's New York. Rather than a wash of black umbrellas, the city pops with domes of red, blue, yellow, purple-stripes, plaid and even beige—all frumpy, eclectic and vaguely Bohemian.

"I see the real world, Nancy. But it doesn't seem real to me."

"How does it seem?"

"It seems like an illusion that nobody notices."

Existential Psychology and appointments with Nancy both fall on Tuesdays, which means I can kill two dress-up marathons with one high-heel. I will never go to Nancy's office dressed in anything less than a perfect outfit, and the same holds true for Ex-Psych. Pyjamas would do for my Jane Austen class, but I must look flawless for Professor Mirtica. I can't explain why. Maybe Nancy could—if I told her.

I hurry up the ramp to the Psychology building, the tails of my knee-length navy coat slapping rhythmically against my legs. I hate walking in after class has already begun, enduring people's stares as the heavy door clunks shut behind me, tiptoeing past the professor as I find a squeaky chair and sit down. Usually if I'm late—even two minutes late—I skip the class. Unfortunately, an assignment is due today.

Juliana saved me a seat. Good.

"What did I miss?" I whisper, pulling out my notebook.

"Well, we strayed a bit off topic at the beginning, talking about synchronicity."

"Jung's theory?"

"Yeah. Did you read ahead?"

"Sort of. I actually read another book on it before."

"Smart ass. Knew there was a reason we got along."

I smile slightly. "So what did she have to say about it?"

"Long and short: meaningful coincidences exist. Most people ignore them. If you want a better life, assume the meaning behind the coincidence will become clear once you start searching."

"Great. Pretty much what the other book said."

"And now we're back to discussing death... again."

I grin. "Shocking."

"You haven't missed much yet," Juliana says, sliding her notebook over. She's already filled in one full page. In any other class, that would be half the lecture material. In Professor Mirtica's class, it's five minutes' worth.

"I'll copy it when Mr. Red Baseball Cap starts talking."

Juliana rolls her eyes. Mr. Red Baseball Cap sits at the front of the class and interrupts the professor about twice a lecture. He irritates me, but he's also deliciously brazen. I can't imagine cutting off Professor Mirtica to say the ridiculous things he does, especially when she shoots him down *every single time*.

"Oh, there he goes," Juliana says. I shake my head and copy out her notes while he drones on. Professor Mirtica nods, listening carefully to his point. She never cuts him off, never tells him he's interrupting, being rude or wasting valuable time. She invariably hears him out, and then, only when his spiel has come to an end, tells him why he's wrong. He's almost at the end... *Okay, Mr. Red Baseball Cap, here it comes*. With three clipped sentences, she deflates his point, and drives on.

"Subjective truth," she returns to the lecture, "is the only relevant reality that exists, according to Kierkegaard. We discover the truth through our subjective understanding of the world. Subjectively, we can find meaning in our lives. Even our suffering has value, because we believe it can. We assign significance to our pain. We ascribe meaning to our 'projects.' But our lives have no objective meaning, don't they? There is no path which we all follow for a purpose we all understand.

Objectively, reality seems rather bleak, doesn't it? We are born, we suffer and we die. Why? For what purpose do we do this?"

I look at Juliana. "Nice topic," she mutters. "No wonder the Existentialists were all so bloody depressed." Professor Mirtica glances up at us, and pauses for a moment. Something like amusement creases the corners of her perfectly painted lips.

"Camus discusses objective reality in relation to life itself. Reality means living in the present moment, not thinking about the 'bigger picture.' Is it possible that an objective reality exists that we, because of our limited capacity as human beings, cannot understand?" She scans the room, looking each student in the eyes. "Yes—if we believe in a reality that transcends human life. But we don't know that. We can only understand our current reality."

We've all leaned forward slightly to hear her. Nobody moves as her voice gets lower because the slightest squeak booms through the hall like a hammer against metal. *Are people engrossed in what she's saying, or simply in her?* I don't know which fascinates me more—the idea of life after death or Professor Mirtica herself.

"How can people enjoy life knowing that their existence may come to any number of unceremonious ends? Why live at all? If life is a futile exercise without meaning, full of pain and misery and struggle, all of which eventually culminates in one's *inevitable death*, why bother?"

"But there's more to life." Mr. Red Baseball Cap raises his hand. I hold my breath.

Professor Mirtica tilts her head. "Really? What else is there?"

"The good stuff, obviously. Like joy. Yeah, there's the crap, but the good stuff makes it worth it, you know?"

Professor Mirtica nods slightly. I try to concentrate on Mr. Red Baseball Cap's point, but the professor's deep crimson lipstick draws my attention. Her mouth traces lines in the air like blood. How does she get away with that? If I wore that colour, I'd look like a vampire fresh from a kill. She is an artistic statement.

"Joy," she says, turning back to the class. "Does joy make the struggles worthwhile? Does joy justify unbearable pain? Does joy validate a futile existence?"

"Why is existence futile?" Mr. Red Baseball Cap says.

"*Why* is existence futile?" Her eyes flash. That didn't seem like a rhetorical question—she actually wants an answer.

He looks at his notebook and shrugs.

I speak without realizing it. "Existence is only futile if you believe it's ultimately physical." My cheeks burn as everyone glances in my direction, but I swallow and go on. "Objectively, lives are futile because everything you do, all of your projects and accomplishments, become meaningless when you die. Life is meaningless if you believe existence ends in death. That's why people believe in a Transforma— transcendence." I catch myself. "An afterlife."

She stares at me for a minute, nodding slowly, and then the Mr. Red Baseball Cap turns around. "But your life might have meaning for other people. When you die, the work you've done might mean something to your family."

"It might," Professor Mirtica says. "But what do the projects of the human race mean as a whole? Why are they worth completing? What is the purpose of human life as it stands? Yes, we complete projects to please ourselves and our societies, but why do these have value? *Do* they have value? Why do people spend a great deal of time investing in 'immortality'? Because they don't want to disappear when they die. People hide from the futility of life long before they recognise what they're doing—if they ever recognise it." Her voice lowers once more, until she seems to be speaking directly to her one, crestfallen listener. "And it's amazing how quickly one's family can move on."

"So life is futile because we don't know if our life's work has any meaning after we die?" Mr. Red Baseball Cap's voice has dropped, along with his eyes.

Professor Mirtica hesitates. She looks almost sorry for him— sorry, and somewhat surprised that she has to be the one to tell him. "Death eventually annuls everything you do in life, James," she says, laying a hand on his shoulder. "And so, objectively, life is futile. Is it not?"

Chapter 10

What do you wear when you don't know what to expect? I stand for several minutes in my silk black skivvies, staring at the clothes rumpled on the closet floor. Skivvies—Jackie's favourite word. She used to wander around in brazen, wild underwear all the time, and the sets always matched. She had Monet-printed lingerie, a set with tiger stripes and one with an elephant trunk smack in the middle of the crotch, its ears making up the cups of the bra. Wild underwear made people powerful, she said. Underneath your clothes, no one knew who you really were.

I've never bought lingerie-as-art, mostly preferring black silk, although I do wish Jackie had taken me lingerie shopping with her—just once. Maybe crazy underwear would make me feel more brazen on the inside too. Probably not. Crazy underwear doesn't make you brave; more likely, brave people wear crazy underwear. I'm an ordered person, so I wear ordered underwear. Matching. Sexy. Plain.

Some old jeans, left over from camp, must be hiding in here somewhere. Yes! I find a ball of denim stuffed into the back of the closet. I pull them on, worried they'll be too small now. They're too big. I check the tag to make sure they're really mine.

I usually hide the scale—better not to know. But today, I yank it out from under the bathroom sink and hop on. *Wow. When did that happen?* I stand to the side and check the tag. Size six, and the ass sags. I cup my breasts and squeeze. Are they smaller too? My stomach is flat—way flatter than during the summer of the tankini. And my face is hollowed. Electric tallies in varying shades of red cover the insides of my wrists, forearms and thighs.

This is why I never look.

My reflection stares back at me the same way it does in Nancy's window—transparent, muted and fleeting. Moving without thought, as when I wash my hands or put the coffeemaker on, I take down the alcohol and razor. *You'd better watch it, or you'll start doing this in your sleep.*

The blood swirls into the water, and my stomach unclenches.

Usually I stop thinking about Nancy as soon as we say goodbye, but tonight the image of her crumpled face stays with me. Her naked weakness embarrasses me, and I have to cut deeper than usual to bring order to the chaos in my head.

"Beth!" Lizzie calls frantically as the screen door squeals shut behind me.

"Yes?"

"Moe says I need to have a bath! I am not having a bath!" She catapults down the stairs just as I swing through the door to the kitchen.

"When did you last have a bath?" I ask, taking pity on her horrified expression.

"I don't know!"

"It was FOUR DAYS AGO!" Maureen follows Lizzie down the stairs. "She needs one tonight, and that's it."

"No!" Lizzie screams as she runs into the front hall. "I don't need one! I am NOT DIRTY!"

"Why all the fuss?" I ask Maureen as she collapses onto the couch.

"All the other staff have given up trying to give her a bath. She carries on so much that they just let it go. But it's not helping her any. It might be fine now when she's just little, but it won't be later."

"Why is she so against the bath?"

"Hates having her face wet." Maureen shakes her head. "I don't know what they used to do to her in the bathtub, but she's terrified. She throws up every time—won't let anyone in to help, and if you run the bath and insist she gets in, she sits on the edge of the tub and splashes instead. And she won't go in without a bathing suit.

"Geez." I try to imagine the sarcastic little goof genuinely afraid of something.

"I don't know what to do," Maureen sighs. "I've tried everything—coaxing, bribing, threatening. I've even gone out and bought a child's shower hose—that made things worse. She has an absolute cow every time. And of course, I can't just pick her up and throw her in."

"Do you want me to give it a shot?"

"Please, go right ahead. I will kiss your feet and crown you bath queen if that child takes a bath. I will even make supper *and* clean up, *and* serve you dinner on the living room couch."

"Wow, deal," I smile. "I shall do my best do deserve such a reward. Lizzie!" I call into the front hall, "come on back here."

"No!" she shouts, her voice muffled and distant. I swing into the hall and look around. The closet door is shut tight. "C'mon, please," I call through the keyhole. "We're going upstairs to have a chat."

"I'm not having a bath."

"Did I say bath?"

She considers for a minute. "No."

"Would I force you to do something you don't like?"

"No."

"Well then, c'mon."

Slowly, the doorknob turns, and a tear-streaked, grubby, just-eight-year-old falls into my arms. "Lizzie," I say, rubbing her back. "Why are you so afraid?"

"I... I... hate... hate... the bath," she hiccups.

"But you don't hate the pool." She shakes her head. "So why the bath?"

She juts out her chin and looks away. "I'm not having a bath."

Wow. Maybe I should have taken the dinner/ clean-up shift.

"I'll make you a deal," I tell her.

She looks up. "What is it?"

"You come upstairs with me, and I will teach you a new silly song."

"Is a bath part of the deal?"

"Not for you. But you do have to sit on the edge of the tub while I bathe my stinky black socks."

She squints for second, thinking, then follows me down the hall.

As we climb the stairs, I start singing. "BLACK SOCKS, THEY NEVER GET DIRTY! THE LONGER YOU WEAR THEM, THE STRONGER THEY GET. SOMETIMES, I THINK I SHOULD WASH THEM, BUT SOMETHING INSIDE ME SAYS 'NO, NO, NOT YET!' NOT YET! NOT YET! NOT YET! NOT YET!"

"Sing it again," Lizzie giggles.

"BLACK SOCKS, THEY NEVER GET DIRTY! THE LONGER YOU WEAR THEM, THE STRONGER THEY GET. SOMETIMES, I THINK I SHOULD WASH THEM, BUT SOMETHING INSIDE ME SAYS 'NO, NO, NOT YET!' NOT YET! NOT YET! NOT YET! NOT YET!"

We turn into the bathroom. "It is time to wash these gross, disgusting socks," I say seriously. "I can smell them inside my shoes. Can you run me a bath?"

"I'm not getting in."

"I should hope not. With my revolting socks, who would want to?"

Lizzie plugs the drain, and I help her turn on the taps. We test the water as it churns in. "That's nice. Oooh, my socks are going to like that," I say. "Maybe we should add some bubbles."

"Yeah!" Lizzie grins. "I have some Curious George bubbles here somewhere." She digs around in the cupboard under the sink, and dumps a generous amount of scented soap into the tub.

"You know, 'Black Socks' is really a round. This time, when I sing it, you sing the 'not yet, not yet, not yet,' okay?"

Lizzie nods, and I all but shout, "BLACK SOCKS, THEY NEVER GET DIRTY! THE LONGER YOU WEAR THEM, THE STRONGER THEY GET. SOMETIMES, I THINK I SHOULD WASH THEM, BUT SOMETHING INSIDE ME SAYS 'NO, NO, NOT YET!'"

"NOT YET! NOT YET! NOT YET! NOT YET!" Lizzie bellows.

"You sing the first part," I tell her.

"BLACK SOCKS, THEY NEVER GET DIRTY! THE LONGER YOU WEAR THEM, THE STRONGER THEY GET!"

I take the second part, "SOMETIMES, I THINK I SHOULD WASH THEM, BUT SOMETHING INSIDE ME SAYS 'NO, NO, NOT YET!'"

"NOT YET! NOT YET! NOT YET! NOT YET!" we finish together.

The bathtub is full. I peel off my socks, and hold them away from me. "These socks really don't like the bath," I say confidentially. "Maybe they'd like some toys in there with them?"

"Yeah, I have some of those too." Lizzie reaches under the sink and throws in a floating boat, some squeaking Dalmatians, and some sand toys. She talks to the socks in my fists the way people talk to a pregnant woman's belly. "Ready socks?"

"They're not ready," I whisper. "They really hate the bath."

"It's all right, socks," Lizzie murmurs. "Guys, you really stink. I think you'd better get a bath."

I shake my head. "They won't get in."

"Here, let me try," Lizzie says. She takes the socks and folds them clumsily into her own hands. "It's not so bad, Black Socks," she whispers. "There's bubbles in there. And toys. And I'm going to wash you out real good. I won't let you drown. Okay?"

She looks at me, and I whisper, "I think they're ready." Lizzie eases the socks into the bubbly water like a gentle fisherman releasing a catch that's too small.

"Okay," I say, dangling my feet into the tub and swishing the water around. "Let's get you guys clean."

"What are you doing, Beth?" Lizzie giggles.

"Well, socks like to be washed by feet, didn't you know? Socks don't like hands all that much."

"Oh," she laughs, sitting down beside me. She plunges her feet into the tub, and swishes the water in a circular current. For five rousing rounds of "Black Socks," we douse the tiles all around the tub, and more than a few of the floor tiles as well. Black Socks bob up and down with the churning water as the toys thud against the side of the bath. Then, Lizzie starts to lose interest in our miniature tsunami.

"Hey Liz," I say.

She eyes me warily. "Yeah."

"You know, it's just a bath."

"Yeah."

"It's not so bad. There's bubbles in there. And toys. And Black Socks. I'll stay right here, and won't let you drown."

She looks down at the toys and bubbles bobbing in the tub, and Black Socks lying across her feet.

"What do you think?"

She shrugs. "I just don't like the bath."

"I know it's not your favourite thing."

"You said I didn't have to."

"You don't have to, Liz. But to be honest, you kind of stink like Black Socks."

She smiles a little, and looks at me out of the corner of her eye. "Do you promise not to let anyone else come in?"

"Cross my heart."

Removing her shirt and jeans takes almost ten minutes. We struggle over each button, and she almost changes her mind six times. Finally, she stands shivering in her underwear by the side of the tub. "I'm not getting naked," she tells me firmly.

"Hey, that's okay." I reply, helping her climb in. "Those skivvies could probably use a wash too!"

"What's skivvies?" she giggles, easing herself into the warm water.

"Skivvies? Skivvies are your underwear!"

"Skivvies? Really? I've never heard that before."

"No? That's what a friend of mine used to call them."

Thinking of Jackie awakens the beast, which begins to claw at my insides. One shallow slice usually silences it, but that's not an option right now. I concentrate on breathing.

Lizzie's shoulders relax. Her skeleton looks less likely to springboard out of her body. "That's my new favourite word," she says. "I'm in my *skivvies*. My *skivvies* need a wash. I'm wearing my *skivvies* in the tub with Black Socks."

And with that, we pick up our loudest chorus of "Black Socks" yet. Maureen is probably hovering outside the door, wondering what the heck we're doing. She will not barge in, and ruin it, though. She's smart that way.

"So do you think maybe we could wash your hair?"

She clenches her jaw. "I don't like getting my hair wet."

"What if you dunk yourself, and I put in the shampoo, and then you can use the shower hose to rinse out your hair by yourself?"

"You're not going to hold me down?"

The history behind this question shocks me. "No Liz," I say very seriously. "I would never hold you down."

"Cross your heart?"

"Hope to die."

She takes the quickest back-dunk possible, barely dampening her hair, and then I gently work the shampoo in. She clenches her fists and squeezes her eyes shut.

"There's shampoo in my eyes!" she cries. I shove a damp facecloth into her hand, guessing she won't appreciate me coming at her face while she's blinded. She scrapes away the tiny bit of foam on her eyelids. "Thanks."

I turn on the shower hose and test the temperature before handing it to her. "Just tilt your head back and you won't get any water on your face."

Lizzie trains the hose on the back of her head, sprinkling the shower tiles, floor and toilet in the process. She fumbles with the shower head, and after a few tries, hands it back to me. "Maybe you'd better do it," she says sheepishly.

I have to laugh. "Look at the mess you made."

Lizzie giggles. "It tickles," she says as the shower stream hits the back of her neck.

I suspect that neither of us has spent more time in a bathroom—ever—but Lizzie has managed to avoid hysteria, tears, and best of all, vomiting. She even lets me comb her hair, though she insists on combing it first to get out all the really good knots.

"Hey Beth?" She looks very small in her oversized flannel pyjamas, Sally-Ann issue.

"Yeah?"

"Will you braid my hair? Like Monica's?" Lizzie's never shown any interest in looking like a girl. She looks more like a rough-and-tumble little brother than she does a young lady.

I shrug. "Sure. Why not?" I gather and twist her hair, smiling at her attempts to sit still. She shoves her hands under her bottom, squirming as I take strands from behind her ears, but she doesn't complain. Maybe she's too tired. Or maybe her tomboy routine is as much of a façade as my own disguise, and she really wants to look pretty for once. Without the baseball cap and dirty T-shirt, she's just a tiny girl.

When I've finished, Lizzie pats her head and smiles. She tucks her hand in mine and leads me downstairs for dinner—clean, sweet-smelling, and a little subdued. Maureen's eyes widen, but she keeps her voice casual. "Hey guys."

"Hey Moe," Lizzie smiles shyly.

"There's sloppy joes for you."

"Yeah, great," I mutter to Maureen as Lizzie slips into her seat. "Could you have found something a little messier, do you think? Maybe teach her to eat with chopsticks tonight?"

Maureen bites her lip. "Aw, sorry. I didn't think of it. I could get her an apron...."

But Lizzie's already grabbed the sloppiest joe on the table, and smeared bright red sauce all over her hands and face.

"Never mind," I sigh as a piece of sauce-soaked meat tumbles down her front.

Chapter 11

That day when it
poured rain—
the only day
of that entire summer—
when the fat drops fell
like bullets
on the old tin
roof,
and the air in there
was dry and
damp at
the same time...
we swung from
that decrepit rope,
never getting
the whole way
across.
Scraping our palms.
Swearing. Laughing.
City girls
trying to be funny.
Trying to be campy.
Thinking we had
at least ten more
summers
Just like this one.

When I get like this, even writing to Jackie doesn't help. I can do nothing but sit on my bed and bury myself in the blankets, no matter how hot it is. I hug my body pillow like a shield against the beast clawing my gut. Even my toes quiver, like someone's stuck me with an Epi-Pen and told me to lie still. I want to stop, to shake it off, but I can't.

I hate this. Why can't I control anything?

I try some meditation breathing, but the thing, this alien intestine, writhes in my chest and presses against my heart. The organ responds by pulsing harder.

I open the front door and step onto the landing, but the air is too warm to give me any shocking slap in the face. My lungs fill too fast—like I'm choking on air. My hands shake. The familiar process has run on without me, and I stop fighting it. If I can't prevent it, the least I can do is detach.

My pulse throbs as I walk into the bathroom and close the door. I open the medicine cabinet, take down a bottle of rubbing alcohol and a little blue jewellery box, gauze, tape; rip off the old bandage and throw it in the bin.

The faucet is too loose on this sink—turn it slightly and water gushes all over the bathroom. Cold water cascades over my left arm, numbing my wrist. I leave it under the tap for a few long moments, then withdraw. Out of habit, I let the water run, though no one's home to wonder what I'm doing in here. I don't even want to stop anymore.

Maybe this time I'll cut too deep.

I imagine the gentle slopes of my wrists spilling blood down the drain like a third faucet. First my forehead will go numb and white, then my cheeks, my neck.... My alabaster skin will glow like marble, reflecting my mother's face as she stands over my coffin, staring at me.

And death will remove this choice.

Open the alcohol. Press the gauze to the top of the bottle. Tip it upside down. Cap the bottle. Put it down. Open the jewellery box. Take out the razor. Run the gauze over the blade. Throw the gauze in the bin.

I sink into a vacuum—a chaos of white noise that drowns out all thoughts.

79

Hold the razor in my right hand. Make the cut.

At first the pain is negligible, but water makes skin rubbery at the same time as the cold anaesthetises. A thin line of crimson appears, and the skin around it grows hot, defiant, as though it's clued in to the assault. I could keep going... could go on until my entire arm is a canvas of red lines. But I don't. The rule is one per day.

Some are small, shallow—barely a tally. Some are long and deep. One for every day since it happened.

The beast withdraws—flushed down a crimson river. I stick my wrist under the water again and watch the blood dilute, swirl in the sink, and spill into the black hole where it disappears. I clamp a thick piece of gauze over my arm and press down almost savagely. It's soaked through in seconds. "Fuck." Sometimes the bleeding doesn't stop for a long time, and leaves a brutal scar.

I lay two more pieces of gauze on top, then tape it down tightly and wrap a light bandage around the whole thing.

Elizabeth, for God's sake. Stop being so dramatic.

For a second, I'm afraid it won't stop, and imagine what the doctors at the ER would say. Maybe I *would* go there. I don't actually want to die; I just want to stop the beast. Eventually, the cut clots and congeals. When the first layer of scab tissue forms, the skin grows tight, like a corset being laced.

I close the blinds in the living room and turn on the desk lamp. The sun depresses me. I prefer a darkened cell. My notepaper sits exactly where it should—miraculously. I take out a sheet and my purple pen, and start writing. I finish and fold the letter into an envelope, sealing it with a sticker from the package on the desk.

"You still like stars, right?" I ask the air.

If only she would answer my letters. *Just one.*

A terrible headache grips my temples and travels all the way down my spine into my lower back. I groan, trying to sit up, feeling like I'm about to give birth to a horse. "Christ on a bike."

But despite two prescription painkillers, the agony curls me into a ball on the side of the mattress. Forget the pain pills—I need a sedative. That way I could sleep my way through two or three days of every month.

Hormones beat the shit out of me. That cutting episode was probably my own twisted form of PMS. Bad days. Altogether awful days. But they will pass.

My phone beeps to tell me I have a text message: Mike wants to come over. Why, when I haven't spoken to him in two weeks? I'd hoped this relationship would just fizzle and die without all the usual drama. Apparently not. *Why do boys always need a showdown?* The day's already started horribly—might as well get everything over with at once.

Mike's stuff lies in little piles all over the place, so a box would be helpful. Even a shoebox would probably do, since I haven't let him keep a whole lot here. I start with the bathroom and gather up his deodorant, toothbrush and hair products. *As if he needs hair products!* His boxers sit in a heap behind the bathroom door. God—boys! Apparently I'll need a milk crate for this one, because I haven't even started on his drawer in my bedroom and this shoebox is full. I gather a few t-shirts, a sweater, a small stack of books and magazines, plus gifts he gave me—stuffed animals that I'll never look at again. He should save them for the kids he'll have with someone else.

Those painkillers do jack for me. My uterus still back flips occasionally into my lumbar region, and the headache clings to the horizon of my brain, but at least I can stand up straight now.

Once I've just about gathered his things, Mike barges in without knocking—and leaves his shoes on, too. "Nice of you to call," he sneers.

"Why should I when you call me ten times a fucking day?"

He flinches, like I've hit him. "Couldn't you just tell me it was over?" he says quietly. "Instead of ignoring me? What's wrong with you?"

"What's wrong with *you* that you couldn't figure it out? We haven't really been together for a long time, Mike... or didn't you notice?"

He laughs bitterly. "Yeah, it's hard not to notice when your girlfriend doesn't even kiss you hello, let alone do anything else normal people enjoy."

My cheeks burn. How could I have been so stupid? Of course he would catch on.

"That's kind of a problem, don't you think?" he adds.

He has to shut up. No one can know. A swift, marked wound to a vital area should throw him off. I'm sorry to have to do it, but how else can I derail him? "Did you ever consider that I need more than a bump and grind from a *boy*, Mike? You want to know why I don't enjoy sex with you? Because you're selfish and needy and *fast*. I've found an actual *man* who understands relationships. And now, whiny adolescents just don't interest me."

A bald-faced lie, but I can see from the shock in his face that he believes it.

"Fine," he spits. "If that's how you feel."

"It is," I say grimly. "Now, please leave."

I point to the milk crate on the floor. He shakes his head in disgust. Without a word, he picks up the crate and slams out of the house. A sweater drops on the landing. I throw it down the stairs.

There. We've managed the perfect imitation of a lovers' quarrel. But I'll never cry. I'm glad he's gone—and more importantly, glad that my secret is safe.

"Do you love anyone, Beth?" Nancy asks. It's a question, not an accusation. Who am I supposed to love? My mother? My father? If I could forget my life with them, maybe I could dredge up love, or some shallow approximation.

Nancy waits.

"I haven't a clue." I imagine us sitting in a 1950's movie, and in my head, I light a cigarette. "Don't ask me questions I don't know the answers to."

She smiles wryly and stares out the window. "What about Lizzie?"

That wasn't a fair question. She must sense the walls rising up around me, because she changes the subject. "So your mother's a painter then?"

"Among other things, yes."

At this time of day, my mother is probably sipping tea on the terrace, staring into the ravine to absorb inspiration for her next painting. She pours herself into her art in a way she never can with sentient things. I've spent hours staring at her work, trying to extract meaning from the sweeping strokes of colour, the shapes that almost emerge, then suddenly meld into something else. Other people call her paintings "inspired," but I hate them. I don't understand what she paints, or why. So when Nancy asks "Is she any good at it?" there's only one thing I can say:

"Brilliant."

Nancy rocks a glass of water in gentle rhythm with her tremors. The heat is probably getting to her.

"That must take a lot of time," she says. Not exactly what I was expecting.

"I wouldn't know."

For the next ten minutes, we lapse back into our routine silence, watching the passersby passing by. Finally, she holds out the glass, and I take it from her and set it on the windowsill.

"Nancy?"

"Hmm?"

"I'm tired."

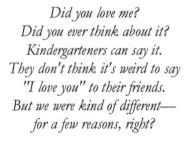

Did you love me?
Did you ever think about it?
Kindergarteners can say it.
They don't think it's weird to say
"I love you" to their friends.
But we were kind of different—
for a few reasons, right?

That summer we spent
in each other's pockets,
blinded by glossy
magazines and the sun
on the lakefront,

and you told me you hadn't
yet decided: boys or girls,
but most of the time,
you didn't care....

Did you think it was weird
that I'd never thought about it?
That I was so dumb?
Did you ever think
you loved me?

Did you ever expect that I'd ask you?

Chapter 12

Nancy closed our last session by asking if loving someone made me vulnerable. I didn't know how to answer. Love makes you stronger because the two of you can face the world together; but relying on somebody so much that you can't feel like a whole person without them makes you weak. Ridiculous—the idea of being half of something when you're alone.

Getting off the subway this morning, I saw Mr. Davidson, my high school chemistry teacher, getting on. As the train pulled away from the platform, he turned around and caught my eye. I held his gaze until he disappeared into the dark.

Seeing him raised something from the dead in me. On my last day at The Hole, he hugged me with tears in his eyes and said he'd miss me. I wondered, as so many times before, if I could make him feel something for me that he knew was wrong, make him do things that would keep him up at night. Something about the way he blushed when I caught him staring at me in class made me think it possible. He had a wife and two young children, but his eyes still followed me as the class performed complex titrations. Mr. Davidson wasn't a particularly attractive man, which made my attraction to him a little strange. A balding crown topped his short, stocky body and his arms the ended in a pair of large, freckled hands. But his genuine eyes and soft chuckle invited me to imagine what it would be like to make love to him. I know he'd thought about it too. Could I have been with him, if I'd just made a move?

I've never dreamed of waking up with Mr. Davidson beside me. In fact, if sleeping with him were a condition of fucking, all bets would be off. Sleep is such an intimate act—lying unconscious next to another person for hours at a time, muttering, drooling, flinging your limbs around, kicking the bedclothes, rolling over: all this while your hair gets messier and your breath gets fouler. And you wake up looking as dishevelled as if you'd just jumped from an airplane.

But something else makes me hate the idea of sleeping with anyone even more: the morning after.

The morning after is always uncomfortable, difficult, awkward. A time comes at night—regardless of whether you've slept with a man or a woman, or your best friend, or your sister, or your cousin, or a slumber party group—that compels you to tell others the most intimate parts of your life.

In the morning you wake up with a confidence-hangover, and you now have to live with what you know about the person you slept with—and they have to live with their new knowledge of you. You never feel the same way about each other again. Ever.

I sit alone in Nancy's office. The door hung open when I arrived, so I came in, feeling like a spy in the Oval Office. So many things in here that I shouldn't see—which makes me want to snoop, of course. *Does she have a file on me somewhere? Would I hear her coming in time to replace it if I found it?*

A large blue tome on her desk catches my eye: gold block letters on the spine read *DSM IV*. I need two hands to pick it up. It's the *Diagnostic and Statistics Manual: Fourth Edition*—a grimoire for psychologists. What kinds of crazy diagnoses do its twisted pages contain?

Crossing my legs, I lean back in my chair and peel open the cover. It creaks—*not well used, then?* Fascinating, all the things that can go wrong with a human mind: psychosis, schizophrenia, bipolar disorder. I leaf through, disgusted and intrigued—like I'm seeing a dead body or a video of childbirth, natural, but still illicit. A scrap of paper saves the page of Borderline Personality Disorder. I'm skimming its nine symptoms when—

"Anything interesting in there?"

I jerk my head up, then slowly look back down and close the book. "Nothing earth shattering." I reluctantly place the *DSM IV* on the coffee table. *Could I borrow it without her noticing?*

"Sorry I'm late."

"Never mind. Gave me a chance to catch up on some reading."

Accompanied by a soft whirring noise, Nancy awkwardly manoeuvres around my chair and into the alcove.

"New chair?"

"Loaner," she says, jiggling a joystick on the armrest. "Trying to figure out if I like it."

"What do you think so far?"

"Bit bulky."

"Can't you get a smaller one?"

She glances at something on her desk. "Maybe. I'll ask Tom to keep looking. How do you like my book?"

"Well, I like the part about my mother," I say, only half-joking.

"Borderline Personality Disorder?"

"Yeah. How'd you know she has it?"

"I don't really. Can't diagnose someone I've never met. But the few things you've said about her make me wonder. And children with borderline mothers are more likely to exhibit borderline behaviours."

"Which would be?"

She looks up—her eyes are warm but unrelenting. "I think you know."

Instinctively, I wrap my hand around my wrist. Her eyes flick down, then back to my face.

"You mean this is all genetic?"

Nancy's deep, hearty chuckle reverberates from her tiny body. I realise that, for the first time, I've told her exactly what's on my mind. She's good. She deserved that point, but I'll have to be more careful.

"Not necessarily. We can classify people with the same disorder, even when their symptoms vary. But the self-destruction is something you both share, I think. The love-hate relationship you have with one another, and with others. Emotional volatility masked by flat affect. Secrecy."

She's never talked to me like this, so frank and self-assured. Usually she lets me believe she knows nothing about my life. I don't know whether to be offended or relieved.

"It's frustrating for you, having an artist for a mother?"

"She's frustrating, period."

"What's she like?" Another direct question. She's a little off her game today—makes me feel like I'm talking to a friend. I pause, trying to find words that will even scratch the surface.

"She's like a tornado inside a hurricane," I say at last. "When you're around her, you live in a constant gale-force wind, so you never hear an approaching disaster until it's too late. And in the eye of the tornado, things seem relatively calm, so you're grateful for the peace—even though a run-of-the-mill hurricane is still trying to knock you down. And you never realise the stress you're under until you finally get away. You know what I'm saying?"

Nancy nods slowly. "She's not always like that, though, is she?" she presses gently.

I frown, shaking my head. "No. Sometimes, when she stops screaming and throwing her tantrums, she's... nothing. You can't get in, can't get through to her."

"So it's either hell or hell frozen over?"

"That's one way to put it. She's so confusing. There's no middle ground with her."

"Everything is black or white?"

"Yes. Something is either fabulous or it's terrible; people are perfect or worthless—and sometimes even that changes from day to day. She's elated or she's depressed. She's screaming, or she's giving the silent treatment. She hates you or she loves you."

"So," Nancy says softly. "She does love you sometimes?"

Slap.

She did love me, once, when I was little. Then, she could dress me up like an angel and stand me in the corner of her studio with my own tiny easel—before my flaws started to show, and I became an awkward, gangly teenager with a mind of my own. Before she could see the neediness, the lack of control, the imperfections.

She did love me once, but not anymore. I abandoned her. I slammed my door in her face, packed my things, and I ran. I never looked back.

And she never tried to come get me.

I stumble up to Second Cup, running a bit behind, but desperately needing a good, strong coffee to survive Beverly today. Thankfully, there's no line. A new person stands at the cash register, so I actually have to verbalise my order.

"What can I get for you?"

"Caramel Macchiato, please." I say. *Wait a sec—that's not my usual order.* When left to my own devices, apparently I can change.

Of course you can change, Beth.

The words are audible, and I'm sure my jaw drops. *E's still in my head?* Most people give up their imaginary friends in early childhood, but mine somehow got blended into my psyche. I still see her sometimes, and every so often, I hear her voice. Abnormal, I know—no need for a reminder.

"A large one, please," I add. It's going to be a long day.

The multiply-pierced barista raises an eyebrow as she hands me my order.

"Thank you." *Could she be as young as she looks? Why isn't she in school? Why am I interested?*

Lizzie and Gina both leave today. Gina will go to live with an aunt in British Columbia, and seems pretty pleased about the whole thing— maybe a little nervous. Lizzie , on the other hand, sits in my lap, trembling, and clutching her filthy stuffed elephant Pootsie—who is even more afraid of the bath than she is. Her mother will collect her at 9:00. A judge sent her father to prison again—for now.

"Did I ever tell you that I had a stuffed elephant when I was little?" I say.

Lizzie shakes her head. "Did it look like Pootsie?"

"Yes. Almost exactly the same. I think Pootsie is a little better loved than Winston, though."

"Winston? That's a funny name for an elephant."

"Oh yeah?"

Lizzie considers for a moment, then cracks a small smile. "I was little when I named Pootsie, you know."

"Hmm."

"Beth, is it going to be better this time?"

"I hope so." I squeeze her tighter. "Your Mom is going to take really good care of you, right here in Toronto. So you can come back to visit anytime you like, okay?"

She nods, and wisps of her fine dark hair catch my cheek. "You have my cell number?" She nods again, and pats the crease in Pootsie's backside where the puppeteer's hand is supposed to go. I smile, despite the hollow ache pressing down on me. Strictly speaking, Lizzie shouldn't have my phone number, but if she needs help, I don't want her to wait for someone to hack through red tape. The courts will parole her dad soon enough, and that scares the shit out of me.

A car pulls into the drive, and Gina gets up. "Hey Aunt Jodie!" she calls apprehensively.

A little woman with an elegant bun and a bright summer dress toddles up the steps. "Hello, my Gina!" she wheezes as she takes Gina into her arms. "Oh, you've grown so big!" Her smile displays a set of perfect white dentures, and her eyes crinkle with pleasure. Gina relaxes into her aunt's embrace, and I breathe a sigh of relief.

Sometimes the kids leave the group home to go on to better lives, and sometimes not. From a detention centre for substance abuse, to a behaviour home, to a residential home and now to a family, Gina's trod a very long road for someone so young.

"Need help with your suitcase?" Maureen asks as Gina lugs it down the stairs.

"No thanks, I've got it."

When the car is loaded, Gina hurries back up the steps. "Bye, Beth!" she says, hugging me quickly.

"You take care. And please remember that corduroy chairs are for sitting on." I smile sweetly at her, and she cuffs my shoulder, grinning.

She hugs Lizzie next, then Maureen.

"Bye guys!" she yells up to the top balcony. The other kids rush out onto the top porch.

"See ya, Snobbo!" yells Kenny.

"Yeah, I'll miss you too!" Gina calls sarcastically, but her lower lip trembles. We all wave as the car disappears down the road.

And then another car pulls up. Lizzie stiffens in my arms. She must have felt me start as well, because she slips her hand into mine and whispers, "Don't worry, Beth. Everything's going to be okay."

I squeeze her shoulder as a mousy woman with untidy brown hair alights from the beat-up old sedan and walks slowly up the drive. Dark hollows shade her sad eyes, and she shuffles along as if carrying far more weight than her tiny frame.

"Hi Liz," she says, cracking a wan smile as she approaches.

"Hi Mom," Lizzie whispers.

"Ready to go?"

"Uh-huh."

I pick up Lizzie's suitcase and lead her by the hand to her mother's car. She squeezes me tightly as we say goodbye, and tears well up in her wide eyes. I tap the underside of my chin, and she raises her own chin slightly, attempting a smile.

Only after the car has turned the corner do I bite my thumb and take a shaky breath.

Chapter 13

I run the water, cold and hard, into the sink. The beast has been building the entire day, and it will be brutal. What the hell made me think I could be a social worker? The goodbyes are horrible—even worse than the hellos.

The metal slicing my skin doesn't hurt—I barely even notice the cut until blood darkens the line—but I force myself to look, to concentrate on the sting, so I can stop. A churning, gut-ripping claw in my stomach has replaced my apathy. And even after this, I doubt it will go away.

The blood swirls playfully on the porcelain sink like paint washed from a palette.

As a small child, I loved to watch my mother paint. She would close the door to her attic studio, where sunlight poured in from the skylights and the big round windows facing east. I would drop to the floor, my knees tucked powwow style, and breathe in the freshly treated canvas: the oil paints, the turpentine, the life she brought into the room and her art. Occasionally, she would stand back, squint at the strokes she had just made and tilt her head. When she reached for the paint thinner, I stopped her.

"No."

"No?"

I shook my head. "No. It's pretty that way."

Sometimes later, I would notice she had taken out a section here or there, but never while I sat there in the studio. I don't know when she stopped painting for me. Perhaps when I started to encourage her destruction—"Yeah, you're right. Take it out"—she felt that I no longer saw the work as art, as an expression of her. She may have been right: I saw long brush strokes, short dabs and blobs; meaningless, shiftless shapes; and the mess she'd leave behind.

She closed me out of the studio years ago. I can't even remember the pattern of stains the hardwood bears, or the splattering on the walls. They will have changed by now anyway. What I remember, and what I miss the most, is the little easel in the corner—the one with paper and watercolours and a big fat paintbrush. *Does she still have it?*

My cousin Kate calls at 11:00 pm. "Oh that's all right," I say groggily when she asks if she's woken me. "I only require sleep every fifth night."

"Sorry," she says, although she doesn't sound a bit sorry. "I have news. Therefore you must have news as well."

"All right, go ahead."

"Roger that."

We giggle helplessly. "Okay, what is it?" I ask at last.

"We're having a pah'ty!" she says excitedly. "And guess who's coming to dinner."

"Sidney Poitier."

"No. Simon Mickelson!"

I fall back against the headboards. "Yeah right. He didn't tell me he was going to be in town."

"He wanted to surprise you. But I thought you might want some pre-warning. I know you like to dress for the occasion."

Kate knows me far too well. "I appreciate that."

"He's very excited to see you."

"Is he bringing anyone?" A long pause. "Kate?"

"Well, maybe."

"Who is this girl?"

"How do you know it's a girl?"

"Oh please, I think I know him a little better than that!"

She laughs softly. "Okay, okay. Her name is *Meagan*." She draws out the vowels so it sounds like a porn star name. I smile wickedly.

"Ten to one she won't show up." Simon and I have a silent agreement about bringing significant others along when we're going to see each other. We've never so much as kissed—the whole idea being a little too irrevocable for our liking—but bringing a date erases that tantalizing line of possibility. We flirt. We laugh. I sometimes fantasise about marrying him. But nothing has happened between us. Trust Kate to keep stirring those coals. If we haven't ignited yet, we're not likely to... but I can't let go of the idea. And Kate knows it, which is why she always invites Simon to her little gatherings.

"So how serious is he about Meagan?"

"You'll have to ask him when you get here. Next weekend. Mom's cooking dinner... will your dad be back?"

I snort. "Yes, I'm sure he'll fly in expressly for the occasion."

"Just making sure. Heaven forbid family gatherings."

"Or at least complete ones."

"See you there!" she sings, and hangs up.

I hold the phone in my hand a minute longer. *Simon Mickelson. Hmm.*

Simon and I met in middle school—the first day of the seventh grade. He was cool, even then. Not in a football-jersey or black-leather kind of way, but in a calm, ripped-jeans, earnest smile and steady hands kind of way. He knew how to settle people's arguments without getting involved. He'd also figured out every quirk and trick of every gadget in the school. Whooping cough or mono or something had knocked him out for half the previous year, and so he had to repeat seventh grade. He never complained about it, and he didn't advertise it. Everybody knew, and nobody really cared.

When we moved up into eighth grade, seventh graders went to him for advice.

And though we safely guarded the boundary of our friendship—never even suggesting that we date—he always put my needs first. I practically lived at Simon's house during middle school. His mother Francine bought me my first bra and tried to befriend Heather. No such luck.

I really missed him when Heather decided I should go into the academic track at The Hole. We would have been separated anyway, because by the tenth grade, he had caught up with the rest of his class. He went to university on time, and I haven't seen him since.

It doesn't matter though. Our friendship is like a ball of Plasticine: it remains exactly the same until one of us comes along and moulds it into something else. He just never changes. Occasionally he gets his hair cut, and grows taller—and taller—but he's still the same, and when I'm with him, so am I. He transcends my past, and sees the good in me—what's left of it, anyway. I know it's crazy, but I have a feeling that he's the one I should be with. When everything's over, when my Jellicle Transformation is complete, I'll be normal enough to make a life with him.

I wear my favourite dress—way too thin for the weather, but its flowing print hugs and ruffles and swirls in all the right places—with a long coat over top. A sheer shrug covers my arms to the palm, concealing everything underneath. The shrug has been a very convenient trend for me because it helps me stay hidden in vogue. I've straightened my hair and glossed the frizz down, and I finally feel ready to go. If everything goes according to plan, the extra time spent primping will be well worth it.

Fourteen subway stops and a three-block walk later, I arrive at Kate's mother's house. "Beth!" Kate rushes down the stairs to squeeze wrinkles into my perfect dress. "Hi!"

"How was the trip?"

"Not bad. I took an extra long route to avoid The Tower."

Kate winks. "Good plan."

"Where's your Mom?"

"In the kitchen." Kate drags me through the hallway. "Mom! Beth's here."

"Would you care for a megaphone?"

My cousin shoots me an apologetic look.

"Oh, Beth, I'm glad you're here!" Aunt Caroline envelops me in a perfumed and amply-bosomed embrace.

"Hi. Sorry I'm late," I say into her flour-dusted apron.

"Oh, don't be silly. You're right on time."

An amazing smell wafts to the front door.

"Mmmm.... What are you cooking?"

"Everything." Kate grins.

Aunt Caroline sighs and steers me toward the kitchen. "Come along. You need to eat. I see your father still hasn't managed to put any meat on your bones."

I smile and exchange a quick look with Kate, who ducks her head and stifles a snort. Aunt Caroline has no idea how much my father is away. She thinks her brother's trips last a week or so, and even that she finds hard to digest. If she knew that he left for months at a time, she'd hurry over by nightfall and start packing my suitcase. In small doses, like an hour at a time, I find her maternal air comforting. As a permanent guardian, though, I'm fairly sure she'd smother me. To death.

She thrusts a paper plate into my hands. "Now, eat!"

Kate and I heap our plates high with ham and pineapple, potato salad, bread rolls, and veggie sticks. We find a quiet corner in the living room and tuck in, carefully avoiding Uncle Tim, who has already darkened the doorstep of intoxication—he is a well-known patron. Along with my father, Uncle Tim plays the part of middle child, sandwiched between Aunt Caroline, the oldest, and Uncle Beck, the youngest. Tim served in the armed forces for years, and once, when drunk, he confessed to killing a guy at close range. It was an accident, I'm sure—the confession, not the killing—and Kate and I have been wary of him ever since.

"Ooooh, guess who's here." Kate glances past my shoulder.

"Oh no," I whisper. My stomach clenches.

Kate catches her breath. "And he's alone," she says pointedly. *Of course he is.*

Any other person would go over to say hello, but Simon and I follow a strict routine. With fluid grace, I set down my plate and cross my legs, pretending to be very engaged in a conversation with Kate. She plays along, muttering ridiculous nonsensicals with a serious expression. Simon approaches. At just the right moment, I turn toward him.

"Simon!" I say warmly, standing to greet him. I'm the epitome of femininity and grace. Even my mother would have to give me a nod tonight.

"Beth, how are you?" He embraces me tightly. I feel his heart pound against my chest.

He scans the room. "Are you here alone?"

"Uh-huh."

Kate winks at me from her seat.

"Hi there, Kate."

"Hey, yourself. What's up?"

"Nothing much. Are you enjoying university?"

"Shut up. I'm going next year and you know it."

Simon laughs. "Sorry. I had you confused with Beth."

"Whatever," Kate says. "I'm the only normal one around here. You two braniacs are skewing the curve."

Simon laughs again, and Kate smiles. "I'm just going to see if Mom needs any help," she says, flashing a smile at me as she passes.

Suddenly, I feel sweat breaking out on my palms. *Could I slip to the bathroom to put on some powder?* "Where's Meagan?"

"She couldn't make it," Simon says, avoiding my glance.

"Oh that's too bad. I would have liked to meet her."

"You would?"

"Of course," I say wickedly. "I wanted to learn more about the future Mrs. Mickelson."

He actually blushes! I decide to be kind and switch the subject. "So, are you hungry?"

"Starving."

"Here," I set my plate between us. "I can't eat all of this anyway."

Simon hasn't changed since age twelve, with his head of sweaty, tousled hair and pink cheeks that made his freckles explode. I remember him in seventh grade, churning an old and dented ice cream maker and frowning so hard his lips puckered. We added chocolate chips, blueberries and maple syrup to that batch. *God, that was a long time ago.*

Simon looks up suddenly, as if he's just had the same memory, but the humour in his eyes gives way to something else. I can't read him as well anymore—maybe it *has* been too long. He looks out the window beside us, and for a second, the sunlight glances off the faint freckles on his cheeks.

He's here, so he obviously wanted to see me. But what does that mean?

Has the future we always expected arrived?

What if it's happening now?

Chapter 14

The phone rings shrilly as I climb the final two steps to the front door. After scrambling with the locks and handles, I shove the door in and sprint full speed across to the kitchen to grab it in time. "Hello?"

"Hi, Beth?" At first, I don't recognise Maureen's voice.

"Oh, hi. What's up?" A pause. "Maureen?"

"Yeah... listen. I know it's not your night, but would you be able to come over?"

"Sure, what's going on?"

"Lizzie's back."

"What? Why?" Dread creeps up my chest.

"Dad paid her and her mother a visit nice little tonight. Drunk out of his skull—he put her head through a sliding glass door."

"I thought he was still in jail."

"I guess he got parole earlier than anyone expected. Apparently *they* didn't even know he was out until he showed up on their doorstep. He's split now though, of course. CAS is looking for a new home for the Emerys to relocate into, and the police are out looking for him."

"Why doesn't someone just take the bastard out and shoot him?" I kick the kitchen chair closest to me, and it careens into a wall. "How's Liz?"

"She's not doing so well...."

"Yeah, I guess not. Fuck! Okay, I'll be there in a bit."

"Okay. Thanks."

I slam down the phone and throw my purse across the room onto the futon. I want to cry—I feel the awesome pressure in my chest, tightening around my lungs. Releasing it would feel really good right now.

Garlic and onions waft to my nose as I run up the stairs to Beverly. I don't bother to take off my boots or hang up my coat as I clomp through the door and down the front hall.

"Beth, is that you?" Maureen calls.

"It's me."

In the kitchen, pots clutter the counters; tomato sauce spatters the stove and the tiles of the backsplash. Kenny sucks his spaghetti in strand by strand, like a play dough spaghetti factory in reverse. Rachel has separated her plate into four equal portions and concentrates on eating one bite from each wedge. B.N.E. has two bowls—one for the spaghetti, and one for the sauce—and Monica picks gingerly at her plate, which makes me wonder if anyone's been watching her today.

"Where's Lizzie?" I whisper to Maureen. She nods toward the stairs.

"In her room. She wasn't hungry."

I squint as the staircase's dim shadows replace the warm light of the kitchen. *Why have we never bothered to install a light fixture on the stairs?* Outside Lizzie's door, I pause. She's going to look terrible, so I freeze my face into a neutral expression.

"Lizzie, it's Beth." I knock quietly. "Can I come in?"

Silence for a long moment. "Yeah."

A large scrape has begun to scab across her left cheek, and a dark purple bruise forces her eye closed. A gauze bandage lies across her forehead, and her fine brown hair straggles to her shoulders. Her face is gaunt—*did her mother not feed her enough?* Her one visible eye stops me in my tracks. Behind the curly lashes lurks a new, unfamiliar shadow.

She looks up at me as I close the door.

"Hey," I say, smiling softly.

"I didn't know you were coming today," she whispers.

"Well I didn't know *you* were coming today." I sit down, take off my coat and boots, and lean back against the headboard of the bed. "I brought someone for you."

"Who?"

"Look and see."

I pass her my purse, and she unzips it to pull out a grey flannel elephant.

"Is this Winston?"

"Yep."

She hugs the elephant tightly. "Thanks Beth. How did you know I'd forget Pootsie?"

I just smile. "I've met you once or twice, kiddo. What did the social worker pack for you?" She points under the bed, and I lift out a small pink suitcase to find a change of clothes, two pairs of underwear, socks, a hairbrush and a toothbrush. Everything is almost the same colour: essence of worn dishcloth. I take out the hairbrush and put the suitcase back under the bed.

"Are you going to brush my hair?" she asks.

"I'll be gentle. Promise." If we leave it unbrushed any longer, we'll never untangle it. She turns around and bows her head. Despite the tangles, her soft hair slips through my fingers elusively. I start at the very bottom, brushing out the first inch or so, careful not to yank. The process is slow, but neither of us has any place to go. As the minutes pass, her fists unclench and she begins to remember what it feels like to have someone touch her without inflicting pain. Four inches up, and it gets easier. A matt of hair sits like a clot at the top of her head. I prod it—dried blood. I bite my tongue hard to keep from gagging and force my voice to be light. "Lizzie, does this hurt?"

"A little."

"I'll be right back. Don't go anywhere."

Walking at a normal pace takes a vast amount of control. I want to run, to wash all traces of that man's hands down the sink in a single, powerful blast. But she's a child. She doesn't need such a quick and intense solution. In fact, that's the last thing she needs. When I return with a washcloth and a bowl of warm water, she is still sits with her head bowed.

"Lizzie?"

"Yeah?" sleep has crept into her voice, but it carries a slight edge.

"How long were you at the hospital?"

"Mmm... a few hours?"

"You didn't stay overnight?"

"No. The nurses wanted me to, but then lots more kids came in because of an accident...."

"What kind of accident?"

"A car accident, I think. At a crosswalk."

I rub her shoulder lightly. "And then they said you could go home?"

"Uh-huh."

I squeeze some water onto her head and run the washcloth through her hair, teasing out the flakes of blood until it comes clean. Half an hour later, I've combed and braided her hair.

"Close your eyes tight and count backwards from forty-four," I say.

By the time I return from dumping out the bloody water, she's reached eleven. She holds her hands over her eyes and crouches by the bed, her voice muffled by her shirtsleeves and Winston clutched to her chest. *What will she dream about tonight? Will she wake up crying? Has she even cried at all?*

"Lizzie," I whisper, gently touching her shoulder. "You can stop now."

She opens her eyes, and turns around. "My hair looks nice, doesn't it?"

"Yeah. It looks great."

"It didn't hurt at all."

"No? Good."

"Beth?"

"Yeah."

"How long am I going to be here this time?"

She's struggling. I can tell by the way her eyes try to meet mine, but fall short. She's growing up, and she hates it.

"I don't know, Lizzie. As long as you need too, I guess."

She nods, mollified.

I gesture to my bag, and she opens it again, grinning as she extracts her two favourite stories. My breath catches; she has such a sweet smile. "This one," she says, thrusting it at me. I shift into a more comfortable position and open to the first page.

"In the Rediford valley, the children don't go to school. There has been no school there for generations."

She inches closer to me, first sticking her legs out, then lying down on her side. By the time I arrive at Chapter Two, her head is on the pillows, and her eyelids droop.

"The children gathered around the centre of the courtyard where something was rustling the leaves of the Atwood tree." The pillow inches its way onto my lap, followed by a braided head of hair. Soon, her eyes have closed, and her arm rests lightly across my knees. I brush the stray strands from her forehead and rub her back, feeling it rise and fall as she relaxes into sleep. On the back of the bed hangs a raggedy quilt, and I lay it over her before turning out the light and leaning back against the headboards. If she wakes up in the night, she'll be scared, and I'll be here.

Through the open curtains, the moon and its stars watch us. The stillness of the day has given way to the cool softness of spring nights. A breeze carries the jubilant scent of dew-drenched grass through the windows. I love it, but I want to hold my breath against it.

Outdoors.

Freedom.

Moonlight and sand and lake water and campfire. The memories stir something that I would rather not feel. It's just easier not to feel.

The rodents are awake. Shadows scurry past the windowsill and merge with the larger shadows of the garden. A tiny body curls beside me, confident that I can protect her. But I can't. A pang of guilt twists my stomach—nothing I do will fix her life.

She has to pick up the pieces alone. Because if she can't, she'll be crushed.

*Why did you
have to go to
arts school, anyway?
You could sing at home,
or in lessons,
or even on stage,
if you wanted to.*

JELLICLE GIRL

Why was there a
special school
for you?
It made you a little odd,
you know...
humming to yourself
all the time,
composing
melodiesduring the cacophony
in the mess hall,
tuned out
to the idiocy
around you.

That's what I liked
best about you.

You let me
lie with my
head in your lap,
and you played with
my hair
and said that
attraction is
just attraction,
is just another
form of friendship.

And I believed you.
Because you seemed to
know.

Chapter 15

"So Beth, how have things been going lately?" Nancy asks.

Subtext: How closely do your arms resemble a butchered chicken right now?

"Not bad," I reply guardedly. "Why do you ask?"

"Just curious."

Never, in the entire time I've known Nancy, has she asked to see my scars. Never, in fact, has she mentioned the cutting at all. Strange? Or just part of her approach? I know she knows. The Hole probably printed it in black and white on my form that they sent over. Maybe she's waiting for me to volunteer the information to her—but that's never going to happen. She must have some other reason.

"Beth, how did you react to what happened to Lizzie?"

"How did I react? I don't know."

"You didn't cry?"

"No. I don't cry, Nancy."

"Ever?"

"No."

"Why not?"

"What do you mean, why not? It either happens or it doesn't. And with me it doesn't."

"What happened the last time you cried?"

Slap!

I didn't expect that. Probably should have, but this woman has an endless arsenal of surprises up her sleeve. With effort, I keep my face neutral, but turn my gaze out the window. Nancy stares at me; I can feel her eyes on my face. "Beth, I can't help you if you don't tell me the truth."

"You can't help me anyway," I snap. "I don't know why you bother to try."

As I leave Nancy's office, a flag ad catches my eye: *The Toronto Art Gallery presents Heather Sarandon: April 3rd to 25th.* I stand for a moment, staring at it.

Well done, Mom. I whip out my phone and dial Kate.

"Hey, you'll never believe it," I say drily.

"What?"

"Heather's got an exhibit at the Toronto Art Gallery."

"No way!"

"Yeah, I just saw the ad."

"Wow. Are you going to call her?"

"Uh, no."

"Oh, c'mon Beth. Be a sport."

"Yes. That would definitely describe me: sporting all the way. If I called her, she'd expect me to turn up, and I can't think of a single nice thing to say about her work, Kate. I don't get it."

"Yeah, well, she probably doesn't understand you either."

"I would say that's a given. But me turning up at her art show won't change that. But it's still pretty amazing, what she's done."

I stare at the ad for another minute before continuing to the subway. All these years, my mother has been hard at work painting, rubbing things out, painting them over. I always knew she was brilliant; I've just never understood why.

Once my mother creeps into my head, she stays for an irritatingly long time. My childhood rears up in my memories—the terrible silences between us, the miscommunication, the cold and stealthy secrecy, derisive looks, hostile lifts of the eyebrow, snide comments. Ludicrously, I can't even remember how it started.

She has this desperate need to be perfect—crystalline in appearance, sharp, classy, harmonious—but inside she's a raging mess. I do recognise part of myself in that, though. My game began with her. And now I don't know how to stop it, this insane fear of vulnerability. I can't let go any more than she can.

You'll never believe what Heather is doing now! I've been gone more than a year, and she hasn't so much as picked up a phone to call me, but her career is well underway. What could she have painted that has everyone flocking to her exhibits? I ran into Simon again at Kate's party. Wish you could have been there too. But that probably wouldn't have gone over very well, for obvious reasons.

I've been seeing Nancy for an eternity now, but to be honest, nothing much has changed. We keep playing cat and mouse. I know that keeping secrets won't help me get better, but I can't seem to let go of the game. What's it going to take for me to let go of you and latch onto normal life?

I wish I could grow up. And I wish you were here.

Still miss you like hell.

Love, Beth

A familiar Mountain Equipment Co-op bag—fire engine red—bobs above the heads of the crowd, and a shag-haired Simon lopes through the doors of the train station.

"Hello!" He wraps me in his famous hug, his biceps twitching against my shoulders.

"Hi," I manage breathlessly. "How was your weekend?"

"Great. I spent some time with my mom. She tried really hard not to nag me. Hey, I saw a flag up for your mother's exhibit. That is her, right?"

"Yep that's her. The one and only Heather Sarandon."

"Well, I figured. But there could potentially be more than one."

"Please, no! One's quite enough."

106

Simon grins. "Thanks for picking me up. You didn't have to. Where are we going to eat? I'm starving—"

"Paccelli's" I say quickly. "I'm starving too. Let's go."

We have linguine, and Simon gets away with ordering red wine. I've never felt nervous around him before, but suddenly this niggling grain of doubt in the back of my mind tells me we're not on the same wavelength, and that the only way I'll figure it out is to make the first move. That thought nearly makes me drop my wine glass. But then he smiles.

"I've missed you," he says seriously, as if he's just become certain of it.

"Me too."

"I'm moving back to Toronto for good at the end of the semester. B.C. was fun and all, but I'm ready to come home."

"That's awesome. I'm glad."

"It'll be nice to see you more often, Beth. I miss my old friends and everything."

I always knew something would change and make me better. Is Simon the key? It would make sense. When I see him, I become the person he thinks I am—altruistic, intelligent, driven, kind. Could he make my Jellicle Transformation finally happen? No one person can change you forever—but they can help.

It happened in reruns of *The Facts of Life*. Blair always gave Cindy flack for hugging girls, until one day, she met a cute boy at the dance and her "time clock" ticked on. Of course it can happen to me. I glance away, feeling a grin forming. Maybe Simon holds my time clock. Finding out would be the best thing—or the worst. I've always felt safe to love Simon, because he never looked at me as a girlfriend. Loving him from a distance gave me a trump card: "things aren't working out with the flavour of the month, because Simon, your true destiny, awaits." But now, if dating Simon doesn't work out, then I'll know absolutely for certain that what happened with Jackie wasn't a fluke—that I have an irreparable flaw.

I'm not ready to know.

And yet, I hear myself saying, "It'll be nice to spend more time with you, too."

Chapter 16

"Hello!" I breeze into Nancy's office.

From her position in the alcove, she raises a hand in greeting, but strain lines crease her forehead.

"You look cheerful," she says.

"And I am!"

"So, tell me then."

"Tell you what?"

"What has you in such a good mood?"

"Just the weather, Nancy." I lean back in my chair. "It's gorgeous outside."

She tries to smile despite the tiny beads of sweat dotting her grey face.

"You're not feeling well, are you?" She looks like shit.

She presses her tongue into her cheek and tilts her head. "To tell you the truth, no, not really."

"Nancy, I can go. We can meet next week...."

"Nice try," she says, then catches her breath sharply. Her hands grip the armrests of the wheelchair so tightly that blue veins pop out along her forearms.

"What's the matter?" I ask.

As if in answer, her legs begin to tremble violently. She closes her eyes. "Don't you dare feel sorry for me, my girl."

I roll my eyes. "Fine. I'll just ignore you completely. Maybe throw you out of your wheelchair and kick you while you're down. Would that make you feel better?"

She chuckles. "Just get me my purse." I grab her purse off the desk and open it.

"The blue bottle."

I root around and pull out her medication, instantly recognizing the prescription: Ativan, 0.5 mg—a fabulous cure-all for everything from anxiety to seizures to whatever the hell is wrong with Nancy. Her hands tremble too much to open the cap, so I do it for her. The pills have no immediate effect. Her feet sound like helicopter blades against the footrests.

"Does this happen a lot?"

She studies me for a moment, and something shifts in her gaze—maybe hostility, maybe denial. For a moment I don't think she's going to answer, but I swallow and wait, never dropping my eyes from her face. Finally, the tremors stop.

"It's normal, to a point." She hesitates, as though deciding whether or not to tell me the rest. "I have multiple sclerosis. The rapidly accelerating kind. It's normal for it to get worse. Only, in my case, it's getting worse all the time. Four years ago, I was diagnosed, and got a cane soon after that. Two years later, I needed a walker. Now, I have this chair."

"Doesn't MS make you tired? I thought it was one of those really exhausting diseases."

"It is," Nancy says shortly. "But I'm not dead yet. I'm not going to sit around and wait."

"Don't you have other things you want to do with your time, like spend it with your family?"

She smiles. "Sure I do. My husband drops by between clients. He has his own practice upstairs. I also like my work. If only some people would let me do my job...."

She doesn't mention her daughter, Bethany, but I don't have time to ask because she jumpstarts the game. "Beth, tell me something."

The suddenness of her request takes me aback. "What do you want to know?"

"When you imagine your life in ten years, what do you see?"

I do her the courtesy of considering it; turfing out a flippant reply would be rude, and I doubt she'd want to hear it. I frown and lean back in my chair. *What if I told her about the Jellicle Transformation?*

"I imagine a life that belongs to someone else. I don't imagine me in the future, because a decade is so long that I'll have completely transformed by then."

"How do you expect change if you don't undertake the process yourself?"

"I don't know, Nancy. I can't even think about tomorrow, let alone ten years from now."

"Beth." She frowns, perplexed. "If you don't believe that tomorrow will bear the consequences of today, you have no reason to make changes."

I sigh and lean back in my chair. "Yes. You're starting to see my point."

I lean back in my chair, determined not to say anything else. I should have told her about Simon, not the Transformation, but I try not to dwell on that—she's like a shark that can smell blood from miles away. She can sense an emotion with her eyes and ears closed.

Stop thinking about it!

"All right, then." She leans forward. "Something's happened. So tell me, what is it?"

Too late.

"Why? It has nothing to do with my classes!"

"Beth...."

Why not give her a break? We both know we danced over that boundary some time ago. "Nancy, it's no big deal," I sigh. "I ran into an old friend, and we had dinner. He's moving back to Toronto after living in B.C. for a year, and I'm in a good mood. Okay?"

"He?"

"Yes, he."

"Who is he?" Nancy wants nothing but a stream of facts today, so I relate the Simon and Beth saga thus far. It takes the better part of the hour, seems relatively harmless to me, and keeps Nancy occupied. All in all, a successful endeavour.

"So you took an emotional risk," she says at the end of my story.

"All right."

"Well, did you?"

"I guess—although risk doesn't factor much into spending time with somebody I've known my entire life."

"Beth, what do you hope to accomplish with this relationship?"

I stare at her for a second. "What do you mean, accomplish?"

"Well, do you want to be friends? More than that? Do you want a lasting relationship?"

My face grows hot, and I drop my gaze to my hands.

"Beth?" Nancy's voice is quiet, gentle. "Have I offended you?"

I swallow hard, and shake my head without lifting my eyes. "No," I say as firmly as I can. "I'm not offended."

"But I did strike a nerve?"

"No."

"Do you really have feelings for this boy, Beth? Does he have the same feelings for you?" *What does she mean by that?*

"I... I don't know." I fight for control of my voice, which I hate. The conversation wasn't supposed to go like this.

Nancy sighs. "Never mind. I don't expect you to know right now. We'll talk about these things if and when they happen."

What the hell is the matter with her? Is she totally losing it?

"Then can we change the subject?" I snap.

She nods and stares out the window with me. Without warning, a dark cloud opens, and fat raindrops begin pelting pedestrians. Women in grey suits cover their heads with their hands and dash to take cover. I make silent bets to myself about who will slip next—smearing *eau de street sludge* on her hand-tailored blazer.

Nancy watches the women running and a shadow of sadness passes over her face. They duck under an awning, dripping and laughing. Ringing out their straggling hair. She must sense me looking at her, because she turns and catches my glance.

"Beth, what do you want to do for a career?"

God! Why does she have to bother *me so much?*

"Nancy, do you listen when I talk to you? I don't think about the future. I don't have a clue what I want to do after school. All I want is to graduate from The Hole and get on with university. I want to study everything out there. I want to get the hell away from my life. Okay? After that I *don't know*. And it doesn't matter right now."

"Why doesn't it matter?"

I throw my hands up in the air. "Why would I plan for a future I can't control? What if I change my major at the last possible second, have to make up classes, and end up doing something totally different?"

"So you see yourself changing your mind?"

111

"Christ on a bike! I don't know!"

"Why are you getting upset?"

"I'm not upset. I'm frustrated that you're asking me irrelevant questions."

"Why irrelevant?"

"What is this, an interrogation? Why don't I ask you some questions? Where do you see *yourself* in three years?"

She raises her eyebrows. "Dead," she says flatly.

I swallow hard—determined not to look away from her. She sighs.

"You know, you do have a point, Beth," she says after a while. "The world all seems to have the same idea about life—you must live today for the sake of tomorrow, even though tomorrow may never come."

"Exactly," I mutter, slumping down in my seat. The fight drains out of me. "So why are you always pushing me to think about my future?"

"Because I don't expect that in three years, you will be dead."

All right. That's a good point too. Honestly, I don't know why I resist planning the future so adamantly. The truth is, I *have* thought about my life after graduation. What should I major in? Should I study part time and try to get a job right away? Maybe succumb to being an artistic nutcase like Heather? I've even thought about teacher's college. Simon's worked since he started university, and he gets paid pretty damn well. Maybe I'll just marry him and relax for the rest of my life.

But if I'm being completely honest, I'd have to admit that living the present takes so much energy that there's nothing left for imagination. I just have to survive this stage—this horrible in-between, powerless, "prostrate to the higher mind" stage—to access my future. By the time I graduate from university in three years, I will have become a confident, humorous, well-educated career woman with a diamond ring on my finger and a down payment on a condo. You can't plan someone else's future, and I fully plan to become someone else.

Nancy hasn't said anything. For a long time. I turn away from the window to look at her. She stares out the window too—but half-focused, like someone in a waking dream. *Is she thinking about her future too?* How long will she continue to be a therapist? How much longer before she's too sick to continue?

"Nancy?"

"Mmm hmm?"

Not daydreaming—falling asleep. It must be the pill. Hell, that's what I take Ativan for—to blot out thoughts and force my body to relax. I don't usually take it in the middle of the day though. She probably doesn't either.

"Beth," she whispers. I lean forward to hear her. The edges of her words slur together.

"What is it, Nancy?"

"The future has a funny way of becoming the present—real quick. If you don't take care of the problems you have now, you'll carry them with you into your future, and we'll be having this same conversation ten years from now."

She just told me she won't be around for another ten years, but I keep my mouth shut. She can have this round. Something tells me she won't be playing very much longer. Her eyes are closed now, and she's passed the point of half-dreams. Session's over. I stand up quietly and ease Nancy's sage shawl off the back of the couch, draping it over her sagging shoulders.

"Thank you, Bethany," she murmurs, her eyes closed.

"See you next time," I whisper.

Her head nods onto her chest as I shut the door.

Chapter 17

An eerie quiet has settled over Beverly House on Saturday. I actually have time to take off my shoes and coat before footsteps careen along the upstairs hallway.

"Beth? Is that you?" Lizzie calls, running down the stairs.

"It certainly is. Where is everyone?"

"Come see." She's shoved her tangled hair back in a hair band that must have belonged to Gina. Orange lines stain her top lip— looking more like permanent marker than anything edible—and the little yellow tag of her shirt pokes up under her chin. Before I can say anything, she leads me by the hand through the kitchen and into the upstairs hallway.

"Monica's sick," Lizzie says, and sits down by the door. A bum print in the carpet tells me she's already spent considerable time there.

Fabulous.

"Monica?" I call to the bathroom door. "It's Beth. What are you doing in there?"

A muffled sob.

"Monica? What's the matter?"

"Nothing!" she screams.

I raise my eyebrows. "Oh, I'm sorry. I often lock myself in the bathroom when I'm feeling great."

No answer.

"Can I come in?"

"No."

"Why not?"

"Because you can't."

"Are you sick?"

114

Another muffled sob.

"Monica," I repeat gently. "Are you sick?"

"Yes!" she screams.

"What's the matter?"

There is a loud pop as she unlocks the knob. Slowly, I open the door. The reek of vomit is nauseating, and I push open the window. *Shit. I really thought she was getting better.*

Monica kneels over the toilet, resting her elbows on the seat. Her sweaty hair straggles around her face. Wordlessly, I run a soft washcloth under cold water, and ring it out. "Come on," I say, helping her sit on the side of the bathtub, closer to the open window. Crusts of vomit ring her mouth, and her breath reeks. I run the washcloth over her face, around her mouth, and rinse it out again before starting on her hairline. When she's cleaned up, I put my arm around her waist.

"Come rinse out your mouth." She leans unsteadily against me, this waif of a child, as she wobbles the three steps to the sink. When the water hits her mouth, she gags, and I hold her upright. "Spit it out."

She swishes the water around and lets it dribble out. Her body trembles, and a putrid shade of greyish green tints her face. Her pyjamas hang loosely off her frame.

"Are you okay, Mon?" whispers Lizzie from the doorway.

"Get her out of here," Monica moans.

"Liz, why don't you go hang out with Debbie downstairs?"

"She's not here," Lizzie says in a small voice.

"Did she call in sick? Is Mack here instead?"

"No. Nobody's here."

"There has to be somebody."

"There's nobody," says Monica. "Really. Maureen switched days with Debbie because she wanted three days off. And Mack got the flu so he had to go home before he shat himself. Debbie should have come, like, right after Mack left, but she didn't show up."

"Really? That's not cool. Sorry about that, guys. But Mon, why didn't you call somebody?"

"Like who?" Monica sneers. "Our social worker? Give me a break. I don't want to be moved again, thanks. I kind of like it here. Besides, I knew you'd get here eventually."

"Yeah, but I'm not even... never mind. Liz, go see what the boys are doing—and if they're playing video games, tell them that the front yard is a disaster and they promised to clean it last weekend. And when they give you a hard time, tell them I'll bake something good when they've finished."

"Brownies?" Lizzie asks hopefully.

"Maybe."

"Ugh, don't talk about food," Monica groans and bends over the toilet again.

"Ew." Lizzie watches in fascination as Monica pukes, then turns toward the stairs. "Okay, I'll tell them."

Monica rinses her mouth and sits back down on the bathtub ledge.

"Can we tie your hair back?" I ask her.

She shrugs. "Whatever."

I run a comb through her fine hair, and the rhythmic motion calms her.

"Just braid it," she says. "It's in the way."

I start at the top, and gently gather and twist, gather and twist, until a French braid hangs halfway down her back. "It's getting long," I say.

"Yeah."

"Come on, let's get you in bed." I lead her toward the door. Tears roll down her cheeks, but she lets me take her to her room. I put a towel over her pillow and fetch the barf bucket from the closet. Her forehead feels hot.

"What did you eat today?"

"Cheerios."

"With nobody even telling you to? That's great." "Did you throw it up on purpose?"

She shakes her head. "No. And I thought that the reflex vomiting was over, but I just feel so sick right now. Why now?"

"Monica," I say sympathetically, "I think you might have the flu."

"The flu? I have the *flu*?"

"You have a fever. And you have the shakes too. And I'll bet you'll feel a whole lot better tomorrow."

She groans, and starts giggling hysterically. "Great. Just great."

"I'll get you some ginger ale. Try and go to sleep." She's already slipped into that cold hazy doze that only sickness can offer.

Winston trips me on my way out the door. "Lizzie," I whisper loudly. She sticks her head out from under Monica's bed. "Come out here." She drags herself forward and grabs the stuffed elephant from my grasp. I hold out my hand, and she walks with me out into the hallway. "What were you doing in there?" I ask as soon as the door closes.

"Hiding," she says matter-of-factly.

"From what?"

"The boys. They said they were going to hunt me down with the garden rake. They're outside cleaning the yard."

"Good." I lead her down the stairs. "Come hang out with me." She nods, and follows me into the kitchen where dishes lie haphazardly around the kitchen, cluttered with various food stuffs. A spoon in the middle of the kitchen floor dribbles a pool of brown liquid. *Chocolate ice cream?* I pick up the spoon and hand Lizzie a rag to wipe up the mess.

"Is Monica going to be sick again?" she asks.

"Maybe. She's still looking a little green."

"Green?"

"Yeah, you know. Vomitus. When someone looks like they're going to puke."

"Vomitus," Lizzie giggles.

"Ginger ale should help. Would you take this to her?" I hold out a glass of the fizzing amber liquid.

She nods and takes it upstairs.

"Hey," B.N.E. strides into the kitchen. A bit of pink highlights the tops of his cheeks, and he pants a little.

"How's that work coming outside?"

"Not bad. Need another garbage bag, though. Wouldn't mind a drink, either. Want anything?"

"Milk, if you're going to get it for me."

B.N.E rolls his eyes. He knows I only drink milk so they'll drink it. But that doesn't stop him from pouring a tall glass for himself as well. He downs it in one long gulp.

"What's a-matter with Monica?"

"She's got the flu."

"Aw, gross. Got enough barf buckets?"

"I'm pretty sure I can manage."

117

"So who's on t'night?"

"Don't know yet." I really should call somebody.

Lizzie reappears at the bottom of the stairs, and looks around. "Come on in," I beckon. She comes and puts her thin arms around my waist. I pull her into my lap, and she leans her head onto my shoulder. Her hair smells like black liquorice.

"What's for dinner?" she whines.

"Food, I expect."

Lizzie rolls her eyes. "Really, what is it?"

"Actually, I hadn't thought that far ahead," I confess. "B.N.E., what's in the fridge?"

He stops halfway to the door, and lopes back over to the fridge. "Ketchup, milk, oranges, sour cream, relish, hamburger meat, processed cheese, juice, apples, cantaloupe, eggs, margarine, cottage cheese, corn, sauerkraut, tzatziki—"

"Okay. Now what's in the freezer?"

"Ice cubes, frozen juice, perogies, bacon, chicken, pork, uh... a science experiment?"

"Good enough. Can you throw the chicken in the sink with some cold water? Thanks."

"Sure, Miss Brownie Chef. If you're gonna bake."

"How did you know that was the surprise?"

"Cuz that's the only thing that would make me clean up that yard!"

"All right then, sounds like a deal."

B.N.E. salutes as he bows out of the kitchen and back to his chores. The screen door squeaks shut and his footsteps thunder down the outside stairs.

"Do you need a snack, grumpy?"

"Uh-huh." Lizzie nods.

"Okay, let me up." I groan as I stand and place her on my empty stool. "What have you eaten today?"

"Ice cream."

"Go sit at the table. I'll get you some cheese and crackers."

But first, I have to call Maureen.

"Hi, it's Beth. Fine, you? No, I'm at Beverly. Um... I need to talk to you about Debbie." When I finish the story, Maureen swears softly.

"What the hell are we going to do now?" she says. "I'm halfway to Ottawa, and I can't make it back tonight. And Mack's at home with the flu. I don't suppose you'd like to interview for a position, would you? Starting, you know... immediately."

My stomach flips in excitement.

"Wait. How old are you? Are you eighteen yet?"

"Not quite," I reply, sensing that the helium in my balloon has a very short half-life.

"Hmm...." Maureen thinks for a moment. "When do you turn eighteen?"

"September."

"So that's what? Another six months?"

"Yeah. But I'd like the job," I say quickly.

"Yeah? Well, I think you'd be great. I'll talk to Mack and see what he thinks. We might be able to work something out until we can hire you."

"Okay. Um... so what about tonight?"

"Shit. Well... ah, shit.... Seriously, Beth, I'd come back if I could, but it'd take me at least three hours to get there."

Maureen finally decides that I should stay the night alone, and says she'll call Mack to be on standby from his sick bed. I've never been at the home overnight, and as I hang up, the first nerves creep through my stomach. But I feel way more excited than scared. For the first time since that summer, I feel less than miserable about something. Who knew getting paid to work with a group of delinquent kids would make me happy?

When I get back into the kitchen, Lizzie's slumped over the table, her sweaty head cradled on her arms. "Beth," she says in a small voice. "I feel green."

She's working at the cash today.

Someone else steams the milk behind the bar while she punches in my order.

I hand her a five dollar bill. A new piercing loops through her eyebrow, and a rainbow hemp bracelet peeks from under the cuff of her black shirt. She hands me my change and turns to the guy behind me.

"What can I get you?"

Her voice sounds lighter than I expected, almost fluty.

The customer behind me flinches. Something about him makes me uncomfortable, and I move away to wait for my latte.

He's young, maybe thirty, and wearing a tight-fitting casual suit on his lean frame. His attractive dark blonde hair and blue eyes mark him as the kind of guy I'd bring home as a flavour of the month. But he stares coldly, ogling the barista with his head tilted, as though he's trying to decide something. "Are you a girl?" he says, searching her face.

Ah. He must've mistaken her for a boy until she opened her mouth, but up close, her small, delicate face—fine-boned with flawless pale skin and a straight nose—is unmistakably feminine.

Her cheeks flush, but she looks him in the eye. "What can I get you to drink?"

"God, you *are* a girl!" he crows.

"Now that we've cleared that up, are you going to order or not?" she demands. She tries to look tough, but her hands tremble on the keys of her register.

"I don't know whether I'd want a dyke's drink." He stands back and crosses his arms casually—like he has all the time in the world to decide. "Might catch something."

"Probably the other way around, asshole," I snap. "Being a dick is way more contagious than being a dyke." *God! Did I just say that out loud?*

"How would you know?" he rounds on me. "You play for their team?"

He rakes his eyes over me, taking in everything from my smoky blue eye shadow down to my tight-fitting blouse and high-heeled pumps. His face registers confusion, then contempt.

"Well if you do, you hide it well," he mutters, then shoves away from the counter. The barista raises her eyebrows, but says nothing. People point at us and at the idiot ploughing his way through the subway station. I wish they'd quit fucking staring, but they're not actually looking at me. They're looking at her.

So am I, honestly.

She's pretty for a boi.

Chapter 18

McFarter's taken to faxing my graduation requirements to Nancy, adding to my list until I'm ready to strangle him—or, more likely, go into his office to complain, which is probably his strategy. *So not going to happen.* This week, he claims I need five more hours of "community service activities," or he'll have to hold me back.

I've already done forty hours—more, actually—to insure against this exact scenario. But I'd rather do five extra than look at MrFarter's smug face, particularly since Nancy's already gone to the trouble of finding me a placement. She doesn't have to do these things. She could send me back for guidance at The Hole, but she doesn't. I think she pulled a few strings there, but I can't ask her, because then we'd both have to acknowledge my gratitude, and that would ruin everything.

Lizzie left Beverly again last night. CAS moved her and her mother into a different house so her dad won't know where to find them. Not that this will prevent Mrs. Emery from calling him and volunteering the information. Lizzie will never be safe with either of her parents.

I told Nancy about it. She didn't even have to ask me how I felt. "I'm so sorry, Beth." She's genuine. She gets points for that, especially on days when her insight really irritates me. I can only blame myself. I'm the idiot who thought the idea of an Elder was cool. Obviously the universe listened, because I got Nancy. Yippee.

My community service placement consists of five weeks of one-hour shifts at the hospital. As the only student volunteer in the group, I get stuck with Wednesday afternoons at 3:00. *What the hell? My one hour takes up the entire day!*

The stench of disinfectant and puréed mush envelops me like a toxic gas as the elevator jolts and squeaks down to the basement of the hospital. I find it more than slightly disturbing that the volunteer room sits directly opposite the morgue.

The volunteer uniform looks like the top half to a flower costume—a billowing cotton blouse, worn over ordinary clothes, that smells like industrial soap that could eviscerate skin. Next to five racks of pink uniforms sits half a rack of plain blue shirts. I imagine myself dressed in one of the blue shirts with the sleeves rolled up, sporting a pair of soft blue jeans and going makeup-less. A numb feeling spreads through my chest. I take the vision one step further... pulling my hair back, or worse, cutting it off. Short. Boy-short, like the dykes I saw holding hands on the street.

The numbness spreads to my hands.

...replacing my wedge sandals with runners. Doc martens. Construction boots....

For heaven's sake Elizabeth, you look like something the cat dragged backwards through a hedge. Comb your hair and take off those ridiculous cargo pants!

...spiking the tips of my hair blonde like that barista from the kiosk. Putting holes in my ears and stretching them....

Where on earth did you get those vulgar earrings? And is that a dog tag? Christ on a bike.

The numbness takes me over.

...imagining how people would look at me and what they'd say....

No.

My eyes flip back to the mirror, and I'm relieved to see a normal girl staring back at me. Dark blonde hair glossed and straightened, eyes ringed in eyeliner and mascara: my disguise.

That pink cotton blouse will make me look like a piece of overblown bubblegum, and the boys' shirts remind me of my mother's old painting smock. *But if she can get away with it, so can I.* I don the blue shirt, but roll the sleeves up delicately and cinch the hem to flatter my shrinking waistline. It doesn't hurt to reapply my pink lip-gloss before reporting for duty.

Margaret, the volunteer coordinator, scans me up and down in a very unsubtle appraisal. "Here to steal the meds?" she asks, her dark eyes bore into me.

"Pardon?"

She smirks. "Nobody your age volunteers at a hospital unless they're trying to rob the narcotics. They keep them locked up, you know." Her triple chin jiggles as she shakes her head.

"I'm here for volunteer hours," I snap. "You know—community service?"

"Right. Of course you are." She shifts her elephantine bulk on a rolling chair that squeaks in protest. "Object to the ladies' wear, do you?"

My cheeks heat immediately. *You couldn't fit into three of those hideous pink tops sewn together!* She raises her eyebrows as though she heard the words in my head.

"Your 'university liaison' has requested that you work on the twelfth floor." Why is she smirking like that? She obviously lacks a sense of humour, so she must be enjoying something at my expense. She rolls her beady eyes, sunk beneath rolls of baggy fat, and points at the elevator. Evidently, she doesn't think I'm cut out for this type of work. She may be right, but *she's not cut out for anything other than a muumuu.* So, I head to the twelfth floor—toward the patients, and away from her.

As I step off the elevator, a wave of apathy surges over me. Beige walls frame the drawn faces of nurses and PSWs. A harried doctor frowns as he checks charts and performs rounds. Even the plants mime existential crises. Up here, the smell of puréed mush just about overwhelms me, and I swallow hard. "All right, Nancy," I mutter. "This is absolutely the last time I listen to you...."

That's probably not true. I'll listen to her out of force of habit. I've come to trust her, even though I swore not to. I still have hope for her—that she'll wave a magic wand and begin my Jellicle Transformation.

A drawn face looks up from the nurses' station as I approach. "Can I help you?"

"Yes, I'm a new volunteer," I try my best to be pleasant. "This is my first day."

"And they assigned you here?" she says dubiously.

"This is the twelfth floor, isn't it?"

"Yes."

"Then yes. They assigned me here."

"Okay then." She gestures toward a nearby alcove where a tall metal cart stands abandoned. "The meal trays have been brought up. They each have a room number—you can deliver them."

"Sure." I have to clock a full hour—may as well get started. I grab a meal tray and search for the corresponding room number: 1206B. The occupant sits up in bed, reading. Her hospital gown falls to mid-elbow, and white gauze winds around her wrists. *Yikes. Carpal Tunnel surgery, maybe?* "Hello," I say amiably, putting down her tray, but she just glares at me. Silently, I deliver a can of Ensure to her roommate.

The women next door play a game of checkers while a nurse stands outside like a bouncer at a club. One of the women showers me with a torrent insults as I leave. *Christ on a Bike! What the hell is wrong with these people?*

What *is* wrong with these people? I stop short and look around. Patients sitting in wheelchairs in the hallway, drooling; a woman banging her head against the window, singing church hymns; the woman with the bandaged wrists staring blankly at the wall—this is no regular hospital wing. These people aren't normal.

And then I see the sign next to the elevator. Psychiatry.

Fabulous. She sent me to the psych ward.

I refuse to look at any of the other patients as I bang down their trays and march out. Nancy will learn precisely what I think of her asinine idea. Of all the places she could have stuck me, she picks here? Even picking up garbage at the side of the road would have been better!

Rather than puréed mush, the last tray actually looks edible—green salad, chicken something-or-other with a gelatinous glop that resembles gravy. "That can go in the lounge," says a nurse at the desk. I nod and proceed down the hall to a green room decorated with ancient window dressings and patients' "artwork." I drop the tray on the table.

On the far side of the room, a slender woman in blue scrubs sits staring out the window. *If I had to work at this place, I'd stare outside too, and count the seconds until I could get the hell out... oh wait, that's exactly what I'm doing.* I will not be coming back.

"Lousy weather," I say. The woman, maybe thirty years old, with long hair loosely bound in a honey-coloured ponytail, turns around.

She hasn't aged a day in fifteen years.

Hi, Beth, she says.

Funny thing, I'm actually kind of glad to see her.

"What are you doing here, E?"

She leans her arm against the windowsill and appraises me. *You know I always show up where you need me. How's it going so far?*

"Why the hell would Nancy send me here?"

E chuckles, her warm smile completely out of place in this delusive playroom. She's never told me her real name. She's always just been E—like M from James Bond.

Take my advice. Don't come again unless you plan to stay.

"I have a few things to say to my 'university liaison' about this."

She laughs. *Oh, she's a real piece of work, your Dr. Sullivan. Probably the only person I know who might be able to show you a thing or two about stubbornness.*

I shake my head. "Not for much longer, E."

She doesn't answer. That's not unusual.

It's nice to see you, Beth, she says at last, smiling sadly. She stares at me for a moment, considering.

"What's wrong?"

She shakes her head. *Nothing, sweetie.* Her enigmatic half-smile makes me feel about three-years-old.

I glance at the door, judging how quickly I could escape. I could just as easily leave as ask her to go. Maybe easier.

She sits down on the radiator and leans against the window sill. *So, what do you need?*

"I don't need you."

Of course you do.

Of course I do. If I didn't, she wouldn't be here talking to me. "How the hell do you know?"

Beth, she says quietly. Why does that make me want to cry, the way she says it? The warmth in her voice, the way she knows everything and always has—it makes things seem worse than they are.

Why does she have to look directly at me and talk as though she's reading the stock report? And why does her presence comfort me—soothe me—even though seeing her also means I'm rapidly approaching that edge.... The fall from sanity is so much easier than the climb back up.

Beth?

"What?"

Try to relax.

"What are you talking about?"

You look frightened; you know there's nothing to be frightened about.

"I'm not frightened."

She smiles at me, knowingly. *It's okay that you still need me.*

"Do you wish I didn't?"

No. Not for a second. I'm happy to be here for you. I just wish you could move past this. I wish things had been different for you, less confusing and lonely. I wish you didn't hate yourself.

"Why do you always have to show up? Couldn't you go away this time and not come back?"

She blinks and holds my gaze for a long moment. *Is that what you want?*

I hate that I can't say "YES! YES! Leave me alone." But I can't. I've never been able to.

You've struggled so long, Beth. Can you let this go?

I want to cry, but no tears come. I shake my head and whisper, "I can't."

She squeezes my hand tightly.

I don't want her to feel sorry for me; I want her to disappear. Things are bad enough without adding E to the mix. It takes all my strength to walk away from her—away from her comforting eyes, her knowing looks. *God.*

Beth, she calls as I open the door.

I turn around.

Please don't end up here. When you leave, do not come back.

I clench my fists and march out, stripping off my uniform and dashing into the elevator. I glance at the nurses' station as the elevator closes around me, wondering if anyone walked by the lounge and saw me talking to myself.

Would they have committed me?

I rush home and spend nearly an hour in the shower, washing my hair twice, scrubbing every inch of my body—even under my finger nails. I wash the residue of that place out of every crevice of my body. My clothes already spin in a double cycle in the washing machine, the sludge of human waste bleaching away. *No Nancy, I will not feel better by donating my time to others. In fact, it will drive me completely over the edge.*

And with E around, it's happening faster than expected.

"How did it go? At the hospital?"

Nancy sits in her usual position, hands folded delicately in her lap so that I can't see them shaking. Her acrylic sweater almost matches the green flecks in her blue eyes: I only notice because she looks directly at me.

"Why did you send me there?" I struggle to steady my tone.

"What do you mean?"

"Why did you send me there?" My voice sharpens, but I can't seem to rein it in. She's pushed me beyond self-effacement, which is probably what she wanted. In fact, I know it is. But even knowing that doesn't deter me.

"Didn't we discuss this already?"

Sooner or later, one of us has to answer a question. That task will probably fall to me, because Nancy doesn't look well. Her face is pale, and her hands tremble badly despite clutching them in her lap. I don't even bother to get her a glass of water today. She won't be able to hold it.

"It was fine," I say.

"You're lying."

"So what?"

"I sent you there because I thought it would suit your talents better than picking up garbage on the side of the road."

What? Can she read my fucking mind or something?

"Give me some credit," I snap.

We stare out the window. I fidget and she sighs. "Nancy? Tell me the truth."

She scrutinises me.

"I wanted you to see what could happen," she says at last. "I wanted you to know what a dangerous road you're travelling. And I didn't want you to know that I was showing you."

Slap. Her betrayal both hurts and shocks me.

"I didn't need community service hours, did I?"

She shakes her head, still looking me straight in the eye. *Wow. She's better than I thought. Not only can she read people like billboards, she has a damn convincing poker face.*

"Now," she says. "How was it?"

"It was disgusting. Filthy and perverse—like a prison in disguise. Have you ever been to a place like that?"

For a split-second, fear flickers through her eyes.

"You have, haven't you?"

"This conversation is about keeping you *out.*"

"What do you mean? I'm not going back there! You've just told me I don't need those hours. Wait a minute. Do you mean to ask me if I'll go back as a *patient*? Are you fucking serious? You think I'm psychotic?"

She looks at me coolly. In the midst of all this, I have to give her credit for her self-control—not one trace of condescension or superiority marks her face. She is completely calm—on the outside, at least.

"You think I'm crazy."

"No. I don't. But I think you'd like to be."

"What the hell are you talking about?"

"You're running away from something, and you have an easier time believing you're crazy than recognizing that this thing—this huge demon—will continue to torment you until you accept it or let it go."

"How could you possibly know that?"

She sighs as though she'd like to shake me by the shoulders.

"Your only problem is that you're too goddamned smart for your own good!" she says. "Genius is a curse, sometimes. Especially with kids like you who have nobody to teach them to turn their minds *off!* You're alone too much and you think too much about yourself."

I've had enough. "All right. If I'm too smart for my own good, then why the hell do I need to see you every week? You could release me from this stupid programme and let me get on with my life!"

"Because, darling. I don't know what you'd do if I left you alone. And if you hurt yourself, I'd never get over it."

Oh. I want to stop fighting her, but some instinct overrides that desire and I can't drop my weapons.

"You're not crazy, Beth. You're sad."

"How do you know?"

"I *don't* know. You won't tell me. You'd rather die—literally die—than let anyone see your pain. You'd rather have me think you crazy than tell me what made you lose control of your life. You're trying so hard to get that control back that it's suffocating you. Pain does that to people, Beth. They would rather do almost anything other than face it again."

I feel like she's ripped open a barely-clotted wound. "Don't talk about my pain, Nancy. *You're* in pain. I shouldn't be the one thinking of jumping off a bridge, you should."

Her eyes widen in shock, but it's her own fucking fault. She tore into me and awakened the writhing monster I have to sedate every day. "*You* have to live with life's futility. *You* have to outrun death, even though it's sitting on your shoulder."

She looks like I've back-handed her. "Beth—"

"What do you want me to do?" I yell. "Tell everyone I run into about the black hole in my life? I don't want people to know! I won't let them pity me like they pity you. My pain is nobody's business. I don't want to share! It's bad enough that E thinks I'll end up in the psych ward, and now you— I don't want to fucking talk about it!"

The colour drains from her cheeks. I examined her, discovered her secrets and spat them in her face. But she got to me first. She saw so far inside, I'm amazed I never felt her rooting around in my psyche.

I slam the door behind me, shocked to see her crying.

Chapter 19

I run up the steps to my house and throw open the door. Everything looks unfamiliar—the shoes in the front hall, the dishes on the counter, the bathroom tiles. I grip the sink, but can't force myself to look in mirror. My breath catches halfway to my lungs. I sit down on the side of the bathtub; put my head between my knees. Why do people tell you to do that when you feel sick? It just gives you vertigo on top of everything else. I stand up and pace up and down the tiles.

"I hate you Nancy!" I scream at the window.

I hate her most for being right. The thought of dying, rather than living with all the guilt and lies and fear, has tempted me. *Maybe this time I'll cut too deep.* Jackie and my mother and Simon and the Jellicle Transformation....

A complete charade....

I can't tell the difference between reality and what I've forced myself to believe.

I grab a towel from the rack and hold it tightly to my chest.

Elizabeth, please settle down.

I need my mother to smack me. Instead I press the towel to my face, and try to slow my breathing. In a minute, the hysterical whirling will subside, and I'll cut life back into myself....

There. The blood drowns me in numbness. It pours onto the porcelain in crimson swirls. I feel nothing. *Thank God.*

I sit on the couch in the living room and listen to the phone. It's been ringing for a while now.

The noise stops suddenly, and my heart sinks.

I wait another ten minutes, watching the blood soak through the gauze on my wrist, but it doesn't ring again. Nancy can't win this. She doesn't have the physical energy to push ahead and cut me off. It makes me sad, because she's the only person who had a chance of beating me. I can't give her a break, though—can't quit fighting just because she could have won. I'm not strong enough to give in to her.

The phone rings again. I get up from the couch and walk outside. If I stay in that goddamned house, I'll answer the phone. And only because I feel sorry for her.

The school building never changes much—the Canadian flag on the flagpole fades with each passing summer, but the thronging chatter behind the walls still sounds like a giant nest of hornets. Only a few months have passed since I left The Hole, but as I step inside, the dull roar of the students reflects off me, like university has given me invisible armour. If I've timed this right, they should just be leaving for the day.

Slowly, I climb the stairs to the Chemistry lab. Kids rush past, backpacks flying off their shoulders. I lean against the wall and wait for the stairwell to clear. In three minutes, not a single student is left in the whole science wing. Hilarious. They can't wait to get out of high school, and then they sign up for a decade of post-secondary.

I take a little bottle of baby powder from my purse and sprinkle it on my hands. I made sure to look good: a short blue skirt, pinstriped collared blouse, high-heeled sandals and subtle makeup. Quietly, I step into classroom 219. The heavy door closes with a soft thud. The lab is empty. For a second I'm afraid that he already left, but then the back door opens, and he walks in.

Without looking, I flick the lock on the fire door.

His gaze travels from my hand on the lock up to my face.

Not even a full year has passed since I took his class, but university must have given me a different perspective, too. The lab seems small, pokey. And he's changed as well. His stocky muscularity approaches a somewhat less-flattering border, and his hair has crept a little farther up his cranium. But his eyes still gleam with a genuine and kind light, and his freckled hands still look strong and confident.

He smiles, not in surprise, but with pleasure, and opens his arms. "Beth Sarandon."

I step into the embrace, and we hold each other tightly. In a friendly hug, we would have let go now, stood back a little awkwardly, and begun pleasantries. But this hug goes on. His strong arms close tight around me, and I breathe in his familiar scent—a cologne you can taste. My hand presses into the small of his back, and I lean onto his shoulder. His acknowledgment feels so good that I nearly drop my plans. But it has to be done.

"Why are you here?" he whispers.

I don't answer. Instead, I tilt my face up toward him, knowing that he could push me away, humiliate me, reject me. But I know he won't; otherwise I'd never have started this.

When he presses his lips to mine, my body melts into him, every sense concentrated on his touch, on suspending myself in this very second. I curl my hand around the nape of his neck and kiss him gently, pulling him in, and taking him.

I don't care that he has a wife. A kid. A life. This isn't an affair. I don't expect a future with him. I only want him to take me away from my own for five minutes. I want him to find my on switch and press it.

I push him onto a stool and stand inside his open legs, gratified that he's already hard. His hands move gently around my waist and up to my neck. A faint blush creeps up his cheeks. He's obviously had other indiscretions—he knows exactly what he's doing.

I run my fingers down his chest and into the warm crease of his jeans. He takes a shuddering breath as my fingers make contact with something they shouldn't.

"You're sure the door's locked?" he says.

"Dead sure."

I lean in to kiss his neck and undo the top buttons of his shirt. He buries his face in my shoulder and kisses the hollow there, his hands on my hips, eyes closed. I slip his shirt off, running my fingers around the tiny freckles on his shoulders. I straddle him, bringing my breasts in line with his face as he fumbles with my buttons. Quickly, I shake my shirt to the floor and wrap my wrists around his neck so he doesn't see the pink and red lines running up the insides of my arms. I don't need to worry—he pays no attention to my arms.

I hold my breath. *Is it going to happen this time?*

My bra unclasps—I didn't even notice him flick it. *Definitely not his first time.* As it falls to the floor, cool air rushes over my breasts and makes my nipples hard against his hands. He leans me back, and his erection pulses against my groin. It almost makes me gasp.

For a second, I wonder if the block of ice in my chest will finally melt; if, for once, I will finally be able to enjoy normal girl-on-guy sex without shutting down and wanting to kill my conquest.

He kisses my nipples, and I close my eyes, letting him touch me, feeling everything he wants me to feel. His thumbs travel down my ribcage as I kiss my way up to his earlobe and gently nibble it. He gasps and holds me tighter.

Playfully, I run my fingers down his spine, loving his involuntary jerk as I reach the base. He moans softly and I smile. Mission accomplished. I am transforming. My weight on his groin erases every other label—teacher, student, man, girl. We blend together as our bodies arch and slide and stretch.

I lean back to undo his pants, and he lifts himself slightly out of the seat to let them drop. He reaches his hands under my ass, brings me into line with him, and gently rocks into me. He's trembling— that's sweet. I wrap my feet around his calves, and begin to ride him as he leans back against the wall, his hands still guiding my legs. He moans deeply, and I press my fingers against his mouth to keep him quiet. We don't need an audience.

But then it happens.

Somewhere between the moment when he starts pumping into me and his final jerk and groan, the numbness takes over. His sweaty body feels wrong.

Unwanted.

I feel violated, even though I've done the violating. His breath crawls over my neck, too hot. His hands clamp onto my back, too large.

Before he can even wipe himself off, I pull my clothes back on and leave.

Not even looking over my shoulder to say goodbye.

In the middle of the night, Nancy finally catches me. The persistent ringing of the phone, which, in the fog between dreaming and reality, sounds vaguely musical, wakes me up. After a few seconds of blind groping, my hand finally lands on the cordless. I clear my throat, pick up.

"Hello?"

"So you're finally home."

I'm not in the mood for games. "What do you want?"

"Beth, I need you to come back in tomorrow. I wanted to talk to you this morning, but things got a little out of hand before I could. Can you make it?"

She sounds as if she's been up half the night.

"Time?"

"Whenever you can get here."

Something in her voice makes my chest tighten. "Nancy, what is it?"

The tone of her voice—warm, kind—makes me feel like child released from a time-out. "Bethany, just come tomorrow."

I hang up and lean against the headboard, staring out the window at the moon and its stars. She called me by her daughter's name again, and she wasn't even medicated this time. I know why she wants to see me; I just don't think I'm ready.

You never knew I woke up
earlier that night—
in the dark of the cabin
when the other girls

slept.
On your top bunk,
across from
mine,
I saw you...
more than your shadow.

Your knees were bent,
tenting the
blanket
like a pregnant
woman in an
OB-Gyn chair.
I could tell
from the way
you breathed
and twisted your face
into the pillow...
trying not to
make any noise.
I could tell,
and I watched you
anyway.
I couldn't help
watching you.
Fascinated.

I thought about it...
almost did it.
I almost climbed down my ladder
and up yours.
I almost slid into bed beside you
And watched you from there—
put my hands on you...
touched you til
you moaned and sighed
and came with me.

Instead, I coughed
just a little
to let you know
I was awake.
Your legs slowly slid down
And your hands came out
from under the blankets.

You pretended to
go back to sleep.
And I did too—
pretended, I mean.

She waits for me by the window. I set my bag down on the chair by the door, and pour her a glass of water from the tea trolley. She doesn't turn around. She still stares out the window as I place the water on the sill and sit.

"I'm sorry about yesterday," she says quietly.

"Me too. I didn't mean those things."

"Yes you did." She turns to me, her face relaxed, her hands limp in her lap. "You have searing insight, Beth. I just wish you could learn to use it better."

"I didn't mean it to come out like that."

"Maybe not. But you were angry." She glances at the crease of light gauze visible under my long-sleeved shirt. A look of defeat crosses her face. "Oh, Beth."

"You surprised me, that's all." I turn away from her, back to the window. Today, the park is empty. Streaks of watery sunlight bounce off the fountain onto stone benches, and a light breeze ripples waxy green leaves on tall trees around the gate.

"I hurt you. And I'm sorry for that. I have no right to make assumptions about you."

"It's fine. You weren't wrong."

A single cyclist jumps the curb and zips through the gate, around the water fountain, and out of sight.

"Beth, who's E?"

I stare at Nancy for a moment. Even if I wanted to tell her about E, where would I start?

The first time I met E, she was sitting on my window seat in The Tower. I lay on the floor, trying to colour within the lines perfectly enough to show to Heather. Five previous attempts sat crumpled beside me, and the sixth swam behind a haze of my tears.

Nice picture, she said.

I looked up. "Thanks." I never even asked who she was.

Can I have it?

"It's for my mother," I told her.

Not that one. The one beside it.

I uncrumpled the first attempt—a bear on a beach ball—and held it out. "This one?"

She nodded. *Yeah.*

I never asked her where she came from or what she wanted. I never opened that chapter of our relationship. Those things didn't matter.

She would show up every once in awhile, unannounced. Not often. I learned to whisper when she came, because my mother would occasionally rap on the door and demand to know who I was talking to. When she came in and found me alone, she would frown and usher me outside. I'd flutter my fingers discreetly at E on my way out, not wanting to be rude. She never took offence.

In grade school, I learned that E's presence could cause problems, so I told her not to come anymore. She didn't, for a while. But the day after I got home from camp—the summer with Jackie—she was waiting for me in her usual place by the window seat. And then I knew my mind was going to a place where E would be the least of my problems. Her reappearance didn't matter to me much, that day.

Nancy can't know any of this, so I just let the silence answer for me and hold out her water glass. She shakes her head, and I put the glass back on the window sill.

"Beth, I can't do this anymore," she says quietly. "I'm sorry."

"That's all right." I shrug. "I don't need therapy anyway." The DSM-IV lies on her desk; I doubt she can lift it now.

She shakes her head and sighs. "I wish that were true. But to be honest—you need better help than I can give."

"You're giving up."

She smiles wanly.

"Because of what I said?"

She closes her eyes, shakes her head.

"Nancy. If you weren't treating me, you'd still be practicing, wouldn't you?"

She looks at me sadly. "That may be true, but what good could I do—for myself or for my clients? I needed to realise that I.... Beth, there was a time when I would have been able to take you and ten more just like you without breaking a sweat—the kind that needed to be broken to be mended. But I can't help you, and now I realise that. I know it's time...." Her sentences come in chunks and fragments, like her mouth is out of synch with her brain.

I know what's happening. She does too.

"I have to sort out some things in my own life," she says.

"With Bethany?"

She looks surprised for a moment, then nods. "Especially."

"So what now?"

"We say goodbye. And you call me when you feel like catching up with an old friend."

My wrist starts to ache. I knew it would today—the recent cuts are too deep to disappear under light gauze. I can feel every single one.

"Goodbye," I say stiffly, picking up my bag. I look over the room—at the desk, the window, the knick-knacks placed on various surfaces. One looks ready to fall off a shelf, and I readjust it, refusing to look at Nancy. My body feels heavy from my neck down to my feet. I don't want to leave her alone—now that the game has finished, I feel a strange desire to protect her.

Ridiculous.

I turn quickly and leave, careful not to slam the door.

Chapter 20

My secrets are heavy sometimes. I daydream of turning off my monitor and picking up a piece of parchment, a quill pen and a pot of ink, and scribbling away madly—just to see flourishes sprawl over the page like tendrils of zealous ivy.

Then I have a cup of coffee and get a grip.

The blade marks on my wrists have faded to a dull peach. I see that metamorphosis differently now. I used to think that when the cuts turned to scars and the scars faded, it would be the last time. Now I know better—the process will probably repeat over and over. That doesn't worry me anymore. In fact, the consistency comforts me, gives me a pattern to follow.

Especially now, without Nancy. I miss her calm assurance, her protective nature, and the way she tripped me up for my own good, even when it made me furious. Somehow, I expected her to overcome my secrets, but she didn't. Or couldn't. I never told her enough to let her help me.

And now, even if I could find the courage to tell her, she's gone.

"What do you mean, you can't?" Jackie called from the dark water below. "Just shut your eyes and take the plunge."

"I can't," I insisted, staring down from the top of the diving cliff. The lifeguard squinted at me from his tower on the dock. Other J.C.I.T.s lined up behind me, dripping and laughing, resisting the temptation to shove me off so they could "take the plunge" again. Jackie treaded water below, to the side so that I wouldn't land on her head—if I ever made it off this jutting rock.

"Beth, just jump!"

"It's too deep!" I shouted, hating my fear.

"Well, you wouldn't want it to be shallow, would you?"

I laughed a little hysterically.

"Take a few steps back, and just walk forward. You won't even know you're jumping."

"What the hell are you talking about?" I yelled down. "That's the worst way to do it!"

"Hey, want me to jump with you?" asked Jacob—the boy the counsellors had caught me kissing the year before.

I smiled, blushing. "Nah, I'm going right now." I took three steps back then ran to the end. My stomach crashed against my ribs, and I almost vomited before my feet hit the water. Luckily my arms smacked the surface and stopped me from going under.

Freezing water flowed into my mouth, and I came up spluttering. The lifeguard jumped to his feet, but I held my hands up over my head in the boating "I'm okay" sign, and he sat back down slowly, legs tensed at the edge of his chair. Jackie swam up beside me, laughing, and swept the hair off my face. I put a hand on her shoulder. Her powerful egg-beater kick kept us both afloat.

"That wasn't so bad, eh?" Jackie grinned.

"Not enough to kill me, anyway," I gasped.

"C'mon, let's go to shore." She knew the really deep water made me nervous. I followed her, half treading water, half doggy-paddling. She backstroked toward land, her legs moving through the water in a smooth scissor-kick. The sun-flecked waves made her feet look like a school of silver fish beneath the surface, and her bikini top had slid down so it barely covered her nipples—a fact I didn't bother to mention.

The other J.C.I.T.s clambered out at The Rock and ran back up the cliff to jump again, but we swam behind the cliff, out around The Point where the trees jutted out into the water. I had never been this far out before. The deep water scared me too much to have crossed the rope, but of course

Jackie would. God forbid she let anything like boundaries get in her way.

All of a sudden, Jackie slowed, bringing her toes out of the water as she slid into a seated position on the surface. "C'mon up," she said, holding out her hand. We'd hit a smooth rock-shelf on the backside of the cliff where we could sit, or even lie down, and the water would just lap at our knees. I giggled as I floated up beside her, enjoying our getaway. I stared at the forbidden horizon, leaning against the jagged limestone, thrilled to discover some new part of camp after so many years. The rock shelf gave us something we always lacked: shelter and privacy. In the distance, I heard the muted shrieks and laughter of the cliff jumpers, but we couldn't see them, and they certainly couldn't see us. I began to shiver, and Jackie put her arm around me. Her breast brushed against my shoulder, barely covered by the slipping bikini.

"So, how does it feel?" she asked. For a wild moment, I wondered what she meant, exactly, then realised she was asking about the jump.

"Oh, not bad." My voice sounded weird, even to me, and my stomach flip-flopped again. Why did this always happen around Jackie, this unsettled feeling? *Unless... unless she... unless you think....*

Christ on a bike, never mind!

Jackie smiled encouragingly. "You want to do it again?"

I froze.

Get a grip! She's talking about the cliff!

"God, no!"

She laughed like that day when I'd admitted I'd never kissed a girl. "Don't worry, you'll get there."

She looked at me, and I smiled back. Glistening water droplets beaded her face, and water streamed from her hair in rivulets across her shoulders and down her semi-exposed breasts. If ever there was a time, this would be it.

A smile crept onto her face. "Do you want to kiss me, Beth Sarandon?" she teased. I blushed and looked away from her, but when I looked back, she was still watching me. I bit my lip and gave her an embarrassed smile. She shrugged and closed her eyes, tilting her mouth toward mine. After a moment, I pressed my quivering lips to hers, and she kissed back—softly, sweetly.

I liked it.

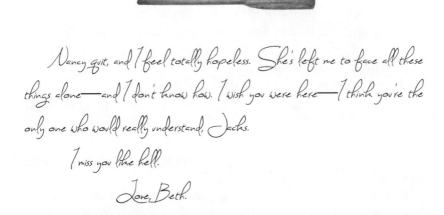

Nancy quit, and I feel totally hopeless. She's left me to face all these things alone—and I don't know how. I wish you were here—I think you're the only one who would really understand, Jacks.

I miss you like hell.

Love, Beth.

I seal the envelope with star stickers, and place it on the shelf next to all the others.

In the middle of the night, I wake up terrified. My hands ache from gripping something—what is it? The pillow? What was I dreaming about? Dark water enveloping me... torchlight... someone screaming... *oh fuck.*

I stumble out of bed and pull on a dressing gown against the night's chill. Streetlamps light my way to the window. Moonbeams reflect off the birch trees across the street, and the neighbour's lights spill yellow squares onto the sidewalk. It's too still. Lonely.

The open windows allow me to sit on the sill without having to hunch my back, so I dangle one foot out and lean back against the frame. I take deep breaths, and pop an Ativan out of the bottle in my dressing gown pocket. It doesn't help, so after ten minutes I take another one. When my eyes begin to close, I climb back into my bed and curl into a ball under the covers.

Cold and dreamless sleep.

Someone knocks on the door, and I fight to open my eyes. The numbers on the clock refuse to focus.

The knocking continues.

11:58.

In the morning? *Oh my God, it's almost noon.* A suffocating cocoon of covers binds my feet as I force myself out of bed.

"Beth?"

Still struggling between sleep and waking, I stumble to the door and peer out the peephole.

Simon.

I haven't brushed my teeth and I have total bed-head. *What is he doing here?*

"Hang on a sec! I was just getting dressed."

"Okay!" he chuckles.

I run to the bedroom and change out of my sweatshirt and boxers into a slip dress. Applying deodorant and brushing my hair leaves no time for teeth-brushing, so I stick a wad of peppermint gum in my mouth and pull on a shrug.

Barely decent, but better than pyjamas.

"Hi!" he says as I let him in.

"Hi. You're back. I wasn't expecting you."

"I wanted to surprise you. Hope you don't mind."

I shake my head, still recovering.

"No, not at all. C'mon in. I just have to wash my face—"

He catches my arm.

"Beth, I need to talk to you." His eyes bore into mine, and his fingertips close on my arm with a surprising jolt. His heartbeat throbs against my skin.

Is he going to kiss me? God, I'm so not ready. I pull my arm out of his grasp and nod, backing slowly toward the bathroom. "Just give me a sec."

As soon as the door shuts behind me, I run the water and splash my face and hair. He was going to kiss me, I'm sure of it. God, Simon! I've thought about this day—what it would be like to kiss him, to feel his lips and his hands and the fair stubble along his jaw. Would I hate him like I hated Jacob? Mike? Mr. Davidson? Would I hate myself afterward as well?

I spit out the giant wad of gum, brush my teeth and put on a little makeup and perfume. *Do I want this? Really? Shouldn't I be sure?* Maybe all that stuff about knowing Destiny when it creeps up on you is a total croc. Or maybe we all need to be smacked over the head with a grand piano hammering out Prelude No. 9: *Signal of a Great Change.* Simon's supposed to be my future. We've known it since we were twelve years old. He's the one I've been waiting for, the reason no other relationship has worked for me.

Right?

By the time I've covered the zit on my chin, I've convinced myself to let him kiss me—to let things happen like they're supposed to. I'm ready to let the past die, and confront my future. Simon can make that happen.

I open the door and watch him jiggle his foot against the floor as I creep down the hall and into the living room.

His eyes darken when he looks up. "Beth—"

"Simon, never mind explaining," I say softly. "I know why you're here."

"You do?"

"Yeah."

He leans back on the sofa and sighs. "We haven't been dating that long, but she seems so sure."

What? Who seems sure? Meagan? I try to sort through his unspoken thoughts while retaining a neutral expression.

"Mmm hmm."

"She's going to university next year, and I can see her point. It doesn't make sense for us both to take out separate leases, you know?"

"She wants you to move in with her?"

"Yeah."

"Okay. I guess I didn't realise things were so serious between the two of you."

"We're really right for each other, you know? It's just weird because she's been right in front of my face for so long."

I take a deep breath. "Wow. I guess I've been a little out of the loop."

"It's not your fault. We didn't really tell you before. I thought I should be the one."

Well yeah. I've never met Meagan, so her showing up here would be a little weird. "Why didn't you?"

"I guess...." His hands tremble a little.

Tears well up in my eyes, but I'm not afraid to cry—I know I can't, even now.

"I guess I didn't want to hurt you."

Because *I'm* the right girl for him? Does he think so too? Has he been waiting for me as well?

I know it's not the right thing to do—he's with Meagan, and I should encourage him to follow his bliss—but when he looks at me, and our eyes lock on like magnets again, I know I've never felt anything close to this with any other boy, and no one but Simon will be able to make me forget her....

I lean in and brush my lips onto his, smooth and soft next to the stubble of his chin. Gently. Sweetly. Chastely.

And then it's over.

Confusion flickers in his eyes. He leans back and brushes his fingers over his mouth. I reach for the remote and turn on the T.V., wondering if I've just made a total fool of myself.

Like a wish puff, I float, disconnected from my mother dandelion, just beyond the hands that wait to trap me, to whisper their dreams into my ear and blow me away. But wish puffs are like butterflies—touch them lightly, or they collapse, never to fly again.

I sit on the edge of the tub and run my hands through my hair. Shouldn't I be happy? Shouldn't I feel whole now? My life is moving down the right path. I kissed Simon and he kissed me back.

So why do I still feel so off-track? Jackie would get this. She understood everything about complicated relationships. Shit, she was

the one who made relationships complicated. I could write about it,
but I'm too scattered, too confused. Tomorrow. Tomorrow's poem
will go like this:

The showers
should have closed
at ten,
but we never listened
to stupid rules like that.

Do you ever think that
maybe we should have?

Maybe they were there
for a reason?
Like, to stop things like this from
happening?
And why did you come into
my shower?
Why didn't you
stay in your
own?
I could barely see you
through the steam.
My hair was full of
shampoo
when you came behind me
and put your hands in the
frothy strands to
rinse them out.

Your breasts brushed
against my back
and then
against my breasts.

I caught my breath,
and you laughed before

JELLICLE GIRL

putting your mouth on
my nipple,
making me lean against
the cold shower wall.

Why did you have to
kiss me again?
And why did I have to
like it?
And, what made you think
that it was okay?

Chapter 21

A month of exams follows this last week of classes. I leap over puddles on my way to the Psychology building. Everyone complains about the constant April rain, but I find it romantic. Besides, it suits my mood—distracted and cold.

My phone rings and vibrates. "Hello?"

It's Kate. "Listen, I can't talk long, but I'm dying to know what you said to Simon."

"What do you mean?"

"Oh, c'mon." My cousin pants softly, and I hear a shrill whistling in the background. She must be jogging. "As if you don't know."

"What?" I repeat, genuinely perplexed.

The whistling stops.

"He said Meagan wanted him to move in with her," I say.

"*What?*"

"Yeah. Crazy, right? They're way too young."

"Beth—Simon and Meagan broke up."

Shit! "When?"

Kate sighs heavily. I imagine her doubled over, catching her breath. "Beth, I love you, but sometimes you can be so dense. This is obviously going to be a long conversation, so let's just have it later, okay?"

"Yeah okay. See ya." I say, and hang up.

Shit! Why would Simon break up with Meagan? It has to be because of me, because of our conversation. Is that self-absorbed? But that's not how it's supposed to go. I'm not ready. He's not supposed to be available. Ever!

Berating myself will have to wait until later. I rush into the Psychology building for my last class of Ex-Psych, but, suspiciously, few people move through the hallway. I glance at my watch, 2:30.

Shit. Thursday lectures begin at 1:30. I've missed almost the whole damn thing! Simon must have been weighing more heavily on my mind than I thought....

A notice pinned to the auditorium door reads, Class Cancellation: Existential Psychology. Students, please pick up papers at Professor Mirtica's office: Psychology Building 546.

I breathe an audible sigh of relief. *Would having her mail me my paper count as pathological avoidance?* Yes. It would. I check my reflection in the glass of a snack machine and find everything in order. My hands shake as I get off the elevator and walk to Professor Mirtica's office. The door is ajar.

No, the door is a door... a jar is a jar.

Have I found the right room? The dark hallway makes the numbers beside the door almost invisible. Should I knock? *Get a grip! All you have to do is walk in, tell her your name, and collect your paper.* I knock—too loudly.

"Come in." The door—actually a fire door—thuds to a close, reminding me of the chemistry lab, and the morning after, and the sick feeling Mr. Davidson's hot man breath gave me.

I threw up on my way home that night.

Professor Mirtica sits at a little table near the window, pouring tea. I almost smile. I don't know what I expected, but afternoon tea never crossed my mind. Framed photographs of the Existentialists hang on one wall of her bright and well-decorated office, while several tall wooden bookshelves line another. Her desk occupies one corner. A tea table and chairs sit beneath narrow shelves that hold stone Native artefacts.

"Hello," she says, rising gracefully. "You're from my Existential Psychology class."

I nod. She's asking without asking, as usual.

"I thought everyone had already come." She picks up a folder and rifles through.

"Beth Sarandon," I say, but she's already found it. She hands me my essay, then watches me I take it. Does she expect me to look at it now? I don't want to look at it now... what if I got a bad grade?

"Here," she hands me another piece of paper. "It's a take-home exam, due on the day that the final was scheduled." Maybe she expects me to ask why we're having a take-home, but I don't.

She's dressed entirely in black—*is this artsy or funereal?* Up close, she's as flawless as she is from a distance, but not unapproachable. Why, when I can to talk to anyone, no matter how intimidating, have I avoided Professor Mirtica all semester? Why does she scare me? I need to hurdle that ridiculous barrier in my mind. Kindness brightens her eyes, which I can't see from the back of the auditorium, but also grief—unmistakable and profound.

"Did something happen?" I ask gently.

A flicker crosses her face, but she holds my gaze. "My partner died last night."

God. "I'm so sorry."

"It was a long illness," she says simply.

Something in her face makes me think she used "illness" very loosely.

She looks down at the desk and swallows imperceptibly. No tears well in her eyes, but this has moved her profoundly. Some losses in life have layers beyond the reach of tears. The deeper the loss, the more hollow the ache, and the less tears help.

"You did very well," she nods at my paper. "One of the best I've seen."

Going along with the subject change seems like the kindest thing to do. "Thank you," I manage.

She smiles wanly and sits back down at her tea table, indicating the seat opposite her. I take the seat, crossing my legs gracefully... I hope. She hands me a flowered china cup and offers me milk and sugar but I don't trust my ability to manipulate tiny instruments right now. Better to drink it black. Why has she asked me to sit down? Maybe she needs someone to talk to—maybe she thinks I do.

I remember that day in the lecture hall when she asked us about the futility of existence, and how she seemed to need that question answered herself.

"Do you think everyone believes their lives are objectively meaningless?" I ask, fingering the tiny china handle.

She sets down her teacup. "No, I don't. I don't think everyone thinks about these things. Some people go through their entire lives doing exactly as they should, almost dogmatically. They never stop to ask themselves why."

She tilts her head thoughtfully. "You mentioned suicide in your paper, that when a person recognises his ability to end his own life, he experiences anguish. And the knowledge that he can harm himself is the precursor to recognizing his freedom—his control over existence. But not everybody considers suicide."

"Only perfectionists," I say wryly. She smiles, but that knowing look creeps back into her eyes. This time, it doesn't make me uneasy. If she can read me, that's only fair. Some people are naturally gifted that way.

"The idea of transcendence interests me," I say. "And death is the only way to find out for certain whether or not it's possible."

Professor Mirtica nods, absently, as though a memory is pulling her. "Camus even argues that the choice between life and death is the only philosophical question worth undertaking."

Her words falter, as if weighted with something heavier than they can hold. But she feels compelled to discuss this subject, like a persistent mosquito bite that begs to be scratched, even though it will bleed.

"Well, perhaps he was right," I say carefully. "If someone can't decide whether or not to live, what's the point in examining anything else?"

"And as long as one is alive, the decision has never been irrevocably made," she agrees. "Imagine the anguish that causes. Almost better to kill oneself and get it over with."

Her eyes flash. She doesn't believe that—why would she say it then?

"Unless you don't believe in transcendence," I say. "Then you'd be wasting your only sentient experience. You'd think you could make that decision irrevocable as well."

She glances over at the pictures on her wall. "You'd think so." Grief clouds her face, and silence settles over us.

Eventually, she speaks again, her voice heavy. "Even if you understand these things 'objectively,' that doesn't mean you can live with them 'subjectively.' Subjective reality mires us in emotions that take precedence over logic and reason. You can understand things you cannot accept...."

Words could shatter her, but the question hovers over us like a bread basket in a French bistro. All I need to do is reach up and pluck it down.

"What can't you accept?"

She absently fingers her wedding ring. Her words fall like lead weights at my feet. "That she chose death."

The world pitches to one side. *She?*

I keep my face blank—no reason to be surprised. Apparently some lesbians are gorgeous university professors in thigh-high boots.

My mind reels with the unbelievable betrayal her partner has dealt her. All her life, she's striven to make sense of life in the face of death, and chosen life. And now her partner—her intellectual and spiritual equal—has scorned that.

I wish I could empathise without revealing too much of myself, could explain that for some people, death seems like the only way to shut that incessant mind loop off.

"You can only live in some people's minds for so long," I say. *Jackie's, for instance.* "I don't think we can fully understand someone else's subjectivity."

She glances up sharply. "And yet we have to live with their decisions."

"You said she was ill?" I ask softly.

For a long moment, I don't think she's going to answer.

"She was obsessed," she says slowly. "With death. The afterlife, transcendence, mortality... totally fixated on it. She was a writer. She collected methods of death. Her preoccupation fascinated me, at least at first. I was drawn to her existential wounds, I suppose. We understood each other in a very spiritual way. The difference was that my fascination with death was philosophical. Intellectual. Hers was real. Her obsessive mind could not turn off, no matter how many times it cycled through the same scenario and arrived at the same decision. I think she could have killed herself fifteen different ways and still not have been satisfied."

I feel like a novice vampire handling her first vial of blood—vaguely sickened, but nonetheless captivated by the thick crimson liquid, fascinated with the morbidity.

"Every day for forty-one years, she went to bed having made the same choice," Professor Mirtica continues. "And then one day.... The compulsion was always there. I don't know why it surprises me. Maybe it doesn't, really."

"Does it make you angry?"

Bitterness twists her mouth. "She acknowledged her freedom. I understand that... but some things are better grasped theoretically."

"Like finality?"

"And cowardice." She catches her breath, as if shocked with herself for saying it out loud. "Living with the uncertainty of life takes incredible strength. You have to have commitment, courage. There is a world of difference between knowing you're going to die someday, and knowing that you're going to die today. Faith lies in making plans for a tomorrow that may never come."

I let her words hang in the air so she can hear them again. "I'm sorry you have to find your way without her."

Her teacup remains on the table. She crosses her legs and folds her hands on the tabletop, staring over them without seeing.

"I'm having difficulty wrapping my mind around the idea of never," she sighs. "Never seeing her again."

One hand moves to cover her mouth; the other trembles near her saucer.

"Never only lasts as long as you're alive. We don't know what will happen when we die. Maybe we will transform, transcend. Maybe something will bring us back to them—the people we love, I mean. Maybe faith is just as important in facing life as it is in facing death."

She looks up, and her dark eyes see farther into me than I would like. Like Nancy. She nods slowly. "Thank-you."

I meet her gaze. "Good luck... with everything." I stand up slowly.

She rises gracefully, smoothing her pencil skirt, the grief in her eyes suddenly veiled. "Your exam will be marked by the end of May. You can come review it then, if you like."

I open the door.

"Beth?" she says.

I turn back.

"Who was she? For you?"

I freeze.

Concentrate on breathing.

I haven't said her name out loud in almost two years.

"Jackie," I whisper. "Jacqueline Sykes."

She looks at me sympathetically, then turns to her desk, as I close the door. She's going to cry. I have a gift for unlatching floodgates in other people. Too bad I can't do it for myself. I can read people, for better or worse. Nancy was right about that.

I wonder if Professor Mirtica's partner and I had similar childhoods—choked by the choices that churned in our brains. Did she sneak down to the kitchen in the dead of night to ease open a drawer and stare at all of the options? Did she wrap her hand around a cool metal handle, and slip a knife from its resting place? Maybe hold it to her heart or to her gut? Did that precipice, with no one to watch her or call her back, fascinate her? Did the minutes play aloud in her chest cavity? Did she have to count to ten and force herself to put the knife away? Then, did she tiptoe back upstairs, her stomach heaving as she sank to her knees beside the bed, weeping with relief because she had escaped herself again?

I wonder how it happened with her, if not like that—if her obsession was powders or pills or guns. And I wonder how she lived with it, day after day. Mostly though, I think of what Professor Mirtica said: "Living with the uncertainty of life takes incredible strength."

Chapter 22

I stand awkwardly to the side to let Simon shuffle through the door. "Hey," he says, shifting his weight from one foot to the other.

"Hey yourself."

He bites his lip, avoiding my eyes. *Damn it—I've done this to him. And I'm about to be an even bigger jerk and tell him it can't happen again.* "Listen. I'm really sorry about last time," I say, trying to keep my voice steady.

He sighs in relief. "Yeah. I really wasn't expecting that."

"I'm sorry."

"Don't be."

"Did you tell Meagan? About what happened?"

He looks at me quizzically. "No. Why would I? We broke up."

But they were talking about living together—why didn't he explain it to her? "Right. Okay. Well...."

"You didn't tell Kate, did you?"

I frown. "Of course not. Why would I?"

Simon's grabs me by the shoulder and steers me into the living room. Is he going to kiss me again? He stares right into my face, and his jaw twitches. "I figured you felt guilty about kissing me, and that's why you've been avoiding my calls. I just want you to know that we can totally forget it ever happened."

I look at the ground. He knows me way too well. And he's so kind to let me off the hook. I'm just not ready yet. The Transformation needs to happen at the perfect moment, and right now isn't the time.

"Yeah?" I look up at him. "So we can go back to being friends, then?"

He laughs. "Well, yeah. Of course! We've always been friends. One little mistake doesn't change that."

I grin, and let out a sigh of relief. "Well good. C'mon then, there's a *Jaws* marathon on T.V."

I scoot to the far end of the couch as Simon grabs the popcorn. "Which one is this?"

"The first one." I squint at the screen to make sure. "It's just starting. We've got all four to get through."

"Well I guess I'd better order some pizza."

"Nah. Mrs. Continiso will be up with spaghetti soon. Just wait."

Simon settles back on the couch and digs his hand into the popcorn bowl. I haven't seen this movie in years. I used to love it as a kid. The scary music starts and I bite my lip. Oh God. I forgot about this part. *Why do people swim at night?* Dread creeps around my collar, threatening to choke me. *Shake it off.* My head begins to swim and a lead ball crushes my stomach. I can't watch this. I have to turn it off.

Suddenly the scene ends and a commercial for laundry detergent blares across the screen. Thank God for ad-focused network television. I thumb the sound down as Simon turns to me.

"Beth, do you want to go to your mother's art exhibit?"

I frown. "No. Do you?"

"Not if you don't want to. I just thought you might like to go. It opens tomorrow, right?"

"Yeah, I think so." I know it opens tomorrow—and Heather will be there for the opening. "I haven't seen her in so long Simon... I don't know how things would go, you know? Besides, there's a reason we haven't...."

"Yeah, I understand. I just wondered if it might make you feel better. You know—closure and all that."

I cuff him on the shoulder. "Yeah, thanks for the analysis, Dr. Mickle. Maybe I ought to make an appearance... even if she just throws me out."

Simon laughs. "I doubt it. She'd probably have one of her bodyguards do it for her." I smile, but wryly—more far-fetched things have happened.

Hating my mother is easier than missing her. Maybe a divine understanding will magically fall from the heavens one day— another Jellicle Transformation—and I'll finally understand what goes on in that woman's head.

I don't know why I need to understand her. Maybe it's because our shared genes make us far more alike than I would ever admit, especially to her. The brick wall that stands between us blocks out anything she might reveal of my own future. I feel cheated, cut off from important information because she's closeted herself away from everyone except her fucking, nonsensical paintings.

Simon tucks his arm firmly in mine as we walk up the path to the Gallery.

"You're sure?" he asks as we approach the door.

"You mean I have an alternative? Great, let's go home."

He winks and opens the door.

Inside, the gallery hums with patrons. Art-lovers murmur ridiculous comments to each other as they make the rounds, and the more they talk, the less they know. I remember their type from my mother's previous, smaller-scale, exhibits. The ones who actually know something about art keep quiet and look at it.

Simon stands on tiptoe and looks over the crowd. "It's upstairs," he says, finally catching sight of a poster. We take the ramp up to the second floor. I feel like I've had an abdominal lobotomy—something's severed my stomach from its surrounding organs. It writhes around, looking for an exit.

Less of a crowd has formed upstairs, but enough people mill about that we can blend in. Simon keeps close to my side as we navigate the rows, giving perfunctory nods of appreciation, and the occasional murmur of interest.

"This way," I whisper. We bypass some very morbid sculptures and head straight into the enormous space they've given my mother. Astounding. At least fifty pieces—only a fraction of what she must have painted—line the walls. I recognise her trademark 12"x14"-sized images, but pillars and heads block my view of the larger pieces over to the right. *What was so important that she'd paint it on an 8'x10' canvas?*

To my left stands a table where a bowl of dark pink punch sits nestled between trays of champagne flutes. A tuxedoed caterer sets down a doily-lined platter of shrimp, and I stare at it for a second, imagining art enthusiasts picking up the delicate crustaceans, putting the sweet flesh into their mouths, dabbing the juice off their fingers with a paper napkin... and greeting my mother with a warm hand clasp.

She'd wonder why her palms itched, why hives crept up her arms and face, why her throat felt thick and dry, and her breath came only in shallow gasps. I've seen it happen before, and sometimes, when she made me crazy, I'd fantasise about slipping a shrimp into her dinner....

The catering company didn't realise they were playing Russian roulette with their appetisers.

I grab the platter from the waiter's hands and empty it into the garbage can.

"Hey!" he protests.

I hand him back the empty tray. "Just trying to save you from a manslaughter charge." I wink disarmingly. *Never pass up the opportunity to practice flirting.* He stares at me in confusion.

"Manslaughter?" he asks. "From shrimp?"

"Shellfish."

He slaps a hand across his forehead. "Someone's allergic?"

"Yeah. Your star attraction."

"I almost killed Heather Sarandon?" he whispers.

I nod, wondering just how many *fruits-de-mer* are on the menu tonight. "You could have done it with Lobster, too. Also, crab."

"Shit."

From the panic on his face, I guess the kitchen teems with poison morsels.

"I'll get rid of it all," he promises.

As the waiter hurries away, Simon tries unsuccessfully to cover up a snort. "Think she's got life insurance?" I give up and giggle helplessly, mostly from nerves.

We make a slow circle around the room. The first collection are landscapes full of densely-packed gardens, waterfalls, ivy trellises—a crying garden gnome. "Look at this one, Robert," gushes a heavily-perfumed woman to her bored-looking husband. "I love the texture of her roses. I feel as though I can actually smell them."

"Yes, indeed," says the husband in a monotonous undertone.

Oh, please. We move past the other garden themes and onto her earlier work. "She painted this when I was four," I say, leading Simon toward one of the smaller paintings. Two distant figures stand on either side of a stream running up toward a mountain. They're too far in the background to see their faces, though one is clearly a child, the other an adult.

I have never studied art. I don't know what makes one painting brilliant and another terrible. I don't know anything about colours: juxtaposed or blended. In fact, I have made a conscious decision to avoid fine art altogether. The less I know about Heather's artwork, the better—because I hate it. Sometimes I just want to rip it all off the walls and punch jagged holes into it with knuckle blades.

Her paintings are beautiful, so beautiful they're almost painful to look at. Not just for me, but for everybody. People are drawn to her art. They stand for hours, staring at the delicate lines and strokes, the rich, vibrant colours, the compelling subjects. I wish I could hate it for its ugliness. In reality, I hate her work because she pours all the beauty she should keep in her soul onto these godforsaken canvases, while she remains a cold, hollow shell.

"What about this one?" Simon asks, turning me around. I stand back, astounded by the enormous canvas on the opposite wall. A sky of constellations wink down at us, all of them to scale, all painted in inky indigo, and all framed by the roof of The Tower.

"How did they ever get it down the stairs?" I whisper.

In the next painting, people face all different directions, looking confused and searching for someone, I guess, in a dark forest. The trees look positively smug—she's given them faces, personalities—and they whisper to one each other as they conceal a small child in their branches.

"This one's nice too." Simon leads me to an easel by a glass case. "Is this a self-portrait?" It certainly looks like Heather—but much younger. No lines mar her face, and her complexion is clear and pale. Dark brown hair falls in untangled waves down her back. She turns away from a mirror, looking past the painting, past us, beyond the wall. An even younger version of this girl looks out of the mirror, expressionless. *Echoes of the Future* reads the caption.

As I try to figure out whose future she's painting, a hush falls on the room.

"Beth," Simon whispers, looking over my shoulder. "It's her."

I turn around. Heather makes her way through the crowd, unobtrusively, standing back from the paintings and appraising their position and lighting on the wall. Is she satisfied?

She doesn't look any older, and certainly no less composed. How can she have remained the same all this time? Fragile bones, flawless porcelain skin and hair like dark maple syrup.

Beyond her looms another giant canvas, bigger than all the rest. People mill about in front of it, nodding, murmuring and pointing. I edge my way into an opening next to an elderly couple, and my heart skips a quick and painful beat.

The image is so familiar I could close my eyes and fill in the details she missed. In the background, illuminated by moonlight, an island floats in the centre of a lake, an earthen hump of green and brown. Brightly coloured finger paintings splay over the walls of a small cabin on the left. On the dock, torches cast shadows on a tangle of people running and diving into the water, but illuminate a lone girl, waist deep in the lake, her hair dripping down her back, who gazes out toward the island.

The blue-black water freezes my feet; its frigid waves lap my waist.

How could she paint such a clear picture? She only came once, the day she dropped me off on my first day at camp, and we never even went down to the docks. I would have been eight, which was nine years ago.

She must feel the electricity move around her, because she turns. Our eyes lock, and she freezes. I can barely breathe. Everything around us fades away—even the chatter of the art viewers deadens.

I was wrong before. Something *has* changed about her. She seems smaller, farther away. And the warm glow of the gallery softens her face, making it look as though time and distance have worn away its hard edges. She never could cross distances. For her, emotional barriers are physical, as impenetrable as slabs of steel—even if her heart begs her to take the first step. She sees chasms where only fissures exist.

Her hand catches a flash of silver at her throat. I recognise it, the necklace of amethysts and rose quartz she made for me, and I left behind. She leans forward slightly, and I think she is going to take a step toward me. But her feet stay rooted to the carpet.

I know, as I have always known, that *I* will have to bridge the gap.

Only the gap is too big for me as well.

I can't.

Not today. Not when my sanity seeps from every crack and orifice.

I should never have barged in on her show. I should leave.

I crash through the door and run down the corridor, down the steps and into the street.

"Beth!" Simon's voice rings out behind me.

I bolt into the busy core of downtown, whistling with activity and traffic. A streetcar clangs, inches from me—and I leap across the tracks, barely missing it.

"Beth!" Simon catches up.

"Please," I choke breathlessly. "Please."

Simon runs with me down the street, clutching my elbow.

I shake, inside and out, during the entire subway ride home, ignoring Simon who sits across from me. *God, just like Nancy.* Thinking of her makes me want to scream. Fuck—if someone else had given birth to me, I wouldn't have needed Nancy in the first place. Now I've got my mother to deal with, and Nancy's gone.

Elizabeth, please sit still and stop thundering through the house like a bull in a china shop.

The subway screeches through the tunnel, and each time the doors open with their cheerful jingle, my stomach turns over. I have to get away from here. Now.

As soon as the train pulls into our station, I dash to the exit. The cool outside air soothes the beast a little, but not enough to stop.

I hate this feeling—this intense, anxious, horrible feeling.

"Simon, would you leave me alone?" He's followed me all the way to the steps of my dad's place, but he can't come in. He can't see this. I don't look back, just shake him off and fall into the house.

I hurry into the bathroom, strip off my dress, and pull on shorts and a zip-up sweater. I pull my hair back, take off my makeup. *Stop. Stop. STOP!* I know this is dangerous, but I can't stop myself. I need help. Jackie would understand. She'd wrap her arms around me and hold me until I could breathe again. But she's not coming.

She'll never come.

That painting.... Stark terror shivers through me as I remember the siren across the water. *How the fuck did Heather know? Who told her? God, if she did know, somehow, that day I came home, and she still she said nothing to me.... Fuck!* I didn't think I could hate her more.

Water gushes into the sink. It spills over my wrist, numbing the skin. I let the water run, staring at the criss-crossing blade marks running from the base of my left wrist all the way up to my shoulder. When is this ever going to stop?

I pat my arm dry. Reach for the alcohol. Disinfect my wrist, and the blade.

My hand dangles in the water. It's soothing. Tranquilizing. Better than Ativan, some days. But I need an antidote, not a tranquiliser.

Not Simon. We're not going to work. I love him, probably more than anybody, but he can't cure me. I can't expect him to. I won't use him like that; I won't abuse our friendship.

Friendship?

Yes. Friendship. Of course friendship. How could I ever expect Simon to fall in love with a—

"Beth!" With a start, I drop the razor. *What the hell is he still doing here?*

"Yeah?" I don't recognise my own voice—strained and high-pitched.

"It's Lizzie on the phone. Can you come talk to her?"

I stuff everything back in the medicine cabinet, throw open the door, and take the phone from Simon. "Lizzie?"

I can barely hear her voice as she hiccups, trying to talk. "Speak up, sweetie," I say, standing as still as possible. "Just tell me where you are."

"Get me out," she whispers before the line goes dead.

Chapter 23

The house—if you can call it a house—consists of four walls of tumbling vinyl. The roof appears to be held on with thumbtacks, and chalky paint flakes from every window frame. The neighbouring houses crumble into heaps of rotting wooden porches, grimy plastic siding, overgrown yards and weed-claimed walkways. *What the hell kind of life is this to send a child into?* A single cracked pail sits on the bottom step, filled with popsicle sticks. Lizzie's favourite.

Glass shatters, and someone yells. Sirens scream in the distance, but we've beaten them here.

How will we get inside?

Without hesitating, Simon leaps up on the sagging porch and rings the bell.

A man staggers out and leers at us. The reek of alcohol washes over me when he opens his mouth, "What in the hell—"

Simon shoves past him, and the man loses his balance. He trips down the stoop and falls face-down in the grass next to me, passed out.

"Jesus." Simon whistles.

"Lizzie!" Gingerly, I hop over the man and into the house. Simon follows. "Lizzie!"

Lizzie's mother suddenly staggers down the hall as if in a viscous dream.

"Mrs. Emery," I say, clutching her arm. "Where's Lizzie?"

"What?" She stares at me blankly.

"Elizabeth! Where is she?"

"I... I don't know," she says hollowly. "I don't know."

"What's wrong with her?" I ask Simon.

"She's stoned." His face twists in disgust.

"Lizzie!" I yell, running through the tiny kitchen. Insects crawl along every counter, swarming the back door. *Is that a dead rat?* "Lizzie, it's Beth!" The bedroom sits empty, the bathroom rank in the summer heat.

"Beth!" Simon's voice comes from behind a thick heavy door that leads into the garage. Under a pile of junk huddles a little dark-haired girl, clutching a cordless phone.

"Lizzie!" I rush over to her. She extracts herself from her hiding space and throws her arms around me. She neither speaks nor cries; she just shakes, chalk-faced and terrified, in my arms.

"I'm so sorry," I whisper, hugging her tightly. "I'm so sorry." Her cold silence frightens me almost as much as her emotionless face. "Lizzie, it's going to be okay."

She tightens her arms around my neck, burying her face in my shoulder. "Please take me with you," she whispers desperately as sirens draw near, car doors slam, and two enormous police officers charge into the garage.

When the police have finally handed Lizzie over to waiting the paramedics, they lead us outside to meet with a social worker. "You're Beth Sarandon?" she asks, appraising Simon and me. *Is she going to ask why we're here? Why Lizzie had my phone number?*

"Yes, I'm from the youth home on Beverly." I leave out the fact that I'm the co-op student and not an actual counsellor.

"She just came from that home, didn't she?" The social worker leafs through a thick file.

"Yes."

"Well, I guess she might as well go back there," she sighs. "Until we can work out a more permanent arrangement."

"Don't worry about it tonight," I whisper to the tiny girl, her arms tight enough around my neck to turn my lips blue. "Let's just go home."

"C'mon, Elizabeth," the social worker says. We both look up, not sure which of us she's talking to.

When Lizzie sees the woman's outstretched arms, she buries her face deeper into my shoulder. The social worker takes her gently by the waist and tries to pull her away.

And then Lizzie loses whatever measure of self-restraint she has managed so far. "No! No, no, no, no, no, no, NO, NO, NO!"

I set her on the ground, the gravel digging into my knees as I try to pry her arms away from my neck. I want to reassure her that she'll go back to her old room, in a house where she knows all the people and the routine, and where she'll be safe and happy. I want to tell her that I'll come in the car with her, but she clings so tightly that I finally give up and sit down on the hard, gritty pavement. I can feel her tears and snot smearing into my hair, the mud and rocks digging into my skirt, and for once, I don't give a shit.

The concept of *home* has ended for her, and she knows it. All her hopes for a nice family—of a sober father and a doting mother who made chocolate chip cookies—rooted themselves in this house, this stinking pile of rotten siding, where she had to hide in a garage and call for help. And as bad as it was, and as much as the people at Beverly will take care of her again, she just can't let go of the possibility that she could have a normal life.

I totally understand.

For half an hour, she processes this loss.

Finally, her sobs reduce to gulps, then to sighs, and finally, to silence. She pulls away from me and sits up. The social worker waits. She doesn't try to pick Lizzie up and chuck her into the car, and for that, I give her credit.

"Beth," Lizzie's small voice is urgent.

"Yeah, Liz?"

I gear up for some hard questions, but as usual, Lizzie is a bend in the road.

"I need Pootsie this time, okay?"

I ruffle her hair. "Okay."

Simon's already heading toward the door. "A bear?" he guesses.

"Elephant," Lizzie and I say together.
"Looks like Winston," I stage-whisper, and Simon laughs.

I keep thinking maybe.
Maybe if I hadn't kissed you,
we wouldn't have
had to talk.
We wouldn't have
gone down to the lake
in the middle of the night
so no one
could hear us.

Maybe we wouldn't
have been so giddy
that we forgot
one of the paddles.

God.

I'll never understand
why we had to
talk about it then.
Why I decided then,
in the middle of the
lake,
in a canoe with one paddle,
and no moon....

I'll never understand
why I felt afraid then.

Maybe because I knew
I wanted to kiss you
More than I'd wanted

to kiss Jacob
or even
Mr. Davidson.

Maybe I was
afraid
that kissing girls
wasn't normal,
if you wanted to kiss one girl
more than you wanted to
kiss any boys.
Maybe if I hadn't told you....
Maybe if I'd waited....
Maybe if you hadn't looked at me,
confused—for once—
and you hadn't said
"It doesn't mean anything, Beth."

Maybe if I hadn't told you
I couldn't do it
anymore.

Maybe...
It wouldn't have happened.

Someone has fixed the porch light, which shines like the North Star. Maureen greets us at the door and shakes hands with the social worker, who kindly dropped Simon off at the subway station on our way to Beverly.

"Thank you for accommodating her again on such short notice," the social worker says.

"Hey," Maureen greets Lizzie, who barely looks up before burying her head in my shoulder. "Your room's all ready for you."

"Let's talk in the kitchen." Maureen invites the social worker inside, and I carry Lizzie upstairs. She sniffles quietly as I run the bath.

The warm water flowing onto the porcelain tub reminds me of what I didn't do this afternoon. I look down at the faded lines of silver, peach and pink on my wrists. Lizzie's gaze moves from the door toward me, and I shove my sleeves down.

What would she think if she saw them?

Simon calls again, but I refuse to answer. He's come by, but I pretended not to be home. I feel bad freezing him out, but now that I know he's not the one, I'm afraid I'd treat him like any other flavour of the month, and then hate myself for hurting him.

Kate's called, and I've ignored her as well.

I feel like a scarecrow with ten different arms standing in the middle of an intersection, each hand pointing at different road. If any way led directly to sanity and happiness, surely I would notice it.

But none of those roads leads to my Jellicle Transformation.

Even wide awake, I can hear the scream of the alarm, driving people down to the shore, carrying the waterproof flashlights.

They plunged into the water in waves: one, two, three, up for breath, two strokes back, and pike-dive under. One, two, three, up for breath, two strokes back....

My lungs exploded as I dove again, and again and again. The lake at night shimmered like a pot of ink, impossible to tell up from down. The murky water grabbed my waist when they finally dragged me to the dock, shrieking.

Suddenly, my stomach heaves, and from my bedroom window, I vomit into Mrs. Continisio's flower beds—what a way to repay her beautiful lasagne.

This memory, this dream... it consumes me, overwhelms me. I wait until I'm exhausted to tumble into bed at night, afraid of being afraid to go to sleep. My consciousness hovers on the edge of something darker than insomnia, another existence in the world of sleep and dreams. It is as real as this one, just as arresting, and it rests below the surface of my mind when I'm awake, just waiting to pull me under.

I sit for a long time on the sill, leaning back against the frame. I wipe my mouth with my t-shirt, and spit a few times into the garden.

That fucking painting... that huge disgusting, horrible painting. Why would she do it? Why would she paint that for the entire world to stare at? The most horrific day of my life, and she's displayed it on an 8'x10" canvas. What possessed her?

Slowly, I climb down from the window and reach for an Ativan. I don't care what time of day it is—this waking nightmare has to stop. In the living room, shadows mark the walls. I turn on the light and sit down at the desk. My computer hums—a constant friend, this mute machine—but I take out notepaper, a pen, and start to write:

Jesus Christ, I miss you. You were the only one who could ever beat me, you know—the only one who could ever get close enough to ground me permanently—because you could make Heather seem ridiculous. I hate her for what she's done—hate her more because I don't understand why she's done it. Why would she paint that? Why?

Jackie, I think I'm going crazy—I can't function this way, I just can't. I need someone to help me.

After staring at the phone for half an hour, I finally dial.

The effusive, pink-haired secretary from Nancy's office practically shouts, "Bloor Street Mental Health Centre." An awful vibrating noise, like roadwork, drowns out her voice.

"Hi, this is Beth Sarandon calling," I say loudly.

"Beth? Bethany Sullivan? How are you sweetheart? How's your mom?"

"This is Beth *Sarandon*," I shout, but the drilling swallows both my clarification and her reply.

"Pardon?" I yell.

169

"Sorry, Bethany. The noise here is awful. The water mains are being repaired. Listen, tell your mom that I cancelled all her appointments for the next few weeks. Has she come home from the hospital yet?"

Another screeching noise assaults my ears, and I hold the phone away from my head.

"Listen, I have to let you go Beth. I'll call you back later."

"Okay." I realise it's pointless to try to explain to her. "Thank you. Bye."

Nancy's in the hospital? She didn't look well when I last saw her, but not on death's door. Yet.

Maybe she got a bad flu. Maybe she had surgery. Or maybe this is really it.

Chapter 24

I sleep all day, and through the night into the next afternoon. When I wake up, my head pounds. I turn the pillow over and find the other side surprisingly cool. Chills rack my body, and my stomach still hurts. Breathing shallowly forces the bile back down my throat and clears my head until I can sit up. Three pills were obviously too many.

Light bathes the room, and even as I look, objects fade and trade places. *God, it's really happening. I'm officially nuts.*

Biting my lip, I rise slowly from the side of the bed. The phone rings. Whoever it is can wait. What good could I possibly be to anyone? The thick swamp of mental sludge finally mires me down. Why struggle through it day after day, collapsing into hell at night, only to face the same thing again tomorrow? No point fighting it. Admitting insanity is the only sane thing to do.

I want a white room, cool clean sheets, puréed food. Silence.

I brush my teeth in even, methodical strokes, and I have to remind myself to spit out the foam and rinse my mouth. In the mirror, my eyes are shadows, my face a pale, untreated canvas bouncing light. Disembodied hands take down the alcohol, but I don't even have the energy for that. Instead, I head into the bedroom.

Clothing. I want to dress in cotton—in cotton balls, if possible—something that will wrap me in a cloth hug. Or, better yet, I don't want to feel my clothes at all, just as I don't want to feel my life.

Why bother with my disguise today? What's the point, when the person I've dressed up for saw through me the whole time?

I pull on the softest jeans I own—faded, stained and full of holes—and a white, threadbare t-shirt that once belonged to

Jackie. Somehow, her perfume still rises from the weave of the fabric. What would Jackie say... what would she think? She wouldn't say anything. She would just hand me my socks, and take me by the hand like a small child.

Loneliness is physical. Don't believe anyone who says it's all in your head.

I want my mother.

I hate my mother.

In the back of the closet hangs my first smock—my mother's old painting shirt that reminds me of the volunteer uniforms at the hospital. When I was ten or so, Heather was going to throw it away, but I begged her not to, and she gave it to me instead. I wore it a lot, back when I wanted to imagine we were close, the kind of mother and daughter who shared clothes and bags and gossip. I haven't put it on in years.

The paint on the sleeves marks out a roadmap of my life. The swirls and streaks, the lines and colour hold more memories than any scrapbook. A light rose from that time she made me sit for a portrait. The marigold she spent three days mixing, and caused her to burn Christmas dinner. The azure that dotted her hands when she slipped into the back of my grade five play.

Shakily, I roll the left cuff, a heavy button-up band that hides years of half-healed scars. The forearms carry no memories—she always rolled the sleeves up to her elbow. Time to go. I pack nothing, carry only my wallet and keys. Why do I even bother to bring these things? I won't need them where I'm going. They're an anchor, an illusory tie to my other life. The one I'm about to leave behind.

In jeans, without makeup, I leave the house. It doesn't matter what people see, whether they whisper about me and or call me names, because I'm escaping.

Walking slowly down the steps and across the street, I can't feel my feet. Am I even really awake? The world recedes, seeming to continue normally, but on the other side of a thick plate glass window. One foot in front of the other. Onto a subway. Down darkening streets....

The rain starts in earnest just as I arrive outside the hospital.

I should have guessed my feet would bring me here. Anarchists. My body seems determined to undermine me, having no interest in self-destruction. I hesitate for a long time at the entryway, watching the automatic doors open and close, but then the stench of disinfected mush accosts my nose. *Might as well go inside. Where else could I possibly go?*

In the lobby, I hold my breath and step onto the elevator. The lift dings for floor seven, then ten. *Wait a second. You can't just waltz onto the psych ward and demand a bed. You have to check in at the Emergency Room.* The elevator stops at 12.

And there she waits, just outside the door, as if she expected me.

I knew it, she says as she steers me away from the nurses' station and into the lounge. Her voice sounds like it comes from the other side of the thick glass window, but at least sound can penetrate.

"What are you talking about?" I demand. She wears the same blue scrubs as the first time I met her here, her makeup-less face taut with anxiety. I vaguely notice her hand on my shoulder.

Beth, we have to leave.

My throat vibrates in what would be laughter if it weren't so strangled. *I just got here. I came for help, and she wants me to go? Why? I thought she wanted me to get better.*

E shakes me by the shoulders. I break away and move toward the door. "Leave?" I echo in an incredulous whisper. "To go where?"

She catches my arm and yanks me around. The look on her face—so ridiculous, so intent—evokes that choking, half-whispered gasp that seems to be the only communication I can manage.

She slaps me. Hard. The glass shatters.

The stinging heat in my cheek drags me out of myself. I become aware of the nurses' low voices and the hum of various hospital machines, the creaking of beds, the grinding of chair legs on linoleum, E's cool hand on my arm. I am here. I am back.

My breath comes in deeper, calmer intervals. I look at E. Her steady grip on my arm relaxes, and she points me to the couch. I sit, obediently, like a child. She smiles and takes my hand into her own.

This will change your life, she says, her grey eyes glowing warmly.

"What will?"

What you're about to do.

I stare at her kind, expectant face. Who is she? Whenever I flirt with the edge of self-destruction, she appears. I've fought with her, warred with Nancy over her, and come back to her again, now that the edge has crept so close I can feel it crumble around my feet. Why do I keep leaning on crutches if I really want to fall?

Beth. Are you ready?

"I have to stay. I don't have a choice."

To my surprise, she laughs. *You always have a choice.*

"Not this time."

Beth, you don't belong here.

"Why? Why do you say that?"

Because you still have a life to live. But you're not living, you're hiding.

I can't even muster enough energy to feel angry. I just feel cold. Defeated.

"No."

Jackie isn't part of your life anymore, she says, jerking my chin up to meet her relentless gaze. *You need to stop writing her letters and admit that she will never pick up a pen. You have to get on with living.*

I reel, as though cracked across the face with a two-by-four, tearing my eyes away from her.

You're not supposed to live in this place. You're not even supposed to be in this place.

"Why are you here?" I hiss back. "Stop trying to talk me out of this. I'm tired, E. I'm so tired of running, worrying about the future, if I'll ever be normal, if I'll ever have kids. And if I do, will I be the kind of mother Heather is? I'm tired of not sleeping. I'm tired of missing Jackie. I'm tired of walking along the edge of crazy, and forcing myself to stay on the right side. This is the best place for me, because at least here, I don't have to worry about going crazy. I'm already there."

Beth—

"You tell me to keep fighting for something I don't want. I don't want this life anymore, E! I just want silence. Please. Just... let me stay." I plead with her like she's the Goddess of Psychiatric Mercy.

Some desperate part of me conjured her. She seems so real that I forget she's in my head. I can let her go.

I can let myself go.

She regards me for a long moment. The air around me closes in, even as a vast expanse opens up at my feet. E walks to the edge—then takes three more steps, hovering over the abyss. *You can't "fall off the edge," Beth, because the edge isn't real. There is no line. Only degrees of reality. Shades of grey.*

I reach for her, but stop at the cliff edge. She comes back toward me, still suspended over the dark chasm. I need her. She can't die.

Come, she says.

"I can't."

Yes. She grabs my hand and pulls me to her, then wraps her arm tightly around my waist. She stands on something solid. It bends and sways beneath my feet, and I want to scream, but instead cling tightly to E's waist. What are we standing on? It feels like a tightrope. But where is it rooted? She inches her way back, pulling me with her. How am I not dead?

Look at me. Not down.

I strain every muscle in my body to keep my balance as I dangle over the dark, cavernous gulf.

Just let go.

"No! I'm not ready."

Let go. What's other choice do you have? You can't live like this, remember? You want the nightmare to end. Just get it over with. Let go and see what happens.

I hear it: the sound of the rushing water, the screaming, the splashing. I see the torches flaming in the night, the moonless sky bright with stars. Nancy's face after I slapped her with words. A social worker handing Lizzie over to her parents to abuse again. My mother shaking her head at me. My father rushing to hang up.

The darkness closes over me. The beast writhes in my stomach. No razor can cut through to this monster. I need to kill it permanently.

I pull away from E, just enough to see her face. She nods and lets me go. I teeter for a moment, arms flailing, then I close my eyes, and fall....

A light goes on.

The abyss disappears.

I fall to my knees on a bridge—a wide one. The tightrope isn't a tightrope at all. It's wide and solid. I stand, put my feet side by side, and jump a little, testing it, like I did once to the sewer grate, daring it to open. This doesn't crack either. I don't fall off.

I collapse and let my head rest on my knees, laughing with genuine relief. A lightness fills my chest, erasing the crushing weight from earlier. E slips down beside me. We rock to the gentle swaying of the bridge.

"Has this been here all along?"

E nods, her face breaking into a brilliant smile.

"I haven't been walking the edge. I just couldn't see past the cliff."

I know. You've been this way your whole life. Black and white. Real or False. Present or absent. But that's not how life works.

"So how can I tell when I'm getting close to crazy?"

Sanity is like reality—different for each person. Your reality is not the same as others'. Here I am. You hear me and see me. But I am not here. Can you explain it?

"No."

You are one person, but you fear yourself. How is that possible?

"I don't know."

Her eyes burn with empathy and intelligence.

You're frightened of yourself because you believe that you have no control over the future.

She speaks directly to my neurosis: my sane side already knows all this. *Your future self connects to your present self, Beth. The future self will make decisions for you. Does that scare you?*

"The Jellicle Transformation," I whisper, shaking my head. "It hasn't happened."

She squeezes my hand and shakes her head. *Why would you want to be different from who you are?*

"Because of what happened to her." My throat tightens. "Because of what I did."

She doesn't even blink.

What happened to Jackie was not your fault.

E cups my cheek in her palm.

Forcing yourself to love a boy who will never make you happy won't fix that. It won't change what happened between you. All it will do is make you miserable.

I swallow hard and sit, just staring out the window. From this height, I can't see the passers-by passing-by. Why couldn't I tell Nancy these things? I wanted to. I almost did, at times, but I never gave in. I kept playing the game, and in the process frustrated her, manipulated her... hurt her.

She had an agenda. *There was a time when I would have been able to take you and ten more just like you without breaking a sweat—the kind that needed to be broken to be mended.*

That's why she sent me here. She tried to break me so I could be mended.

Are you ready to go? E says at last. I look around as though I've just arrived. Some broadcast in Spanish or Portuguese blares from the television, and bored patients, who would rather play with their food than eat it, smear the remnants of their breakfasts across the table.

The silence and whiteness and mush suddenly terrifies me.

"Yes." I jump to my feet. "I am."

Good, E replies. *Because this is probably your last chance.*

"For what?"

To see her.

I want to laugh, but not the unhinged hysteria of earlier. Of course. The real reason my anarchistic feet dragged me here. To make amends. I feel such a relief to be doing something, to be thinking clearly.

"She's here? Where?"

You'll have to find her, E says as if nothing could be simpler, as if people wander in from the streets unnoticed all the time. Hell, let's just hop on an elevator and meander up and down the halls.

E tugs at the sleeve of my shirt, a wry smile on her face.

The blue shirt. I look like a volunteer, which is why they let me in here—and the reason they'll let me out.

"You're always in my mind, aren't you?" I whisper.

She just smiles.

And I accept that.

Synchronicity.

She squeezes my hand tightly, and walks away, leaving me staring at the elevator—and categorising, just for the comfort of it, all the reasons she couldn't possibly have been here.

When the nurses' station buzzes me onto the lift, I press the button to the ground floor and start forming a plan. I will go down to the front desk and pretend to be Bethany Sullivan. If the front desk person gives me the room number, I'll go. If they throw me out of the hospital for fraud, I'll go home.

The elevator stops on the eleventh floor before continuing its plunge down. A teenage boy shuffles closer to me as the doors close, making room for a Chinese family who enter quietly and fold their hands in unison. The teenager wears a wrinkled t-shirt and pants that do nothing to hide his purple underwear. A vague drum beat emanates from his enormous headphones. The lift stops again, sending my stomach plummeting, and an elderly couple get on, moving to the side away from the boy. I can't tell whether it's his music or his underwear they are avoiding. This time we go three floors. On seven, a heavy nurse with a long, dark ponytail squeezes in and holds out a hand to keep the door open.

"Mrs. Sullivan is due for meds, Jill," she whispers to a slight wisp of a nurse pushing a med cart down the hall.

"Do you mean Dr. Sullivan? Room 707?" the other nurse asks. As unobtrusively as I can, I move to the front of the elevator to hear better.

"Is she a 'Dr.'? Well, I've been screwing that up all day. Can you get it for her? I'm off."

"Sure."

No wonder the signs posted all around the hospital say *Shhh. Respect patient confidentiality!* It's so people can't do exactly what I'm about to do: barge in on a sick person who isn't my family member.

The elevator buzzes, and the heavy nurse takes her hand away from the door. Just as the doors start to close, I step off.

I catch a glimpse of E watching me from down the hall, that enigmatic smile playing on her lips.

I listen for a moment at the door to room 707—if anyone is visiting her, they're not speaking.

What the hell am I doing? I can't go in there. She's sick, maybe even dying. What can I possibly say? "Hi Nancy. I was just hanging around at the hospital today and decided to stop by and nose in on your private business. Nice to see you."

I have to see her—I have to apologise for the last time we spoke. We both said things we shouldn't have, and dying people shouldn't have any regrets. Is it self-centred to think she regrets what happened between us? Because she lost her final round? Am I being kind or cruel by coming to see her now?

I take a deep breath and look down the hall.

E nods.

She said I could stop by when I felt like catching up with an old friend.

That's what she is to me now.

So I steel my shoulders and knock.

Chapter 25

"Come in," says a warm, gravelly voice. I didn't know how much I'd missed it until this very moment.

"Hi there," I say, stepping inside.

Years of practice help me hide my surprise at her appearance. Her thick grey hair straggles around her pale face. She's lost at least twenty pounds—pounds she really couldn't afford to lose. She waves feebly with bent fingers, her hand too weak to open, but she smiles at me anyway. Warm. Genuine.

"How did you know I was here?"

What can I say? If I tell her about E, she'll have me committed.

"I have my sources." I wink.

"So, how are you?"

I can't believe her! "Nancy, you look like hell and you're asking me how I am? How are you?"

She laughs—a husky sound somewhere between a chuckle and a cough. "I'm dying."

The thought had crossed my mind, but hearing her say the words out loud still jolts my stomach. She said she'd be dead in three years, not three months. But her words show that she takes no comfort in self-pity, and she'd kill me for feeling sorry for her, so I just nod. Echoes of Professor Mirtica's words come back to me. *There is a world of difference between knowing you're going to die someday, and knowing you're going to die today.*

"I'm not dead yet," she says, as if reading my mind. "Sit down, will you? Tell me what's new."

I sigh and take a seat in the hard burgundy chair next to her bed. *Quit fidgeting with your rings and look at her. Pick a topic—not her impending death.* "I went to the art gallery."

"To see your mother's work?"

"It was enormous, Nancy. You should have seen all the paintings she's done. A few of them would have taken up her whole studio while she was working."

"You sound proud of her."

"Well, it's an incredible accomplishment—all that work, getting it displayed like that. Simon says she's big in California right now."

"Hmmm... Simon, hey? How are you two doing, anyway?"

I shrug, and Nancy smiles knowingly. "Friends at least?"

"Yeah. We'll always be friends."

Nancy struggles to lift a cup of water from her tray and I reach for it, holding the straw to her lips. She drinks slowly, then asks, "Was your mother at the exhibit?"

"Yeah."

I don't know what else to say, where to start.

"What happened, Beth?"

You're supposed to give her what she wants, and she wants your secrets. Don't you think she's earned them?

Suddenly, the words spill from my lips like rushing water from a spring thaw—Heather's sudden appearance, the 8'x10' painting, running away.... An emesis basin perches delicately on her side table. I may need that before this story is finished.

"Why did that painting upset you so much?"

The memory hits me like a blow to the stomach. I stand up, start pacing toward the door and back.

"Beth," she says quietly. "Don't run away. Sit back down."

My heart thunders in my chest, and an awesome pressure crushes me.

"Beth." Nancy's voice calls me, pulls me away from the canoe docks.

She's at a disadvantage. The least you can do is let her win.

"How did Heather know about it...?" I say. My voice feels weird and strangled. "I never told her the whole story. I couldn't tell her—we were too deeply into the game by then. We never told each other anything."

"What happened?"

"Jackie," I whisper hoarsely.

"Beth, who's Jackie?"

I can't believe how much I kept from her. How could we have filled months of talking without my ever mentioning Jackie? Not once. *God.* Jackie's the only one who ever mattered.

"Jackie," I say slowly, "was my best friend. More than my best friend."

Invisible threads connect my heart to Nancy's hands. She begins pulling the secrets out of me, like tiny silk strands, like a spider's webbing. Reflexively, I jerk them back, but she tugs gently.

"What happened?"

The story tumbles out now, fast, sporadic, in a rush of disjointed pieces.

Our first meeting.

Our giggling, our whispered conversations at the dock, in kayaks. My head resting on her lap as she ran her fingers through my damp hair and over my body. My lips meeting hers. Jesus, that day in the showers. All the days after that in the bunk house when everyone else had gone to meals, in the old tree house, out on the lake in the middle of the night....

"Beth?" Nancy's soft voice brings me back to this room, away from the horror of that night. "You write to her. Why doesn't she write back?"

"She can't," I whisper.

"Why not?"

I swallow hard. The bile rises in my throat. I can't say the words. I have never said them—except once, to Heather.

"Beth?"

"Because she's dead."

"Oh, God," Nancy says. "Oh, dear, Beth. I'm so sorry."

Talking about it has brought me back to that night, to the moment I've avoided all the months since then. Jackie and I tiptoed out of our tent, tripping and laughing in whispered giggles all the way to the waterfront. The darkness of the night enveloped us. Splashes at the shoreline reverberated ten-fold over the water, so we didn't paddle the canoe; we just coasted out to the middle of the lake, without life jackets, caught up in the thrill of our midnight transgression.

No thought about the dangers.

We let the water take us in a long lazy line. The air was cold, far colder than during the day. The dark water lapped terrifyingly close to the gunwales, and it felt like floating in an inkpot—an inkpot that could hold anything: piranhas, Megalodons, the Loch Ness monster.

A shadow of annoyance clouded my mind. Precognition? Why were we even out here? Why did we always do crazy things that could get us in trouble?

When we got to the middle of the lake, Jackie leaned over to kiss me—just brushing my lips with hers. For the first time, I pushed her away. "Why do we have to do that?" I demanded. "Don't you care about what it means?" She didn't say anything, which just made me angrier. "Well? Don't you?"

"I don't know what to say," Jackie said. Strange to see her at a loss for words. "It's just not a big deal, Beth."

"What do you mean it's not a big deal?"

"It's just not. I like you, so I kissed you. It's not like you're a lesbian or something, just because you kissed me a couple times."

My heart ramped up. Lesbian. *God.* "Of course I'm not a lesbian," I said shrilly.

"Okay," Jackie said calmly.

"We can't do it anymore," I said, tears coming to my eyes. Jackie laid a cool hand on my arm, and I couldn't bring myself to jerk it away. "We can't."

"Okay," she agreed. "Relax, Beth. It isn't like we're shooting heroin or something. We're not addicts! We're just kissing and... stuff. We just won't do it anymore, okay?"

"God! This wasn't even your idea. It was mine! How am I supposed to go back to normal life after this? We have to get real, Jackie—"

A fish knocked into the hull of the boat. I gasped, and Jackie looked toward shore. We'd drifted much farther than we should have—all the way around the south end of camp. From the middle of the lake, we could see the cliff where kids liked to dive and the little shelf of land that Jackie had taken me to. The current pulled the boat like strong hands on the gunwales. Buoys normally kept us to a specific swimming and boating area—and for a good reason. A few kilometres from this end of the island, the water cascaded down toward a lower lake. The rapids' undertow had caught us.

It seems so obvious now that we should have just rowed to shore and walked out of the water. We could have taken the boat by its painter and led it around the shoreline to the canoe docks. We could have portaged it right through the middle of camp—to hell with whoever saw us.

Because, if we had done that, Jackie would not be dead.

When I think about this night, I tell myself we rowed to shore. This is what my waking memories believe—but the nightmares know the truth.

"Let's paddle hard, okay?" Jackie said, a faint tremor in her voice. "We'll go back the way we came, and we can talk more about this on dry land."

I nodded. We would take out at the canoe docks, and no one would know we'd been gone.

"Beth? There's only one paddle."

"What do you mean? All the boats have two paddles, two life vests."

Jackie shook her head. "One paddle. No life vests." She dipped the paddle into the water and starting rowing, but the canoe, of course, just went in circles. "There's a way to solo this thing, right?" Jackie giggled.

I giggled too, but my laughter sounded a little unhinged. "Maybe if we'd taken a few lessons, instead of sun tanning all summer...."

We'd watched enough canoe lessons to have grasped the basics, at least. I scooted to the edge of the boat, between the two yokes, trying to make the canoe tip toward the water. The boat hardly moved, so Jackie crammed in behind me. The movement of her rowing kept tipping us dangerously close to the water, and the canoe almost turtled more than once.

"We're never going to be able to go straight with both of us in here," Jackie said. The current had pulled us even farther out, and had started picking up speed. In the darkness, a faint roaring reached my ears. The rapids.

Jackie'd heard them too. "All right, that's it," she said, slipping into the black water. "We have to get out of here fast. I'll tow us."

I moved to the bow of the boat and threw her the painter, which she looped around her wrist. Then, I crawled to the bow and straddled it, trying to maintain my balance, paddle in hand. With Jackie out towing, and me paddling bilaterally—nothing we'd ever seen in a canoe lesson—we could more or less make a straight line for camp.

Jackie scissor-kicked hard to stay ahead of the boat. We started out strong, laughing at how ridiculous we must look—Jackie even made a few jokes—but halfway back, the joking stopped and she started panting.

"Hey Jacks?"

"Yeah?"

"Want to trade places? I'll tow us awhile."

"Oh, no," she said, "I don't mind. We're almost there." She knew the water scared me, especially at night—and especially on moonless nights when everything was so damn dark. Why had I insisted we talk tonight? Why had we come out *here*? We should have gone to the barn, or to the swim docks. I cursed myself and tried one more time to get her to come back to the boat.

"Stop worrying, Beth. I'm okay." But she wasn't. She was tired.

We'd made it pretty far, within sight of the canoe docks, when she said she was dizzy. I couldn't see her face.

"C'mon, get back in the boat," I called, shivering from cold and fear. "I'll pull you in and you can lie down. Just keep your weight centred and it'll be fine."

"We'd tip the boat," she panted. "And then... what the hell would we do...? We're almost there.... I'll just duck under... and cool myself off.... I'm sweating so freaking much...."

A normal person would've grabbed hold of the canoe and held on. A normal person would've splashed water on her face and breathed a little before trying to finish the swim. A normal person would've tied the painter around her wrist, or climbed in and let me help, or anything, really, except gone under the water.

But Jackie lived with her hand on a big red self-destruct button, though she laughed so much playing with it that nobody noticed how dangerous it was.

She dove, her toes flipping briefly at the surface and then disappearing. I waited. She loved to dive, and she loved to freak me out, swimming under water for as long as she could stand it before surfacing behind me and grabbing my shoulders. I waited a little longer, looking all around, expecting her to come up splashing at any moment. I stood up, but the boat rocked crazily—she was right, it could flip so easily—so I sat again, and called to her.

"Jackie?" I held the paddle hard against the gunwales so my shivering hands wouldn't cause any clacking. A moment passed—too long. I listened hard, but she never answered.

"Jackie!" I didn't care that I was yelling. I didn't care if everyone in camp could hear me. "JACKIE!"

I slipped overboard and sank beneath the surface. But I couldn't see a thing. Nothing but blackness. Inky, murky blackness. The water closed in on me, thick and heavy, and I kicked to the surface. I could barely breathe for terror of the unknown monsters lurking under the surface—one of which had claimed my best friend. I started screaming her name, over and over.

Then I remembered the whistle hanging from the bow. I grabbed it and blew. Shrill notes ricocheted around the lake, bouncing off the trees. And even though I felt like I was drowning, I dove again. Even though I knew I'd never find her in that water, I kept looking. And every time I surfaced, I reached anxiously for the gunwales of the boat, just to reassure myself it was still there. That I wasn't going to die.

Deet, the camp director, appeared and shouted at me from the canoe docks, waving a torch. I screamed back at him, "Jackie! It's Jackie!" Panic lit his eyes.

Sirens shattered the night, and every light went on in camp. Counsellors ran down to the docks. They plunged into the water in waves: one, two, three, up for breath, two strokes back, and pike-dive under. One, two, three, up for breath, two strokes back....

I imagined her somersaulting into deep water, and scrambling for the surface when her sinuses began to ache and her chest burned for air. She must have dived down, losing track of which way was up, and kept paddling toward the bottom until she ran out of breath.

Deet dragged me out and wrapped me in a towel. I shivered violently, as I wrestled and screamed, straining against his huge hands, desperate to get back into the water, back to Jackie. He held me tight and, finally, I stood silent.

They found her in the morning. The rapids had claimed her—her stark white body a trophy to the cold black water.

Chapter 26

Nancy holds my hand. Tears creep down her paper-thin cheeks, and drip onto the light blue hospital blanket.

"Nancy, it's all right." I hand her a tissue.

She shakes her head in bewilderment. "Beth, why don't you cry?"

"Because I can't, Nancy. I haven't cried—since she died."

She doesn't understand. Her eyes leap back and forth as if trying to focus on something that darts behind and below her. "But why? Because it's weak? Because it's emotional? Because you're afraid?"

"No." My voice is flat. "I just can't."

Understanding dawns on her face. "How did your mother react when you told her?" she asks suddenly.

"Told her what?"

"What happened."

"I didn't tell her—that's what I'm trying to say. I don't know how she knew about that night. She couldn't have known."

"You must have told her something. You couldn't have just pretended nothing had happened."

"When I came home from camp that summer, she was up in the studio. She came down when she heard the door open. She said 'Elizabeth, you're looking rather pale. Are you eating well?' And I just said 'Jackie died.' I didn't cry. I didn't even blink as I said it. She didn't skip a beat, I swear to God. She looked me in the face and said 'that's unfortunate'... and walked away."

"She what?" Nancy says.

I nod slowly. "That was it. I packed my room and moved out the next week. I couldn't be there anymore."

"Why did she do that, Beth? Why do you think she—"

"I don't know."

"Why do you think she couldn't face Jackie's death?"

"Couldn't face it?"

"Yes."

"It's not that she couldn't face it, Nancy. She didn't care."

Nancy shakes her head. "No. I don't believe that's true. There's something about it that she couldn't face." I just stare at her for a second. My mother never even met Jackie. What could some girl's death possibly have meant to her?

Nancy bites her lip. "How old were you?"

"Almost sixteen."

"And when did you start... hurting yourself?"

"I don't know. A few days later, maybe less. As soon as I figured out I couldn't feel myself anymore. When I couldn't even cry for Jackie. I started marking the time—like a ritual, I guess. One tally for each day. I lost count somewhere along the way. The scars disappear, you know. And then it just kept escalating. I kept going deeper and deeper. I would bleed for hours, and it would never hurt. I could never cut deep enough to make it hurt—until later."

"You loved her," Nancy says quietly.

I run my hand through my hair. "I don't know. I don't know how I let that happen."

"It confused you."

Confused me? There's a grand understatement. Confused is what you feel when you come home to no milk, even though you swear you just bought a carton. Confused is when you agree to meet a friend at 10:30, and arrive to find they've been waiting half an hour. Kissing a girl in a canoe when you're fifteen and then watching her die is not confusing. It's something else altogether.

Of course, it never confused Jackie. Not uninhibited, free spirited Jackie, who did just as she pleased, and damn the consequences. I should have reined her in. If I'd done that, she'd still be alive.

"You know it's not your fault," Nancy says. It's not a question or a platitude. Just a statement—like, You know the weather is warm in July, or, You know you need to eat dinner before dessert.

No, I didn't, actually. I never put myself on trial long enough to be acquitted. I just posted bail and ran—and ran and ran and ran.

"It is." I say. "It is my fault, Nancy. *I* didn't check the boat. *I* made us go out in the water. *I* freaked out on her. I didn't act responsibly, and I killed her!"

"No." Nancy says in a calm, but firm voice. "You didn't. You acted like the confused fifteen-year-old that you were. You made a choice. Jackie made a choice. One choice led to another led to another. Sometimes people make fatal mistakes. That's the nature of life, Beth."

"I should have protected her."

"You tried."

"She died!"

"Yes. But you're not responsible."

God. Why is it so easy for everybody else? Nancy's eyes hold me. She won't let me get away with anything anymore. Thank God. I'm so tired of running.

"No matter how much you try to control the world, a time will come when you realise how futile that is. It doesn't matter how perfect your clothes are, how perfect your grades are, how rigid you try to make your emotions. You will seep out the cracks of your own life, Beth. And even if you manage to never make a mistake, it doesn't matter. Tragedy will befall you, nonetheless. Life will go on, nonetheless."

I feel as though she's holding my head underwater to prove that it will drown me.

...me, promising Lizzie I'd never hold her down. The terror in her eyes when she made me swear.....

"You gain power over your own life when you learn to bend and flex and ride the waves that come. Because your fear doesn't hold you hostage."

...coasting in the clear, blue California surf, riding the waves on my foam board....

"You know I can't."

"Yes. But you'll learn. Once you stop being so terribly afraid."

She says none of this with malice, but still, I am ashamed that she knows. "How do you know what I'm afraid of?"

"You spend too much damn time alone. You don't know who you are. You don't know where you end and somebody else begins. Not Jackie. Not your mother. Not your lovers. You blend into them, and that makes you anxious, so you push them away. But a piece of you goes too. No wonder you're terrified all the bloody time."

"That's why I like to be alone," I whisper. "So I always know who I am." I've never admitted that before, that being with other people feels like riding a G-force ride at the carnival where I fight to feel myself, to see my own limbs, and raise my head.

"You thought shutting everyone out would keep yourself intact," Nancy says. "But I'll tell you something, my girl—isolation makes your fear worse."

"I'm not very good at being honest with my feelings."

"Because telling the truth opens you up to rejection?"

My cheeks flush hot.

I know you think you're perfect, Elizabeth. But you're far from it.

"I can't stand people making fun of me. Have you seen what happens to kids in high school who are different? Queer? Why do you think I got the hell out of there?"

Elizabeth, please don't use that word. It's vulgar.

"Didn't you have someone to talk to? Someone you could be honest with?"

Get out of my sight. I can't stand to look at you.

I shake my head. "No. I don't want anyone to know. I'm already difficult enough to—"

What is wrong with you Elizabeth? Don't you have any common sense?

"To what?" Nancy presses gently.

Stop grunting like a Neanderthal and speak up.

"To love."

Nancy pats my hand lightly—like butterflies landing.

"That must be very lonely and frightening for you."

I wipe my nose with a Kleenex, then crumple it in my hand. No tears of course, but this is a start at least.

"Nancy...?"

"What, darling?"

"Do you think she knew?"

"Who, your mother?"

I nod. "Is that what she couldn't face? What Jackie meant to me?"

"I don't know." Nancy's eyes are far away. "People are complicated. Sometimes you think you know what drives them to do the things they do. But you'll probably never know for sure unless you ask her."

"I couldn't ask her."

"Do you need to? Does it matter?"

Yes.

Yes it matters. This is why Heather holds me at arms' length, twisting and turning me in front of her mirrors; scrutinizing my hair, my face, my nails, my shoes, my clothes, my speech, my gait... me. Did she know something I didn't? Could she name the flaw I only guessed at?

Maybe she saw the tiny child painting in the corner of her studio one day, and knew she was different, damaged. I was her only daughter. The cracked diamond. The scowling girl who would never grow up and find Prince Charming.

"Nancy, I don't think I'm ever going to love a boy."

She laughs—then coughs a little. "So what? So you love women then."

It can't be that easy. If not men, then women. Just an alternative. Another fork in the road. She doesn't see the hateful words, the laughs and snickers, and the innuendos. I've never been afraid of the love. Only the stain. The judgement.

"People will laugh at me."

"Yes." Her eyes grip me intently. "They will. I'd like to tell you otherwise, but I know you see it. Some people will judge you. Some will be afraid. Or rude. Or worse."

"I hate that."

"I know. But you must hate hiding more than you hate judgement, or you wouldn't be struggling so much."

Is that true? Given the choice, would I rather hide and be safe, or fly free and be judged?

Suddenly, I find myself telling her about my disguise and the Jellicle Transformation and Mr. Davidson and Simon and how neither of them could turn on my normal time clock and how yes, I am afraid of what people will think of me... but mostly, I'm afraid that Heather hated me because she knew, and since I'm never going to Transform, she'll never love me.

"I hope that isn't true," Nancy whispers. "I can't say for certain, Beth, but I hope that isn't true."

I tell her about Heather's words, her looks, her contempt. I tell her about when it started and how. And I tell her how it ended.

She shakes her head. "I'm sorry. I'm sorry you never knew your mother."

I stare at Nancy for a long time, revelling in her wisdom. It's true. I regret pushing her away for so many months.

The room seems to have sound again. The clock smacks out seconds, and somewhere down the hall, a lunch tray rattles along the linoleum. Just outside the door, a nurse swears.

Nancy squeezes my hand. "I'm so glad you came to see me. I'm just sorry we won't have more time."

"I guess I'd better find another therapist," I joke weakly.

She laughs. "Don't worry, my girl. I think you're going to be all right."

"God, I can't believe you," I mutter. "You're dying, and you tell me I'm going to be all right."

"I'm not dying today."

Out in the hall, someone shrieks, and footsteps pound along the floor.

Security to nurses' station seven, please. Security to nurses' station seven.

"I guess someone tried to rob the Oxycodone." Nancy smiles. I meet her eye and we both giggle.

"I think they're getting away."

"Maybe. Imagine their faces when they realise they have to wait for the elevator."

I laugh again—a real laugh—but then I cover my mouth, because every time Nancy laughs, she coughs, and it looks like it hurts her.

"Can I get you anything? A glass of water... some Oxycodone?"

Nancy chuckles. "Do me a favour."

"What?"

A nurse in floral scrubs bustles into the room. "Lunch, Mrs. Sullivan," she says with mock enthusiasm. She passes an indestructible tray onto Nancy's meal table. It smells like it's already been digested.

Nancy's nose flutters reflexively. "No, thank you," she says quietly.

"Now, Mrs. Sullivan, you need to eat to keep your strength up." The nurse coos at Nancy as though talking to a four-year-old.

"I will not eat that. Please take it away. The smell is nauseating."

"Mrs. Sullivan, don't be silly. Everyone needs their lunch."

I snap, "It's Dr. Sullivan, actually. And if you were dying, do you think a pile of puréed chicken with grey salty slop would give you the will to live?"

Nancy's chest quivers as she suppresses another laugh.

The nurse stares at me as though she'd like to give me a good slap, but she does leave, and takes the foul-smelling tray with her.

"My husband Tom's bringing me some soup."

"Thank God."

"You promised me a favour." She looks at me gravely. "If I give you an assignment will you do it?"

I nod, and Nancy coughs again. Her chest rattles with every inhale. "Pneumonia," she rasps. "Don't worry, darling. It's not a bad way to go."

"You can't die from pneumonia," I say.

She raises her eyebrows. "Sure you can. Especially if you're flat on your back for a month. They want to drain my lungs and put me on medication to stop the congestive heart failure, but I said no."

"You said no?"

"It's my right."

"Nancy, it's going to kill you."

She looks at me hard. "Quality of life." The edge to her voice swipes negotiation off the table. "I don't want to live this way—having Tom hold a tissue to my face when I sneeze because I can't even blow my own nose. You can only stand so much of this. And I'm through. It's my choice now."

"Nancy...."

"No. And don't you dare go dragging around guilt from our last conversation either, my girl," she says sharply. "I've chosen this. And nothing you said to me that day changed the way I see myself."

Professor Mirtica's partner should have seen this—real strength, real challenge—not a ridiculous flirtation with death, an obsession with a theoretical problem. If she'd really understood life and death, maybe she wouldn't have done what she did.

And maybe I should get out more too.

I take an oxygen mask from the back of the bed, but Nancy holds up one hand to stop me. "No. I don't want that."

"Just beside you," I say firmly. "Don't worry, it won't slow down the Grim Reaper any. It'll just make you more comfortable."

She rolls her eyes and allows me to adjust the mask so the oxygen blows on her face. "Are you ready for your assignment?" she says.

"Yeah."

"It's harder than you think."

"Harder than what you're doing?"

How can two people understand each other so well when they've spent months avoiding real conversation? I don't know how this happened. And I don't know how I'm going push on when she finally does get her way.

"Stay home," she says gently. "Write. Not about other people, but about yourself. Write your life the way you see it, the way it happened for you. Don't leave anything out. Be strong enough to be honest. And then read it to yourself, alone, in your favourite place with your favourite things. Just dive into your own mind. You're going to meet yourself this weekend, Beth."

That doesn't sound so bad. And yet, the idea of spending that much time inside my memories sends a block of ice skidding to the bottom of my stomach.

I have to trust her—just this once.

"Okay," I say, after a moment. "I'll come visit you on Monday."

"Yes, please. And tell me how it's going." She pulls me toward her, and I bend down to kiss her cheek. "Goodbye, darling." Her smile shines bright into the darkness the memories have left. She's beautiful.

"Goodbye."

A knock sounds on the door, and a middle-aged man with greying hair and warm eyes walks in. "Tom," Nancy says. "This is Beth. Beth, my husband, Tom."

He takes my hand, and smiles sadly. "Pleasure."

I make a quiet exit. They deserve all the final moments they have. She's brave, this wise witch. She needs time to prepare him, to convince him that his life will somehow go on.

Outside, everything seems quieter. The traffic is just as congested, and the roar of three million voices is just as strong—but somehow not as penetrating. I'm supposed to go to the group home tonight. I've never cancelled, never found it necessary, but I have to tonight.

Considering where I started this morning, home isn't a bad place to end up. I open the curtains and sit down at my computer to write. For as long as I've been writing, I've never written about myself. I could never see myself objectively—still don't. But I write anyway.

The depth of darkness contained in the human mind has never scared me. I swim in it, play with it, let it wash over me. I write to take back possession of myself.

Chapter 27

For years, I've carried my life in a secret bag, and it was too damn heavy. Maybe I'm finally learning how to put it down. When I arrive at the hospital on Monday morning, I feel composed—not a good imitation of composure, but the real thing. Some patterns take a long time to erode, but I'm hopeful that eventually, I can become an authentic person.

I hurry toward Nancy. We don't have many moments left, and I want her to know I'm taking her seriously. She deserves that respect—and the truth—after everything I've put her through. I hope, for her sake, that she considers this a victory, at last.

I ride the elevator to the seventh floor and go immediately to Nancy's room, knocking once.

"Come in," a man's voice answers. I back away from the door, almost bumping into a nurse.

"Excuse me," I say, then catch her arm. "Actually, I'm looking for Nancy Sullivan."

She frowns. "Nancy Sullivan?"

"Yes. She was in 707 on Friday."

The nurse looks toward the room, and back at me, then puts her hand on my shoulder. "I'm sorry, dear. Dr. Sullivan died Saturday night."

What? Already? "Thank-you," I say, and turn away. Without thinking, I head quickly toward the ladies' room, the familiar pressure sitting on my chest.

I can't breathe. I can't stand still. I pace back and forth, holding the counter for support. What I wouldn't give for my razor right now. The mirror distorts my image. My cheeks hurt. I realise suddenly that I'm crying—sobbing, actually. I sink down onto the floor, my back pressed against the wall, and let the tears flow, let the sorrow find gates of its own.

God, it feels so good to cry—I'd almost forgotten....

An hour must have passed, possibly longer. People have knocked, knocked again, and in exasperation, gone to find other facilities. They can wait. Nancy is gone. I'll never get to tell her what I discovered this weekend, what she pushed me to find out. God, I'm going to miss her. I sit for a few minutes more, letting grief wash through me and over me—a salt-water cleansing. I don't know how she managed to corral me onto this path.

But I do know she saved my life.

Who would have ever thought I'd grow to love the person I spent so many hours running from? All the time I spent testing her, hiding from her, when I could have got to know her better. I missed out on so much by not being honest with her—and myself. Still, I'm glad it's over. I'm glad she won. I was so tired of playing.

No guilt. She made me promise, and I gave my word.

Simon and Kate came with me to Nancy's funeral. They sat in the front of the car, and I sat in the back, my cheek pressed against the window. Halfway through the drive, I looked up and saw Simon's hand squeezing Kate's.

Kate's.

His hand squeezed Kate's?

When she saw me looking, she quietly slipped her hand from Simon's grasp.

He looked at me in the rear view mirror.

Beth, I love you, but sometimes you can be so dense.

Oh my God. How blind had I been, exactly? He'd been dating Kate? Not Meagan?

"I'm so sorry," I mouthed silently.

Kate just shook her head and smiled. "It's okay."

Did she know I kissed him? More importantly—did she know I'd never do that again?

He never belonged to me. I would never have made him happy.

He deserves to be happy, and Kate will treat him as well as he'll treat her. When I saw their hands together, I actually felt a little relieved, like the Universe had taken a heavy decision off of my shoulders. Of course he should be with Kate. Why shouldn't he?

The casket was closed, which gave me some comfort. The sight of a dead body has a finality that imprints permanently. I don't want to remember her like that. I'd rather remember her as she was the first day I met her—dynamic, brilliant, confident. I don't want to see her corpse. To me, she's still so alive.

I talk to her sometimes when I wake up before dawn. I sit on my window sill and watch the sun come up—but not like before, when I used to clamber up there in the middle of the night with my heart pounding, trying to clear my head of the awful images. Being up there comforts me now, as I imagine Nancy sitting next to me. In these midnight meetings, I tell her everything I never said when she was alive. Her words keep coming back to me, and now that I'm listening, her wisdom serves as a compass, not a dagger to avoid.

You have searing insight, Beth. I just wish you could learn to use it better.

What does that mean? I have so many other questions, so many things I don't understand.

The minister recited Bible passages, but I didn't really listen. Simon kept squeezing my hand, and looking over to see if I needed more tissues. I just absorbed the scene, saying goodbye in my own way. Nancy's husband sat in the front row, and a woman sat beside him patting his shoulder. She looked a lot like Nancy, but younger, with gorgeous curly hair that was red where Nancy's had been grey. Bethany?

After the service, we stood in line to greet Tom. The redheaded woman had left.

"Hello, Beth," he said, shaking my hand warmly.

"We're so sorry for your loss," Simon said quietly. Kate stood by his side, her arm tucked into the crook of his arm.

Tom nodded at me. "And I'm sorry for yours." He cleared his throat, and looked at me hesitantly. "Beth?" He said my name like we were old friends.

"Yes?"

"Would you like to meet me at my office next Tuesday, around ten?"

His question took me aback, but didn't really surprise me. Does doctor-patient confidentiality apply when the doctor is dying? It probably does, but Nancy knew that by the time I found out about it, she'd be beyond reproach.

"For 'support'?" I asked carefully.

"A chat," Tom replied.

Nancy thought I still needed a shrink. Leave it to her to set me up with the one person I couldn't refuse. "Okay," I said. "Thanks."

"Oh, here, I have something for you." Tom pulled a piece of blue-lined paper, folded in thirds, from his breast pocket. "From Nancy."

When it's over, I walk to the subway station alone. I want the fresh air and the sun and some time to think. The traffic rumbles like the brass section of a band, low with occasional honks. The smoky smell of hotdogs wafts down the street and makes my mouth water. So does the coffee. I get on the train and gaze out the black windows for fifteen stops. At my station, I get off, my purse already open on my way to the coffee kiosk. I need a latte.

The young barista is alone at the counter, and she glances up as I approach. "Tough day?"

I flinch. "Why?"

"Your eyes are red."

"Oh. Yeah. Funeral."

"Oh. I'm sorry."

"Thanks."

"Latte?"

"Yeah."

"Large non-fat, extra hot," she tells the guy beside her.

She waves away my money and sends me down the bar.

"Thanks," I say, smiling a little.

As I turn to go, she touches my arm—like butterflies landing. I look up, startled. Her eyes are blue, with green flecks.

"Take care," she says.

I turn back. "I will."

Chapter 28

At Beverly, I could hear the kids' laughter from the street, so there's no way they noticed the creaking of the front door as I came in. Without taking off my shoes, I creep into the kitchen. B.N.E. and Monica stand at the counter, covered in flour from their shoes to their hairlines, while Maureen shouts at them to pay attention to the recipe.

"What are you guys doing?" I ask, setting down a few bags of groceries.

Maureen turns from the stove, where she's been spraying the cake pans, and waves. "You're back! Feeling better?

"Much, thank you."

"We're making a cake," Monica grins.

"What's the occasion?"

"Well, we thought we'd better learn this baking thing for ourselves," B.N.E. informs me. "Shouldn't be too dependent on you to get our sugar fixes. This here's our tribute to the Great Brownie Chef."

"Is that it?"

"Hell, yes," says B.N.E. "Isn't that enough? Who else is gonna make the real food?"

"Without burned parts!" chimes in Monica.

Monica wants brownies?

"And real chocolate!" A disembodied voice, its mouth full of food, rings out from the other side of the kitchen.

"Kenny, where are you?" I creep around to the cupboard beside the stove, and fling open the door. He's tucked in there, clutching a bag of chips to his chest. I take the bag out of his grasp and put them firmly on the pantry's top shelf. "No more snacks before dinner!"

He just grins—a chip-crumble smile—and hops out of the cupboard. "So where've you been?"

"Home," I reply. "Taking a rest from you!"

Rachel wanders into the kitchen and smiles when she sees me. *Well, look at that. Eye contact! Amazing.* I kneel and hold out my arms. "You're looking good, kid!"

She bows her head, but doesn't pull away. "Hi," she whispers.

I squeeze her tightly. "Hi."

"So, have you been looking after Lizzie?" I ask Monica hopefully.

She sighs. "Been trying. But she spends all her time alone in her room."

"How come?"

Monica shrugs. "I don't know. She's just... what's that word? A wreck loose?"

"Recluse? She's hiding?"

"Yeah."

After the jumble and bluster of the kitchen, I find the upstairs hallway strangely quiet. The old floors squeak in exactly the same places. Even though I've only been gone a few days, things seem different. I notice details that didn't leap out before, like the tilted blinds on the stairwell window, the chipped blue paint on the wardrobe, and the stains on the carpet outside the bathroom door. Everything is familiar, but also new.

In the front bedroom, Lizzie sits on the window seat, staring out onto the street. I stand and watch her for a while before going in. She looks so little there, clutching Pootsie tightly.

"What do you see? Outside?" I ask gently.

Her shoulders tighten, but she doesn't answer.

"Lizzie?" I whisper. "What do you see?"

"Stupid normal people," she says at last, still not turning around.

I sit on the edge of the bed and finger the stitching on an old throw blanket. The silk tassels remind me of Nancy's sage shawl. "How are you?" I ask finally.

"Fine," she says.

"I don't believe you."

She crosses her arms and draws her knees up, still refusing to look at me.

"When did you start keeping secrets from me, Elizabeth?"

She growls, making it clear she'd like me to go away.

"Lizzie?"

"*When you left!*" she shouts.

"Ah. I'm sorry about that. You don't want to let me back in, huh?"

Silence.

"It's powerful, keeping secrets. Isn't it?" She balls her fists but sneaks a peek at me from the corner of her eye. "You know, Lizzie, I learned something important a little while ago about secrets." A slight lift of her shoulders tells me she's listening. "I thought keeping secrets made sure no one could use them against me. But a friend of mine taught me that's not true. Actually, you find your power when you let go of the secrets."

"Why?" she says, turning around at last. I tuck my legs up powwow style and meet her eyes. "Because when you keep secrets, you live behind a smokescreen. It's like lying to everyone—but especially yourself. If you're honest with your feelings, no one has any secrets to hold over you. Your power comes from the courage it takes to be yourself without apologizing for who you are."

"You keep secrets," she says quietly.

"I know."

She raises her eyebrows—she wasn't expecting that. But then she frowns and turns back to the window.

"Liz," I say. "Why do you think the people outside are all normal?"

"Because they're all on their way somewhere. They're not waiting for things to happen to them. They're probably going to their own homes. To their families."

"What else?"

"And then they're going to make dinner and eat it together."

"Oh yeah?"

She turns to face me, almost defiantly, as if testing out this theory of genuineness—scrutinising how I will react to the tears sliding down her cheeks. "Oh Lizzie," I hold out my hands. "I'm sorry, sweetie."

In a flash, she darts from the window seat and into my arms. She squeezes me as tightly as on the day I found her hiding in the garage.

"Why isn't my family a nice family too, Beth?" she hiccups.

"Some families just aren't. Families are like the weather—some days are nice, some days aren't, and you can't tell today what it's going to be like tomorrow."

"I don't want them back," she whispers, looking a little horrified with herself for saying it.

"But you feel bad? You think you should love them and miss them?"

She nods, her lips trembling. I hug her close, running my fingers through her fine, dark hair. She buries her face in my shirt. "Lizzie, it's all right for you to be angry with your parents. One of these days, you're going to understand them better than you do now, and then maybe you'll forgive them. But it's okay to be mad."

"I hate them," she whispers, not meeting my eyes. "I never hated them before. But now I don't think I can forgive them. Will they make me go back?"

"I don't know for sure, but somehow I doubt it. Your father is in deep trouble with the police, and so is your Mom. Lizzie—I don't think you're going back to them this time."

Tears fill her eyes again. "Beth, I'm sad." Her tangled hair sticks to my own wet cheeks.

Her little fists pound against my shoulder. "Where have you been?" she sobs, her voice muffled by my sweater. I hold her tightly, and let her be angry with me. I know I have to trust her with the truth if she's going to trust me again. For a moment, I stare out the window at the passersby, still rubbing her back.

"A friend of mine died," I say softly. "The friend who taught me about secrets. She was very sick, and when she died it made me very sad. I had to stay home and be sad for awhile."

Lizzie pulls away and looks at me, her eyes full of sympathy.

"You're very sad too?"

I nod, blinking skyward.

"It's okay if you want to cry," she says. I try to smile as I look at her small, serious face, but I can't. She wraps her tiny arms around my neck, patting my shoulder, and I hug her back, letting a few tears spill onto the top of her head. She squeezes me tightly, burying her face back in my shoulder.

Something crinkles.

Nancy's letter sticks out of the front pocket of my shirt. I haven't been able to bring myself to read it yet. "What's that?" Lizzie pulls out the blue paper.

"It's from my friend who died."

"Oh. Do you want me to read it to you?"

I smile. "Sure."

Lizzie carefully unfolds the page and smoothes it between her hands.

"'A List of In-tell-i-gent Suggest-ions,'" she reads, sounding out the words. "'By Nancy Sullivan.' Was Nancy Sullivan your friend?"

"Yes."

"Oh. Okay. 'Number one. Move into res-i-dence.'"

"Residence."

"What's residence?"

"It's a building where university students live."

"All together?"

"Yes."

"That sounds like fun."

I smile. That was the idea. "Probably would be. What's number two?"

"'Number two. Breathe.' I got that one myself, Beth!"

"Good for you!"

"'Number three. Keep a jour-nal.'"

"Journal."

"Oh. Journal. Okay. 'Number four. Stop drinking so much coffee.'"

"Seriously?"

"Yeah, that's what it says!"

"All right, you're right."

"'Number five. Stop farting in public.'"

"It does *not* say that, Elizabeth Emery!"

She collapses in giggles. "It does, it does!" she cries, holding the paper away from me.

I wrestle it out of her grasp. "It doesn't." I scan the page, a little taken aback by what she's really written. "Here, read the real thing."

Lizzie takes the paper back from me, and holds it for a moment while she reads the next line. Her face gets suddenly serious. "It says... 'Hug Lizzie.'"

It does.

So I do.

Two weeks have passed since Nancy died, and yesterday, I had my first appointment with Tom Sullivan. Talking to him went easier than expected. It sort of felt like talking to Nancy, through him.

On Tuesday, I finally told Simon and Kate about everything—the cutting, my last session with Nancy, what happened to Jackie at camp. They both cried. I almost cried too, but somehow I still can't manage to let myself really feel it. I'm working on it—with Tom. Simon has called me every day since, and Kate's slept in the guest room every second night. Sometimes, Simon joins her. I kind of like waking up and making a group breakfast. I guess this is what university residence is like—and what real friendship is like, without years of secrets and control and lies in the way.

"Hey, Beth, did you know Heather's exhibit comes down next week?" Simon pours half a cup of maple syrup over his French toast.

"Is it?" I didn't expect it to be there forever, but still, this surprises me. I'm running out of time. Nancy would say that I need "closure." I say that I need to test myself. Can I look at that painting without screaming? Can I forgive Heather for knowing about that night and never telling me—never looking past her own need for silence?

"When next week?"

Simon shakes his head. "Don't know."

"What are you thinking, Beth?" Kate asks cautiously.

"I have to go see it."

"See what? The exhibit?" Simon turns to me with his plate in hand, staring incredulously.

"Yeah. It might be my last chance. I have to try and make sense of it—I can't explain why. I just have to try. So I can be confident that I've done everything possible."

"Do you want me to go with you?" asks Kate.

"Thanks, but no. It's better if I go alone."

The only way to truly know myself—and to understand Heather— is to start at the beginning.

Chapter 29

The gallery is much quieter this time. The closing chime will ring in half an hour, and even the more avid art-admirers have packed it in for the day. I only can handle a small window of time, so that's all I've given myself. Slowly, I climb the concrete ramp to the second floor. My heart beats faster with every step, but I don't expect to see Heather, and that helps a little. The huge oak doors leading to the exhibit feel like they've been lined with mercury, and I press all my body weight into them. They shut behind me with a satisfying clunk. I have the exhibit all to myself.

I pass through the white brick archway, deliberately keeping my back to the 8'x10'. Why do I feel like I'm breaking and entering? I have more rights than anyone to see these things—these intimate expositions of our life.

The room is set up in cycles, each section dedicated to a particular period of Heather's life. Her very early work hangs directly to my left. Apparently, she used lots of colour in her young adult days. Amorphous shapes shift and merge in strange hues of pink and green, creating an almost psychedelic effect. Was she high when she painted these? *Stop analyzing. Observe.*

The next set have captions from the year I was born. She must have painted them when she was pregnant with me. The tone is different; colour still plays a big part, but it's earthy in nature—large, bulbous fruits in enormous bowls of water; tiny objects floating on the ocean; huge trees towering over tiny ants with enormous rocks on their backs.

I shake my head, move onto the next section. She used a lot of red—red for what? Passion? Anger? Resentment? Why red, Heather?

Over the next ten years, her work becomes more dramatic. Conflict dominates the later ones—clashing colours, intense strokes, attention wars between the left side of the canvas and the right. Critics often commend Heather for painting in such a wide variety of styles. She can do almost anything, from impressionism and symbolism to expressionism and realism. Maybe that's why everyone says she's brilliant. Her work is so rich with emotion, and so at odds with her personality, which is tempered, flat. Cold.

We can classify people with the same disorder, even when their symptoms vary. But the self-destruction is something you both share, I think. The love-hate relationship you have with one another, and with others. Emotional volatility masked by flat affect. Secrecy.

Is that why she always kept me in a box? Why she demanded silence? Order? Perfection? Because any ripples through her life would have awakened her own monster?

The second-to-last set look remarkably real, even though the scenes are implausible. Here's the one with the whispering trees, and there, the two people standing on either side of the river. What else? Behind these two, I find others in the same style—they all seem to be telling a story. The objects are concrete. They take the centre of focus, and remain distinct from the objects behind them. But the figures are as enigmatic as Heather's smile.

I look closely at one picture, then stand back. A girl sits at her desk in the corner, biting her lip as she scribbles away furiously. Tears streak her face. Through a series of mirrors, a woman watches her, trying to read what's on the page.

I can't believe this is my mother's work. There we are, Heather and I. But she would never stand behind closed doors and spy on me. It would go against the very core of our relationship. We kept things flat, cold, and hard, like concrete. She couldn't bear to witness or experience feeling. She poured it all into these canvases.

I move on to a large painting—more typical of her earlier pieces. *Have I taken a wrong turn?* No, the caption says she painted it two years ago. A swirling mass of colour dominates the centre—like a tornado imploding. Everything about this piece is huge, and so contrary to Heather's personality that it completely baffles me.

Until suddenly, it doesn't.

Two years ago, I left her. I walked away and never came back. She never came looking for me, and I took it for granted that she didn't care. But this painting says differently. This shows a person trying not to shatter.

What was Heather like before? How did she cope before channelling her emotions into painting?

Suddenly, I know why she painted that enormous picture.

I understand.

She could never share that moment when I came home from camp, because my grief would have drowned her. Emotions, for Heather, were like razor blades for me: tempting, overwhelming, self-destructive.

Maybe my shutting her out hurt her, but maybe it relieved her as well, because deep down, she knew she couldn't face the depth of emotion I had for Jackie. Loving that girl almost killed me. And acknowledging that pain would have cracked Heather's carefully constructed wall.

Slowly, I turn around. The 8'x10' looms above me, and I catch my breath, forcing myself to stand still and look at it. The darkness, the people running, the canoe docks, the water, the moonlight on its surface. And there I am, standing in the water, screaming for Jackie.

"There was no moonlight, Heather," I murmur. "There was no moon at all."

At the right of the canvas, a jetty runs into the water—not part of the original landscape. There was no jetty at camp. A dark clot of shadows gather in this part of the painting, which contrasts sharply with a white nightgown that catches my eye. I look closer. A woman stands behind the trees, one hand pressed to her mouth, the other crossed over her chest and gripping her arm, as if physically restraining herself from rushing down to the girl in the water.

I sink down to a squat and stare up at the 8'x10', taking in the whole picture, but returning again and again to the ghost in the corner.

Heather never did stop painting for me. Did she want me to know what she couldn't tell me? Did she hope that one day, when I cared to look, I would see all the things she couldn't say?

When she couldn't comfort me about Jackie, did she paint this scene for me? Not because she wanted to remind me of my grief, but because she wanted to share it with me.

Who told her?

And then I realise....

She must have known before I got home.

Deet, the camp director, must have called the parents to let them know. It could even have been on the news. Of course. They would have had to make an official statement. They couldn't have kept it secret.

My grief had blinded me to what was going on outside.

Slowly, I turn toward the last set, almost afraid to look. She's turned to a white palate, using varying shades of non-colour, insubstantial strokes, directionless lines. No essence. She seems to have lost her edge, her message. They're disturbing. Empty. Like leafless birch trees in the dead of winter—sparse, shivering, devoid. Does she struggle along the same brink as I do? Wondering whether the icy plunge is less painful than the frigid winter?

I sit on an empty square of hardwood in the middle of the floor, absorbing the early paintings as a collection. I let my eyes blur. The colours run together and the edges melt; the light mingles with the dark. A haze of energy emanates from the lot—confusion, passion, rage, frustration, love and joy. If she'd never had a child, would she be a different woman? A whole person instead of a shell with painted appendages?

I lie back on the floor, the high domed ceiling encasing me in a giant egg—like being back in the womb, just waiting to emerge into a different world. If I close my eyes, maybe I can float up through the wide empty space and through the stained glass windows into the sky. I could watch for a while, unseen, absorbing humanity before being born again, in this very room, and understand enough at the moment of my birth that I wouldn't lose her this time. Blood rushes through my head and my face tingles. I let the tears fall rapidly, spilling out the corners of my eyes. Will this struggle ever be over? Maybe that's like asking the tide to go out and never come back in.

But what's the use of getting better if you can't be there for the people you love the most? What if I can't ever have children without continuing the cycle? What if I can never have a relationship without remembering Jackie? What if I let my fear and sadness cloud any joy?

You're not ready now. That doesn't mean you'll never be ready, Beth. My mother once said that to me: when we were in the studio at our separate easels. I wanted to use her oil paint, not my watercolours.

"Not yet," she said gently.

"But why not? Why should I practice with these if I'll never get to paint with real paint?"

"You're not ready now. That doesn't mean you'll never be ready, Beth."

I close my eyes against the tears; try to breathe out the sudden knot in my stomach. She was right. Wise, in her own way.

I'm sorry you never knew your mother.

Will I ever see Heather again? Will I ever want to? My childhood is still too recent to be called "past," and my empathy for her is too fresh—too fragile—to be tested face-to-face. Heather Sarandon will probably never be my mother. But she is, and always will be, a brilliant painter. And that is how I will have to know her.

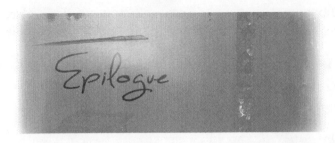

Epilogue

When I get home, I take out Nancy's list, and read it through for the hundredth time.

A List of Intelligent Suggestions
By Nancy Sullivan

1) Move into residence
2) Breathe
3) Keep a journal
4) Stop drinking so much coffee!
5) Hug Lizzie
6) Love somebody

Breathing yoga-style, I concentrate hard on my residence application. Dad said he'd pay for it. He was probably a little relieved to have his house back—not that he ever uses it. Or maybe he just thinks the same thing Nancy thought: I'm alone too damn much. I still haven't decided on a major, but have elected a few psych courses. I think Nancy would approve. And I've been hired at the group home—effective on my birthday.

Yesterday, I put away the coffee machine, and today I'm missing my lattes.

When I've finished the application, I put a stamp on the envelope, and tuck it in my purse. I actually have to mail this letter. Some habits die hard, and standing in the bathroom really tests my resolve. But rather than open the cupboard door to flip open my little box of masochistic treasures, I put on mascara, grab my purse and head out the door.

Simon and Kate want to meet at the coffee shop underground.

When I get there, the two of them are sitting at a little table, frowning over a pile of legal-sized papers. They're cute, signing their first lease.

I smile and wave, then head to the counter.

She's there, taking off her apron.

"Hey, are you off?" I ask.

She looks up. "Oh, hi. Yeah. Just finished." She smiles at me, disarmingly.

Courage. "Do you want to join us?"

She glances at Simon and Kate, then back at me, and the smile reaches her eyes. "Sure. What the hell."

She steps behind the bar to make me my usual latte, but I stop her.

"Actually, if you don't mind, I'm changing things up. I'll just have an herbal tea."

BOOK CLUB GUIDE

DISCUSSION QUESTIONS

1. Although Beth has a difficult relationship with her mother, the longing for her Jellicle Transformation stems from her desire for Heather's approval. Why the seeming contradiction? Is it a contradiction at all?

2. Beth simultaneously attracts and repels people. At one point she confides: "I could talk to everyone, and everyone talked to me, spilling their secrets into my lap like jellybeans." Conversely, she has several moments of deliberately pushing people away—telling off the "dick" at the coffee house, using Dr. Sullivan's pending death against her, and inwardly mocking the "elephantine" volunteer coordinator at the hospital. How do these two aspects of Beth exist side-by-side?

3. Beth accuses her mother for emotionally neglecting her as a child. At the same time, she eagerly anticipates the biweekly awkward phone call with her father, who is both physically and emotionally absent from her life. Why? What qualities do Beth's parents share? How are they different?

4. Beth says, "Time slips. I drop it on purpose sometimes." What does she mean by this, and how does she use this tactic as a coping mechanism?

5. Discuss Beth's cutting. Why does she do it? Is it significant that she describes the blood swirling in the basin with artistic words? The cutting starts as a way to keep track of the days since Jackie died, like a prisoner

ticking away his jail sentence. Is Beth a prisoner? How so? Who or what holds her captive?

6. Why does Beth spend so much time looking out the window? What does this represent? Is it important that she often looks upon a rainy day? When Nancy asks Beth what she sees, Beth responds: "I see the real world, Nancy. But it doesn't seem real to me. It seems like an illusion that nobody notices." How is this thematically important to the novel on the whole? Who else looks out the window?

7. When describing the first time she met Jackie, Beth says, "she always had this look like she knew something about your life that you were just about to discover." Are Beth's memories pure, or are they tainted by time and retrospect? What do we really know about Jackie besides that Beth liked her?

8. Beth left her mother's home after Heather failed to react to the news of Jackie's death. How is this representative of their relationship? Is Heather entirely to blame for the gap? What part has Beth played in their estrangement?

9. Beth is upset when she hears a fellow classmate referred to as a "fucking queer." She also rages against a perceived slight from a teenager toward a butch lesbian on the street, and later, takes the side of the barista at the coffee kiosk who is being accosted by a patron. Although she cannot identify as lesbian, she feels the need to protect the rights of others who are gay. Why?

10. Heather's rules are clearly ingrained in Beth's psyche. From maintaining composure and being a lady to never giving anyone power, why does Beth cling to these rules even when her mother is not around? How do these rules reflect Heather's own insecurities?

11. Beth refers to her makeup and feminine clothing as a disguise. Who or what is she hiding from? Similarly,

she contemplates the barista's wild hair and piercings and wonders if this is also a disguise. Discuss these two styles of dress, and the messages they project to the world. Why might a young lesbian choose to dress in a stereotypical "gay style." What benefit might this have?

12. Discuss the names in *Jellicle Girl*. Beth's full name is Elizabeth, a name she shares with Lizzie and with Dr. Sullivan's daughter, Bethany (Beth for short). Her imaginary friend's name is E, which could also stand for Elizabeth. How does each character represent an alternate side to our protagonist?

13. Dr. Sullivan mistakenly refers to Beth as Bethany several times. Other than knowing the relationship between Nancy and her daughter is complicated, we are privy to no details about the mysterious Bethany Sullivan. How might Beth's relationship with Heather mirror Nancy's relationship with her own daughter? Does Beth's initial combativeness toward Nancy stem from her inner character, or is it more due to Nancy's potential as a surrogate mother figure?

14. Why does Beth write poetry? How does this help her through her pain? Does it help her connect with Jackie, or does it only prolong her suffering? Were they any poems within the novel that you found particularly poignant?

15. During Existential Psychology class, the students discuss the concept of synchronicity. Beth sums it up as, "meaningful coincidences exist. Most people ignore them. If you want a better life, assume the meaning behind the coincidence will become clear once you start searching." Discuss examples of synchronicity in this novel.

16. Later Beth's class discusses the futility of life. Beth can't stop herself from contributing, "Existence is only futile if you believe it's ultimately physical...this is why people

believe in a Transforma—transcendence. An afterlife." How does this statement reflect the reasons behind Beth's desire for the Jellicle Transformation? How are these statements rendered even more powerful in the wake of Jackie's death and in Professor Mirtica's partner's death?

17. From the "Black Socks" bath scene to combing out Lizzie's blood encrusted head, how does Lizzie impact Beth's relationship with herself? Why is Beth tender and forgiving of Lizzie but fails to extend the same kindness to herself? Discuss the similarities between Lizzie and Beth both in personality and the events that happen to them during the course of the novel.

18. Discuss the men in Beth's life—Mike, Simon, Mr. Davidson. What do they have in common? Why does Beth pick each of them? What does she expect from her interactions with these men, Simon in particular? Why does Beth make the conscious decision to return to school and seduce her teacher just weeks after breaking free?

19. Dr. Sullivan catches Beth studying her diagnostic manual. Beth quips that the description of Borderline Personality Disorder sounds just like her mother, and Nancy counters that Beth may also be victim to the disorder. Nancy goes on to say of Beth and her mother, "the self-destruction is something you both share, I think. The love-hate relationship you have with one another, and with others. Emotional volatility masked by flat affect. Secrecy." What other traits do Beth and her mother have in common?

20. Who is E, and what does she do for Beth? Beth claims they were together during childhood, but then E left for several years only to return after Jackie's death. We first meet E while Beth is ordering a Caramel Macchiato from the "boi" barista—not her usual order. E also turns up when Beth volunteers at the mental ward of the hospital, again when she's considering

checking in. How are each of these moments pivotal to the story, and how does E help?

21. Beth refers to herself repeatedly as flawed, broken. Is her sexuality the thing she hates most about herself, or is it something else? How does Beth's sexuality affect her relationship with her mother?

22. Why does Nancy send Beth to volunteer on the psych ward? How did it help or hinder Beth? What is Nancy's overall strategy in treating Beth? Is it affected by her physical decline? How does Nancy's disability affect their relationship?

23. Compare and contrast Beth's teachers, Professor Mirtica and Mr. Davidson. Discuss her attraction to each and how they both ease her toward her Transformation.

24. Describe Beth's reaction to her mother's work. Why can't she see its brilliance? Also discuss the periods of her mother's gallery and how each ties into their mother-daughter relationship. What was Heather trying to tell Beth through her art—particularly with regards to the lake painting—and did Beth receive the message?

25. How does Beth believe her Jellicle Transformation will come about, and why does she cling to the ludicrous idea so desperately? By the end of the novel, has Beth been transformed? If so, how did it happen, and was it like what she expected? If not, what happened instead?

ACKNOWLEDGEMENTS

This book was a village effort. I have many thank-you's to make, so let's roll out the red carpet and put on sequined gowns, because this is going to rival the Oscars.

To the team at Evolved: for parachuting in and helping me navigate the final rapids of publication, particularly my editors Lane Diamond and John Allen, and my amazing cover artist, Mallory Rock. A special thank you to my publicist Emlyn Chand for helping me realise that *Jellicle Girl* was literary fiction.

To Nana and Poppa, for buying me a little chair and desk in the basement, and driving me to school every morning so I didn't have to waste valuable writing time by walking.

Mum, who insisted that I take something practical like a Master's in creative writing... and for giving me piles of tuition money and air miles without batting an eyelash. You were right: education is the best gift you can give.

Lauren—my beautiful little sister, for so many reasons.

Judy and Roxie, my first beta readers, who sat with me for hours to get all the kinks worked out—and then spent hours more kicking my butt to get down to finding a publisher.

To Liz, for always sharing—and for standing by me for so many years. And Lynn, for having Fowler's Modern English handy, and for giving me the listening stool.

Karen Fabian and Karrie Weinstock, who told me at fourteen that if I didn't become a writer, I'd miss my calling. You, and the rest of my remarkable teachers at Branksome, gave me strong enough wings to leave the nest early.

The DE staff at LBP. You are my safe place to fall: my friends and my sisters. Thank you for listening. And for pushing. And pulling. And shoving. Me. In. To. Real. Life.

And to Nancy: because no matter what I do, where I go, and whom I meet, everything truly important to me is wrapped up in you.

ABOUT THE AUTHOR

Stevie Mikayne never dreamed of flying; she dreamed of writing stories that would one day be on library bookshelves. She graduated Lancaster University (UK) with a Master's in creative writing, and immediately pinned up a quotation from Margaret Laurence to deter her from giving into the temptation of a day job. "When I say work, I only mean the writing. Everything else is just odd jobs."

Stevie worked part-time in special education, finance, and at the children's library while keeping one foot in the writing world. She is now a creative writing instructor at the Nepean Creative Arts Centre and at Algonquin College. Recently, she joined Evolved Publishing as an editor and author. Excerpts from her forthcoming novel *Letters to Catherine* can be found in Sleet and Stone Highway Review. She lives in Ottawa with her wife Nancy and their Great Dane, Lincoln.

Jellicle Girl is her debut novel.

WEIGHT OF EARTH

CHAPTER 1

Ella's cell rang. "Hello?" she answered.

"Three guesses." The caller spoke in a low voice, which would have sounded threatening if she hadn't recognised it immediately.

"I don't guess."

"That's too bad."

"How did you get my number?" Ella said.

"I asked Aunt Ginny. Told her I needed some advice on a class for next semester."

"And she believed you?"

"She looks past my spacers and tattoos, unlike some other puritans I could mention."

"Puritans? Are you kidding?"

"Not at all. I'd love to shake up your world. You have no idea." He chuckled—a warm sound. Heat spread to Ella's face, and she was glad of the protective barrier the phone offered. Sounded like he was too.

"You're a lot braver on the phone than you are in person," she said.

He laughed again. "How about in your dreams? How am I then?"

"That's between your dream self and me."

"Yeah? How about if I take you out, and you can see how the two of us compare?"

Ella's heart shuddered. Something about his voice—his hands—made her knees quiver. She was almost afraid to say yes.

"Where?"

"Is that a yes?"

Ella bit her lip, determined not to let her voice betray her. "It's a maybe."

"I'll take a maybe. I'll come pick you up on Saturday at 11:00. If you're not ready, I'll take it as a no."

Ella suppressed a smile. "Deal," she said coolly.

"Okay then."

***

He drove up in a subcompact, fuel-efficient hatchback.

She peeked out the window, her hair gel leaving a tiny streak on the clear surface, and immediately his electric gaze seared hers across the greying twilight.

With a gasp, she pulled away from the window.

Who was this guy? And what the hell was she thinking to get into a car with him?

She ducked into the bathroom to finish applying her lipstick and run her fingers one more time through her tousled curls.

"Ella," her mother knocked softly. "Someone is at the door."

"I know, Mama," Ella said impatiently. "I'm coming."

Her mother caught her arm as she came out of the bathroom. "Who is that boy?" she asked in a low voice.

"A friend," Ella said.

"Are you dating him?"

"No."

"Really? Well you're certainly not studying with that amount of makeup on."

Ella fixed her mother with a cold stare. "Mama, I'm in university now. If I lived on campus you'd have no idea what I was doing or who I was with." She tried to pull away again.

"Yes," her mother hissed. "But you live here. With me."

Ella whirled around. "Which is almost the same thing."

Her mother flinched and let go.

Ella all but sprinted toward the front door. "C'mon," she said, grabbing a set of keys off the rack on the wall. But instead of following, Zeth looked past her shoulder toward her mother, who had just emerged from the hall.

"Hello." He extended his hand and Meredith took it, without smiling. "My name is Zeth Walsh."

"Meredith Casbourne."

"A pleasure to meet you, Ms. Casbourne."

"And you, Zeth."

"I'll be taking Ella to the shopping mall for dinner, then bringing her home, if that's all right with you."

Meredith frowned at Ella, but Ella refused to meet her gaze. "My daughter is a grown woman. She makes her own decisions—wise or foolish as they may be."

Zeth nodded, as though weighing her words. "We won't be late."

Ella shook her head impatiently and ducked outside, dragging Zeth by the cuff of his grey leather coat.

***

He parked in an area of the shopping centre Ella had never seen before: a tiny lot toward the side. Opening the door, he ushered her inside. "Where are we?" Ella said. Usually when she came to the mall, she made a beeline for the stores she wanted, and ducked the hell back out as quickly as possible. Malls exhausted her. Too many people. Too much noise.

Zeth guided her toward a small coffee shop tucked into a remote wing on the bottom floor. Homemade baked goods lined wooden shelves behind thick panes of glass, and a few scattered tables and chairs perched outside the store. A patron emerged, carrying a tall glass mug of dark hot chocolate, swirled with thick whipped cream and sprinkled with cinnamon. Ella watched the mug go by, and Zeth laughed.

"Like?" he said. She shrugged and smiled.

Inside, small groups of people huddled around stone tables. Fused pendant lights cast shadows on three small booths at the back, and a smiling woman in a blue apron greeted them at the counter.

"Fresh apple muffins," she said, winking at Zeth.

"Mmm. I'll take two."

"Black tea?"

"Yes please. And I think my friend would like a hot

chocolate."

Ella smiled.

"Your table's ready," the woman said.

Ella glanced down at her name tag: Sheila. She looked maybe thirty, with a black Irish complexion and a silver pendant hanging around her neck. A Celtic symbol. Well, that made sense. Her dark green eyes lit with amusement as she followed Ella's glance.

"Pretty," Ella said.

Sheila led them to a cosy booth in a shadowed corner and set their drinks down on the cool slate surface.

Ella slipped in across from Zeth. "What's with this place?"

"What do you mean?"

Ella tried to find words to describe the ambiance: the calm patrons, the wise young owner, the Celtic designs... the feeling that they somehow existed outside of normal space and time.

"It's special," she said finally.

Zeth smirked. "Yeah, I know."

MORE FROM EVOLVED PUBLISHING

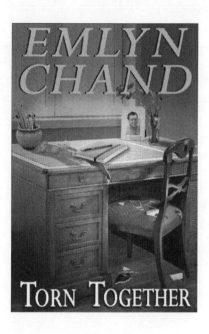

Torn Together, a Literary/Women's Fiction novel, is available at Amazon.

From her cheating boyfriend to her dead father and cold, judgmental mother, Daly knows she can't trust others to be there when it counts. This cynicism begins to melt away when she meets Kashi, a light-hearted charmer from India, who decides he cares too much to let her fade into the background of her own life. After a series of false starts, their quirky romance carries them to India, where Daly must win the approval of Kashi's family in order to seal their "forever."

Meanwhile, Laine struggles to cope with the pain of early widowhood, fleeing into the pages of her well-worn library and emerging only to perform her duties as a social worker at the crisis pregnancy center. Although her daughter wants nothing more than to work as an artist, Laine doesn't know how to redirect Daly to a more suitable profession without further damaging their tenuous relationship.

Can Laine look past her pain to learn from an unlikely mentor? Has Daly finally found someone whom she can trust? Will the women recognize their common bonds before the relationship is broken beyond repair?

Torn Together, Emlyn Chand's first sojourn into Literary Fiction, illustrates how our similarities often drive us apart.

Desert Rice, a Contemporary/Upper YA novel, is available at Amazon.

Samantha Jean Haggert is a beautiful twelve-year-old girl—but no one knows it. All they see is an awkward boy in a baseball cap and baggy pants. Sam's not thrilled with the idea of hiding her identity, but it's all part of her older brother's plan to keep Sam safe from male attention and hidden from the law. Fifteen-year-old Jacob will stop at nothing to protect his sister, including concealing the death of the one person who should have protected them in the first place—their mother.

Sam and Jacob try to outrun their past by stealing the family car and traveling from West Virginia to Arizona, but the adult world proves mighty difficult to navigate, especially for two kids on their own. Trusting adults has never been an option; no adult has ever given them a good reason. But when Sam meets "Jesus"—who smells an awful lot like a horse—in the park, life takes a different turn. He saved her once, and may be willing to save Sam and her brother again, if only they admit what took place that fateful day in West Virginia. The problem? Sam doesn't remember, and Jacob isn't talking.

ALSO FROM EVOLVED PUBLISHING

The Christmas Curse
Cupid's Capture

MEMOIR

And Then It Rained: Lessons for Life by Megan Morrison

ROMANCE / EROTICA

Tell Me You Want Me by Amelia James
Her Twisted Pleasures by Amelia James
Secret Storm by Amelia James
The Devil Made Me Do It by Amelia James

SCI-FI / FANTASY

Eulogy by D.T. Conklin

SHORT STORY ANTHOLOGIES

FROM THE EDITORS AT EVOLVED PUBLISHING:
Evolution: Vol. 1
Evolution: Vol. 2

THRILLERS

Forgive Me, Alex by Lane Diamond
The Devil's Bane by Lane Diamond

YOUNG ADULT

Dead Chaos by T.G. Ayer
Dead Embers by T.G. Ayer
Dead Radiance by T.G. Ayer
Second Skin by T.G. Ayer

And many more to come in the near future.

Made in the USA
Charleston, SC
21 August 2012